T0000596

The Romance Lovers Book Club

By MA Binfield

Never Be The Same

Not This Time

One Small Step

The Romance Lovers Book Club

By Toni Logan

Share the Moon

The Marriage Masquerade

Gia's Gems

Perfectly Matched

Unexpectedly Yours

The Romance Lovers Book Club

Writing as Piper Jordan:

Hotel Fantasy

Decadence: Exclusive Content

Visit us at www.boldstrokesbooks.com

The Romance Lovers Book Club

by

MA Binfield and Toni Logan

2024

THE ROMANCE LOVERS BOOK CLUB

ISBN 13: 978-1-63679-501-0

This Trade Paperback Original Is Published By
Bold Strokes Books, Inc.
P.O. Box 249
Valley Falls, NY 12185

First Edition: March 2024

Credits
Editor: Cindy Cresap
Production Design: Stacia Seaman
Cover Design by Tammy Seidick

Acknowledgments

Big thanks, as ever, to Cindy Cresap for her skillful edits and boundless patience. Big love to everyone at Bold Strokes Books for the support they give us and the work they do. Still very proud to be part of the BSB crew. (Hey, that rhymes).

Sending big love and thanks to Mila and the boys for keeping me sane (during insane times) and making me happy, when it's sometimes easy not to be.

And finally, a massive shout-out to the wonderful Toni Logan, who persuaded me to pick up my pen again and even went so far as to write this book with me to make sure I got back in the groove. Thanks, Toni, it was a lot of fun.

—MA Binfield

A heartfelt thank you to those who make the wheels turn at Bold Strokes Books. What an incredible and talented team, and I am honored and forever grateful to be a part of this amazing family. Thank you.

A huge shoutout to Cindy Cresap, editor extraordinaire. This is my second novel working with you at the editor's helm, and it has been an absolute pleasure.

For my wonderful friends who are always there for me. You guys keep me grounded and smiling. I love you.

A very special acknowledgment goes to MA Binfield. Through email chats and zoom calls, we became good friends. Cowriting this novel with you has been an absolute pleasure. Thanks for taking the leap with me.

And finally, to you, the reader, for taking a chance on this book. I hope you enjoy reading it as much as Michelle and I enjoyed writing it. Cheers.

—Toni Logan

MA Binfield dedicates this book to all the teachers
who showed her kindness…and gave her books to read

CHAPTER ONE

Ladies…ladies." Harper's voice rose above the chatter as she gently tapped the cheese knife against her wine glass. The group of ten women, some seated next to her on the L-shaped overstuffed couch, others on various folding chairs, settled as a hush fell on the small room and all eyes focused on her. "Thanks for coming tonight and double thanks to Brenda for this month's book suggestion." She bent forward and slid a paperback novel off the coffee table and referenced a cover displaying a British princess and an American tourist wrapped in a loving embrace in front of a castle. "I assume everyone's read it?"

There were nods all the way around as books and e-readers were pulled from purses and backpacks. "Great, then let's kick off the conversation. But first a toast to our club." She raised her glass as everyone followed suit. "Here's to romance, love, and all the happily ever afters."

"Hear, hear!" Alice cheered loudly, the curls of her red hair dancing as she bounced excitedly in her seat before taking a large gulp of her wine and then washing it down with another.

"Now then, who wants to—"

"I'll start." Linda, the newest recruit to the book club, interrupted her in an excited voice, shooting up one hand, while the other unclipped a pair of reading glasses from the neck of her shirt. She cleared her throat, fidgeted until she seemed to have found a comfy position on the couch, and began a bubbly monologue referencing plot, character development, and story structure from pages that had been flagged with different colored Post-it Notes sticking out of her paperback.

Harper smiled at her enthusiasm as she leaned forward, sandwiched a slice of cheese between two crackers from the charcuterie tray that sat in the middle of the coffee table, repositioned herself deeper into the couch cushion, and half-heartedly listened. She didn't particularly care about the subtle language nuances in the dialogue of each protagonist, or Linda's interpreted meaning of the scenic relevance in the plot. As long as the book successfully whisked her away into a romantic fantasy that made her forget about her own stagnant life and the characters gave her the *feels*, the novel was a five-star read.

And this one—the tale of an American tourist falling in love with a surprisingly out and proud English princess—had been five stars plus. The plus being the hot-as-hell sex scenes, especially the one in a hedge maze on the grounds of the princess's hideaway castle. She tightly crossed her legs as thoughts of the scene she had felt compelled to read twice replayed in her mind.

Animated and loudly debating voices brought her back to the present, as she focused on the usual suspects in the group who were expressing their opinions as agreements and disagreements about the exposition of the novel volleyed around the room. By the time she finished her third glass of wine, the colorful discussion had wound down, next month's novel was already decided upon, and Harper hugged out a series of good-byes as everyone except Alice headed out the door.

"I'll help clean up." Alice began folding the chairs.

"Stop." Harper waved her off as she tapped the couch cushion. "Come sit and help me finish up the leftover wine." She kicked off her Birkenstocks and rested her legs on the table as Alice flopped down next to her.

"Care if I mix and match?" Alice didn't wait for a reply as she grabbed the two remaining bottles of different varietals and poured whatever was left into their glasses.

"As long as it's red, I don't care," Harper said as she focused on Alice. They grew up neighbors in a middle-class suburb on the outskirts of Phoenix. Best friends since they were ten, had similar likes and dislikes, but their personalities couldn't be further apart. Where Harper was reserved and lacked confidence, Alice was boisterous and outgoing. They were the yin to the other's yang.

"Another fun night with the club." Harper retrieved her paperback copy off the coffee table, brushed off a few rogue cracker crumbs, and flipped through the pages as scenes from the novel came to life in her mind. "Wouldn't it be nice"—she swallowed a gulp of wine and with it the bitter taste of her life—"if our lives really did resemble one of these novels we read?"

"Pfft, I'd settle for a ten percent similarity. Five if there's a hedge maze involved."

"Ha!" Harper wagged an unsteady finger in Alice's face. "I loved that scene too."

"Are you kidding me? Anyone with a pulse would love that scene."

"It was pretty hot," they said in unison, laughed, then leaned against each other until sighs took hold.

"Seriously though." Alice referenced the book. "Why can't we have a life like that? I mean, what's stopping us from just, oh, I don't know, going to London and finding true love of our own like in the novel?"

Harper scoffed. "Sure, because that happens all the time in real life." She giggled at the thought, took another sip of wine, and caught Alice staring at her with an overarching brow frozen in place. "Uh-oh." Harper leaned back. "I know that look. You're about to suggest something weird, aren't you?"

"Look at us, Harps. We're both young…enough…and accomplished…kind of. I mean, you started a book club and have a PhD, and I um…I um…" She waved a dismissive hand. "More importantly, we're good catches. In fact…" Alice cocked her head and held a distant stare. "What if—"

"Nope." Harper cut her off. "The last time you started a sentence with that facial expression, we ended up going on a weekend campout in Flagstaff with the Bear Cubs of Arizona because you thought we'd spend three fun-filled days playing with baby bears, when in fact, we ended up hanging out with a group of hairy gay men."

Alice laughed. "Yeah, we did, didn't we? But you gotta admit, it ended up being a great weekend. I mean, now we both know how to throw an axe and cook a killer omelet over an open fire. Am I not right?" She playfully shoulder-bumped Harper. "But hear me out, this is an even better idea. What if we go to London and recreate all the scenes in the novel and see if we can't find our own impossibly gorgeous princess…or two? I mean I know we're besties and all, but I'm not sharing a princess with you."

Harper blankly stared at Alice as she tried to fully comprehend the complete absurdity of her idea. "You're crazy, and you're drunk."

"True on both counts, but seriously, why not? We've been debating where to go, June is right around the corner, and this would be the perfect vacation."

Every summer when Harper's school was on break, and the Phoenix tourist trolley Alice drove for shut down during the off-season, the two of them scraped their money together and got the hell out of Dodge for three glorious weeks of welcome vacation time where cooler temperatures prevailed.

"No. Absolutely not."

"Come on, look…" Alice grabbed the novel and flipped through the pages. "This could be our itinerary. We could go to all these places, just like our heroine did, and who knows, maybe by the end of our trip, we'll find a happily ever after of our own. And if we don't, well, we'll have had a great vacation."

Harper scoffed, even though she was slowly warming to the idea. She was tempted not for the reason of reenacting scenes from the novel or trying to chase down a fictitious princess. It had more to do with her latest late-night obsession, which included a bowl of popcorn, binge-watching British rom-coms, and falling in love with the English countryside, sexy accents, and quaint little pubs. "Okay, say I did think this was a fun idea, which I don't, but if I did…how are we going to pay for it? London's expensive."

"We'll find a cheap place to stay. It's not like we haven't slummed it in low-rent hotels before." Alice leaned in and batted her eyelashes. "Come on, please. It'll be the perfect adventure. Three weeks walking in the footsteps of the characters from a hot-as-hell romance novel, set in a beautiful part of the world, with plenty of history, good food, and lush green countryside. Unless, of course, you want to think about it. I mean, next month's novel is about two women who meet while climbing Mount Everest, so we could consider that. But hmmm…" Alice extended her hands palms up and jiggled them, as though she were weighing her thoughts. "London pubs and princesses versus frostbite and forced exercise."

"Well, when you put it like that." Harper chuckled. The idea did have a lot of appeal and Alice did make some good points. She cocked her head and strained to think logically through the thick alcohol-induced haze as a thought poked through. Going to London would give her an excuse to try to reconnect with Chelsea. She could reach out and ask her to recommend a cheap place to stay and also see if she, on the off chance, had some time to meet up. After all, how many years had it been since they last saw one another? She glanced at her fingers for mathematical help and was stunned at the answer. Fifteen years. Wow. How could that much time have gone by, when the memory of them together sometimes felt like it was only yesterday?

They had both signed up for the same early morning biology class, and as Harper came shuffling in late, clutching her Starbucks and full of first day college freshman jitters, she anxiously searched the room for a seat. Chelsea locked eyes with her and with a tilt of her head motioned for her to take the one next to her. They immediately hit it off, but it wasn't until the end of that year that their friendship really blossomed. Chelsea was falling behind in a class that Harper had already aced and was worried it would affect her tennis scholarship. So, late in the evenings and every free weekend, they met at the courts, and as Chelsea practiced her serve with basketfuls of tennis balls, Harper sat on the sidelines and tutored her.

Afterward, they would grab a bite to eat, put talk of school and tennis aside, and get to know each other. And somewhere in the mix, the casual friendship they shared deepened, and Harper's emerging feelings morphed into a full-blown crush. A crush that had, against all the odds, been fully reciprocated, and for one glorious night in the back of her pickup truck, become something else. Something exquisite and loving. But something that never had the chance to fully bloom.

She remembered the feel of Chelsea's fingertips on her skin, the warmth of her lips on hers, and the excited tightness low down in her stomach when they came together as one.

Harper grabbed her phone and opened Facebook, as an unexpected tingle shot through her body. She pulled up Chelsea's profile, scrolled to a pic, and extended her arm. "Remember her?"

Alice squinted. "Do I remember a dog?"

"What?" Harper turned her phone around. "Oops…" She moved the photo of the fuzzy-faced terrier down until the profile picture reappeared. "Her."

"Oh wow, haven't seen that face in a while." Alice took Harper's phone and flicked the screen. "She looks just the same."

"Well, that picture was posted about eight years ago, so—"

"Eight years ago?" Alice interrupted her with a snort. "And here I thought you were the only one who kept their page frozen in time. What's up with that?"

"Once I live a life worth posting about, I will. Meanwhile, I live vicariously through everyone else."

"Stalker," Alice muttered as she returned her phone.

Harper focused on the selfie of Chelsea that had been taken at a culinary convention in Phoenix. She remembered the message Chelsea had sent explaining that she and her father were coming to town for a few days and expressing a desire to see her. It had been the first time she had heard from her in years, but in a cruel twist of timing, Harper had to pass on the window of opportunity. She had already booked a Colorado ski trip with her latest girlfriend in hopes of fanning the flames of their smoldering relationship. A relationship that wasn't meant to be, and six months later, they parted ways.

In the months that followed, when despair over yet another failed relationship settled in alongside the regret at missing out on a chance to see Chelsea again, Harper had reached out. When her attempts were met with silence, she had to face up to the fact that saying no to meeting up in Phoenix may have stifled any hope of rekindling a friendship between them. So, with a heavy heart, and for the second time in her life, she stopped trying to reconnect. But as she sat focusing on the selfie of Chelsea in all her dimple-smiling glory, she couldn't help once again wonder if the spark that had once ignited between them that fateful night in college would still be there.

The snap from Alice's fingers in front of her face brought her back to the present. "Are you in an alcohol coma already, because if you are, can I have your wine? It appears as though I already drank mine."

Harper emptied half her wine into Alice's glass. "I was just thinking about Chelsea."

"Oh yeah, what about?"

"I was thinking about that time we made love up at South Mountain in the back of my old truck."

"You two were so hot together."

"Well, we were never really 'together.' It was just something that happened one night, and it was no big deal." But that wasn't true. At the time, she believed with all her heart it was the beginning of something magical between them. Something that was meant to be. But the fantasy quickly faded as the frustration of trying to maintain a long-distance connection with someone who didn't seem as invested as she was sank in. It was her first true heartbreak—and it was one she had never really admitted to.

"Besides, look at her." Harper flipped the screen back around, wanting to lighten the mood. "She was always out of my league. Even if she'd stuck around, it would have never worked." That bit felt painfully truthful. "Don't you remember? Both men and women were constantly hitting on her, and she was always surrounded by that entourage of admiring athletes and coaches. She was beautiful, confident, and worldly. I, on the other hand, was a total bookworm, fashionably challenged, and with the self-esteem of a rock." Harper shrugged off thoughts of what could have been. She, like many, had been unable to resist Chelsea's charm. She should have realized sooner that they didn't have a future. They might have had a fling, but even without everything that happened with Ryan, she was foolish to think Chelsea would have wanted anything more.

"Ahhh, that's so sweet. The Beauty and the Geek."

"Shut up." Harper playfully shoved her.

"Seriously though, I can't remember why Chelsea left so suddenly."

Harper leaned back. "Really? I only talked about it for months. Her brother Ryan got really sick, so she dropped out of school and went back to London to help take care of him. He ended up dying. She took it really hard, decided to stay there with her family, and eventually we just kinda lost touch." She cocked her head. "You don't remember any of that?"

But Harper remembered. Whenever she looked back at her life and wondered how she had turned thirty-four and had never really been happy in a relationship, she found herself thinking about Chelsea, and about the night Harper had finally let herself give in to her feelings—and her desires. In that moment, under the desert night sky, it had felt like the stars aligned and she and Chelsea would be together forever.

"Oh, right. Now I remember." Alice tapped her temple. "But in all fairness, that's when I was with Ruth, so my mind was kinda preoccupied, and we both know it can only retain so much information before I get a headache."

"You mean your body was preoccupied," Harper said. "I seem to recall that I barely saw you when you two were together, so it was a good thing I had Chelsea to hang out with."

"Yeah, sorry about that. Ruth was definitely all-consuming—if you know what I mean?" Alice giggled, hiccupped, then froze in a far-off stare. "Hey…" She turned to Harper. "You know what this is? This is fate. We were meant to read this book, get drunk, and plan a trip to London. You can say hi to Chelsea again *and* meet a princess. It's a win-win."

"Somehow, every logical brain cell that hasn't been killed off by the alcohol doubts that. But…now that we're tripping down memory lane, I will admit that it would be nice to see her again." The daily calls they had promised each other after Chelsea left didn't last, turning instead into sporadic weekly updates and eventually withering to brief texts here and there. Since Harper knew Chelsea had a lot going on with her family, she let her take the lead on how often and when they communicated. But after Ryan had died, their communication dwindled to nothing. Harper had internalized her hurt by burying herself deeper in her studies and blaming herself for ever thinking they were anything more than just two souls that paused at an intersection in life before both moved on.

"Exactly." Alice shook her finger at Harper. "See, it was meant to be."

Harper settled deeper into the cushion as she took another sip of wine. Long ago, her butterflies had stopped taking laps every time she thought of Chelsea and any residual feelings had been whittled down to nothing more than fond memories. The kind of ghost thoughts that sent a momentary tingle up her spine when a certain song played or when she glanced into the night sky in a moment of stargazing. "Nah." She shook her head as she dismissed Alice's latest comment as common sense took hold. "This is silly. We can't afford a trip to London, and besides, Chelsea probably has a busy life with a drop-dead gorgeous wife, and no time to spare. Plus, I don't even know what part of England she lives in anymore, if at all."

"You're kidding."

"No, I'm not. The only things she's posted in the past few years are pictures of her sister's kids and their dog. Nothing really about her life or what she's doing. And apart from a happy birthday message, we don't communicate at all."

Alice stared wide-eyed. "That's fucking nuts." She extended her hand and fluttered her fingers in a gesture for Harper to hand over her device. "Gimme your phone."

"What, no, what are you going to do?"

"Nothing, just give me your phone. I want to look at more of her pictures while you go get me a glass of water. I think the wine's starting to hit me."

"Starting?" Harper chuckled, tossed Alice her phone, and rolled off the couch. "Don't drool on it."

"Ha ha."

Harper fumbled two glasses out of the cabinet, filled them with water, and let her thoughts float back in time until Chelsea's face was front and center in her mind. Could they have really made it work if Ryan hadn't gotten sick? She scoffed at the thought. No matter how many times and in how many ways she had asked the question, her mind wandered down the same dead-end road. No, was the answer. Not even a chance. And it wasn't just that she didn't believe in her own appeal—and as lame as that was, it was the painful truth of where she was at that time in her life—but they'd been teenagers. And what the hell do teenagers really know about life and love? Besides, Chelsea's primary relationship was with tennis. Even if she had stayed, tournaments and practices would have dominated her time, and eventually, they would have taken her away, and the end result would have been the same. Still, there had been moments in her life when she couldn't help but wonder if she should have tried harder to keep the connection between them alive.

Harper sighed. It was ridiculous to be thinking about it fifteen years later. And totally Alice's fault for filling her head with another crazy plan. She grabbed the glasses and headed back to the main room. *What's in the past is in the past.* Revisiting shoulda-coulda-wouldas was no way to go through life, or so she needed to keep reminding herself as that list continued to grow.

"Here's your water." She extended her hand, but Alice had her back turned and her head bowed. "Alice, what are you doing?"

"Nothing," Alice mumbled.

Harper placed the glasses on the table and craned her neck. Alice raised an elbow blocking her view as her fingers feverishly flew across her phone's screen. "Alice, seriously, what are you…Oh. My. God. You are *not* sending Chelsea a message, are you?"

Alice remained silent as Harper gasped. "Holy shit, you are, aren't you?! Gimme that back." Harper lunged at Alice, full tackle, grabbing her arm. "Give…me…my…phone." She grunted as she tried to overpower someone who never exercised a day in her life yet had a physique where, on her worst day, she could probably wrestle most men to the ground. "Alice…Alice!" Harper groaned as they rolled in a ball off the couch and onto the floor.

"There." Alice pressed a finger to the screen.

"Off…me…now." Harper coughed as she lay on her back, sandwiched between Alice and the floor.

Alice rolled off her and scooted against the couch.

"You sent her a message, didn't you?" Harper sat up, rubbed the crushing pain from her chest, and settled next to her.

"Well, I knew you'd chicken out, so yeah, I did…and you're welcome." Alice returned her phone.

"Alice…" Harper grumbled in shock as she glanced at her screen and her stomach bottomed out. "There's so many typos and incorrect words in this message it looks like a five-year-old typed it using a crayon."

Alice waved a hand. "Who cares about typos. Just tell her it was the AutoCorrect's fault."

"The message app doesn't have AutoCorrect."

"It doesn't?" Alice craned her neck and gazed at the screen. "Well, it should. Look at all those typos."

Harper let out a frustrated breath as she banged the back of her head against the cushion. "What if she thinks I actually wrote this? That I've turned into an illiterate moron?" She glanced at Alice. "You are hereby and forever more banned from ever touching my phone."

Alice leaned over and sloppily slapped at her device, hitting it twice.

"Really?" Harper faced her. "Are you four?"

"Oh, forget about the message. Let's talk about London." Alice grabbed the novel and held it up. "Look…" She circled her finger around the two women embracing. "This is us. Well, not really, I mean, I love you and all, but—"

"I know what you mean." Harper pushed the book away from her face, still feeling irritated.

"Harps..." Alice began to grovel. "Aren't you tired of always reading about someone else's adventures? Don't you think for once, it's worth it to splurge a little and go have one of our own? Two besties hanging out for three weeks in the land of fish and chips and sexy as hell accents." She snuggled closer to Harper. "This will be our itinerary." She slapped at the novel. "Everything that happened here is going to happen to us. You and me." She slurred as she wagged a finger between them. "Us."

Harper snatched the book from her and stared at the familiar cover, but this time she saw herself in the arms of the beautiful princess. Why couldn't she have a fairy-tale romance like the characters in the book? Yes, the novel was a complete fantasy, but stranger things in life had happened. Right? Well, to be fair, not in her life, but still...why not? She pinched the bridge of her nose and exhaled a long breath. Why was it so hard to just throw caution to the wind like Alice and worry about the consequences later? Maybe it was finally time to let loose a little and be a bit more spontaneous. After all, Alice had told her since they were kids, she needed to stop being as rigid as a rusty old Barbie doll.

"Come on, it'll be fun." Alice snaked her arm around Harper's shoulder and pulled her close.

Harper gazed into Alice's pleading eyes, and in a moment that tethered between *this is the stupidest idea ever* and *fuck it*, she nodded and said the words that would hopefully shake up her boring and predictable life and maybe bring a little magic to her world.

"Okay, let's go to London."

Chapter Two

It's so great to see you with a racquet in your hand." Denise fixed her with an earnest gaze, and Chelsea hoped this wasn't going to be one of those pep talks her sister loved to give her about playing more tennis. Talks that always seemed to lead to the importance of her finding more joy in life, and finding a woman to be "joyful" with. Her sister always had a lot to say about that.

"Millie wanted to play." Chelsea leaned the racquet against the table near Denise's back door. "To be honest, we spent more time looking for the ball in the bushes than hitting strokes against the wall, but I'm just happy she's well enough to run around again. Even if it is at seven in the morning." She tried to change the subject.

"Oh, God, me too. I can't tell you how much I want her back at school. It's been a long week. And thanks again for watching them last night. We really needed a night off."

"Are you staying for breakfast?" Millie barreled into the kitchen at just that moment, her cheeks red from the exercise. "Mom always does a proper breakfast when you're here. She makes us eat raw porridge the rest of the time."

Denise began to splutter out an objection as Millie ran upstairs offering to wake her little brother. Chelsea smiled. She loved being around her niece and nephew, and most of the time her sister was good company too. And if it was true that she spent a lot of time at her sister's because her own life felt kind of empty, it wasn't something she let herself dwell on.

"Are you staying?"

"I can. Not like I have anywhere else to be." It was a figure of speech. She hadn't meant to sound so pathetic. "I mean, I kind of feel obliged to stay now to make sure the kids get a decent breakfast."

"You're funny." Denise took a frying pan from the cupboard. "Go and get some sausages out of the spare fridge, then. And make us some more coffee. Stronger the better."

"Aye, aye, Captain."

Chelsea busied herself doing as she was told. She was older than Denise by three years, but Denise's vibe had become very big sisterly. It wasn't just that the pandemic had been bad for Chelsea—losing the restaurant she had loved and ending a relationship that she hadn't—but she knew she hadn't coped half as well as Denise when they'd lost Ryan. And everything that had happened since had obviously left Denise feeling like she had to look out for her. The kid sister who'd screamed at spiders almost as loudly as she had when Chelsea won a tennis match was now a fearless, and undeniably bossy, mother of two.

Her phone pinged. Another LinkedIn notification. She clicked on the link. Another job in an office, in front of a computer screen, dealing with unhappy people all day. It wasn't at all what she was looking for. She wanted something that made her want to jump out of bed every day, something involving her passion for food, and somewhere she could be her own boss. But not surprisingly, LinkedIn seemed all out of those kinds of jobs. She finished the coffee and set the machine to brew, annoying even herself with how downbeat she was feeling.

"I saved that one for you." Denise pointed at a paperback on the dining table with her spatula. "I didn't look at it properly when I picked it up at that rummage sale. Turns out it's all about lady loving. And FYI, the ladies do a LOT of loving. Had even me blushing." Denise dropped the sausages in the pan. "But it has a lovely happy ending. Might be just what you need to restore your faith in womankind." She pushed the book in Chelsea's direction.

"You know I don't read romances." Chelsea pushed the book back toward her sister. "Those happy endings you love so much drive me crazy. There should be mandatory sequels to all these books, where we see them arguing about money and realizing they are actually deeply incompatible."

"Wow, that's cynical even for you. I know they say misery loves company, but carry on like that and I'll start to wonder." Denise's tone was a lot softer than her words suggested. "I know it's been a rough few months—"

"Or years." Chelsea couldn't help herself. It had been. She had a right to feel miserable. The pandemic had been the last straw.

"I know. But me and your favorite brother-in-law are still in love all these years later. And look at Mom and Dad. Forty years next year."

"I know, I know." Chelsea relented. "I admit it's possible, but that kind of true love is hard to find. Harder than those books would ever admit. And before you say it, I know I'm not exactly doing much searching."

"And I know that Jennifer was a bitch. But there's—"

"Don't you dare say anything about fish and sea."

"I was just going to say that before Jennifer..." Denise paused. "Before Ryan died actually, you weren't this negative. And I know you even read romances back then, so I don't buy all this cynicism. You're in a funk and you just need something to go right. Something to get you out of it."

The noises from upstairs sounded like everyone was up and would soon be down for breakfast. And they were going to save Chelsea from this conversation. She could feel the tears at the back of her eyes. Not exactly unexpected, but still unwelcome.

Her phone pinged. And then again. Chelsea fished it out of her pocket. This time the Messenger icon told her she had messages. She clicked through to the app to see the name Harper Fallon in bold letters sitting at the top of her feed. She was surprised. She and Harper hadn't been in touch in a very long time.

She read the messages. And then read them again, not sure she wasn't hungry enough to be hallucinating. When she finally lifted her eyes from the phone, Denise was staring at her.

"You okay? I was asking you how many sausages you wanted, but you were so fixed on that phone that you didn't even hear me."

"Harper."

It wasn't much of an explanation.

"Harper?" Denise frowned.

"Yeah. Harper. From college."

"That nerdy one you used to hang out with? From Texas or somewhere like that? I met her when we came to visit. She was one of the few people there that didn't treat me like the nuisance I obviously was at that age. I didn't know you'd stayed in touch."

"Arizona actually." Chelsea shook her head. "And we aren't in touch. Not really. Just Facebook friends. Birthday messages, happy holiday wishes. You know how it goes."

Harper's first message was long—really long—and full of typos. The kind of errors Chelsea would never have expected from Harper. She'd been one of the smartest students in their year. And Denise wasn't being kind, but she was right. Harper had been a little nerdy. She had a book in her hand as often as Chelsea carried a racquet. But Chelsea liked that. Maybe they'd been unlikely friends, but they were close. And Chelsea had fallen hard for her. Really hard. But now she didn't know much about Harper's life, except that she was a teacher, and that she had posted for Hilary Clinton in 2016 like her life depended on it. Harper's Facebook feed was as empty as her own.

When Ryan had gotten sick, she'd lost a lot of friendships. The strain on the family as hope after hope was dashed was immense. They'd closed ranks as they tried to survive first his illness, and then his death. But losing touch with Harper had been the hardest. They had been young, but they had loved each other. And she'd meant to get back in touch when things settled down, but it took years for Chelsea to feel anything like normal again, and by then it was too late.

"And?"

Chelsea realized that Denise was staring at her expectantly.

"She's coming to London for three weeks. For a holiday. Wonders if I might want to meet up, show her around, and she hopes," Chelsea smiled and began reading from the text, "that I might be able to take her to Radclyffe Hall's grave, introduce her to an English princess, ideally a single one. Take her to Whitstable to eat oysters. And help her and her gorgeous friend Alice find somewhere where they can eat teeny tiny cucumber sandwiches and orange marmalade." She let out a breath. "I'm assuming not all at the same time."

"That's kind of weird."

"More than weird—" The penny dropped. Harper was drunk texting. The typos, the odd humor. Of course she was drunk. She did the math quickly. It was close to midnight in Phoenix. Chelsea felt disappointed. She'd imagined that Harper might actually be coming to London, and the idea of seeing her again had instantly lifted her mood.

Her eyes dropped to the last of the two texts that Harper had sent.

I'm sorry about that. Fat fingers getting carried away with wine and wishes. But I have missed you, I even miss watching you practice your serve.

The idea that Harper missed her was nice. Really nice. And not even the stab of shame she felt about not responding when Harper had reached out all those years ago could completely kill the feeling. Chelsea had had a lot of relationships over the years—some of them serious—but none of the women had compared to Harper. It was ridiculous to say it given how young they'd both been, but it was true. And the idea of Harper missing her felt good.

Chelsea checked herself. Harper had sent the texts while drunk—so anything she'd said was meaningless. She probably wasn't even coming to London. Still, Chelsea couldn't stop herself from smiling about all the times after practice when they had sat chatting in her truck together, talking about their hopes, and trying to learn each other's accents. They'd had their first kiss in that truck, and it had been where they finally had given in to their passion.

"Oh my God!" Denise practically shouted the words at her, brandishing the spatula. "I remember now. That soppy look is giving you away. You had a thing for her. You had a *huge* crush on her. You admitted it that one time. Remember when we were drunk and talking about the ones that got away? You talked about her. You said she was the one that got away." Denise spun around happily. "If this isn't the Universe throwing your miserable self a bone, I don't know what is."

Chelsea hated the way her body reacted to the idea of it being true. She felt herself lift—it was almost a physical thing.

"She's not really coming. She's drunk. Look, it even says so... wine and wishes. It's a wish, not an intention."

"You don't know that. What if she means it? Say yes. Go on, Chelsea. Say yes. You're not working right now. You liked her. And you have a spare room in your place. You know London is ridiculously expensive. Offer to put her up at yours. Give the Universe a helping hand."

"We were just kids, Dee. And I haven't seen her for…fifteen years. Don't start with all that. This isn't one of your romance novels."

"Okay, okay. Forget I said that. I just mean that you've been down in the dumps. She seems like a nice person. Someone you used to get on well with. Just take a chance. For once."

The challenge was obvious. And Chelsea couldn't think of a single thing to say in response. Her sister was right—like she often was. Infuriating but right. And one thing that had never changed in her life was her love for London. Her neighborhood was a great place to stay if you were a tourist. And Harper had even put Whitstable on her misspelled list of must-sees—it was one of Chelsea's favorite places. It had to be a sign of something.

She opened the app one more time and began to type a response. Denise, seemingly satisfied, turned back to the frying pan.

Noises upstairs suggested that the family would soon be joining them. She pushed her phone back into her pocket, not wanting to rush her reply. But she knew as well as Denise did that there was a chance that she might overthink it and get cold feet. When Harper had reached out before, Jennifer's ridiculous jealousy had stopped her from responding, even though she'd wanted to. This was a second chance she probably didn't deserve. She pulled her phone back out and quickly typed:

I'd love to see you. It's been far too long. I have a place here with a spare room. London is expensive, so you and Alice would be very welcome to stay here. I can't promise a princess, but I'm pretty sure I could sort you out with your desired (and kinda weird) sandwich choices.

She pressed send and closed her eyes. It was the most reckless thing she'd done in a long time. And if she was honest, she'd only managed to do it at all because she expected a sober Harper to say that she wasn't actually coming.

"They woke me up. They're demanding fried food." Mike came into the room, Nick on his back and Millie at his side. He leaned over and kissed Denise sweetly on the cheek, and Chelsea couldn't keep her heart from swelling with love for them all. Her family. Her safe haven. Safety, a quiet life, and keeping her family close had been all she'd wanted these past few years. She hoped that a reckless text wasn't going to upend all of that.

CHAPTER THREE

Harper woke to the sensation of Simon, her overweight orange tabby cat, flicking his tail in her face and loudly purring. She puffed a breath in his direction, hoping to shoo him away, but when the tickling continued, she lifted a heavy hand in his direction

"Wait. What?" She slurred the whispered words as she sleepily peeled an eye open and focused on her fingers, which weren't in fact wrapped around Simon's tail but instead around a twitching pair of fuzzy turquoise socks dotted with yellow smiley faces. "What the…" She raised her upper body, rested on her elbows, and moaned when her head began to throb in protest at the sudden shift in position.

She slowly glanced down the length of the couch while trying to gather floating bits and pieces of memory from last night. Alice was sprawled out next to her, in the opposite direction, snoring. The puzzle pieces that danced in her head were starting to come together. The book club, the wine, the talks of going to London…wait!

"Alice." She eked her name out through parched lips and a scratchy throat.

Nothing.

She shook her leg. "Alice, wake up."

"Go away, baby, I have nothing more to give," Alice grumbled as she turned to her side.

"Alice!" She instantly regretted raising her voice as her head pounded in protest.

"What?" Alice jerked, rolled onto the floor, and wedged herself between the couch and the coffee table. "Oww." She groaned to the carpet and, after exhaling a heavy sigh, slid her hands to her head and cupped her ears. “Who’s playing the drums so loud?”

“No one’s playing the drums. We fell asleep on the couch, and we’re both hungover.” Harper slowly sat upright, mindful not to make any sudden movements.

“Hungover?” After a fourth attempt that was accompanied by overdramatic moaning sounds, Alice flipped herself over, scooted her upper body against the couch, and sprawled her legs under the table. “And this is how you wake me?” She flopped her head back and gazed at Harper through squinted eyes. “What happened to coffee, a morning muffin, and the gentle cooing of doves?” Alice began rubbing her temples.

“Please tell me you’re not going to throw up.”

“No, I’m not going to throw up. I’m just trying to stop spinning. Why did you let me drink so much last night?”

“Me? You were the one that was all *let’s mix and match the leftover wine*.”

“Remind me to never play that game again.” Alice massaged her neck. “And for the record, your couch sucks as a bed. In fact, I’m giving this whole overnight stay a one-star review.”

“Alice?”

Nothing.

“Alice!”

“What? You’re such a grump in the morning, and could you please talk more quietly.”

“Hand me my phone,” Harper said. “I think something happened last night that we’re both going to regret.”

Alice flopped her hand on the coffee table, slowly spider-crawled her fingers over to Harper’s phone, and tossed it over her shoulder. “Well, considering we’re both dressed, I doubt whatever we did last night was that regrettable.”

Harper grabbed her phone and tapped her screen. Through blurry eyes and an increased pounding head, she tried her best to focus on the open page in front of her. “No…no, no, no.”

“What?”

“Look.” With a flip of her wrist, she presented her screen.

Alice snorted as she pushed the phone away. “And you honestly think I can read right now?”

"You messaged Chelsea last night."

"Chelsea?" Alice paused as she scrubbed her forehead. "From college? Why would I…ohhhh." Her eyes widened.

"Yeah, oh." Harper swung her legs on the floor. "And you told her we were coming to London."

"London? Why would we tell her that?"

"We…" She flopped her wrist back and forth as she pointed her finger between them. "Didn't. You, on the other hand, did." Harper tossed her phone onto the coffee table and cringed at the sound it made. She needed to clear her head, reread what she thought she read, and figure out a damage control action plan. Maybe Chelsea hadn't seen the message yet, and she could send off an *oops, sorry* reply before she felt painted into a corner. She slowly peeled herself off the couch and stumbled into the kitchen trying her hardest not to make the throbbing in her head worse. "Coffee?"

"Is that a question?" Alice said as she snaked her way back onto the couch.

Harper fumbled around her kitchen, then returned with a tray of two oversized mugs full of coffee, four pieces of buttery toast, and a bottle of aspirin. She chased down the pills with swallows of coffee and waited for the caffeine to work its magic before retrieving her phone. She winced as she refocused on the message Alice had sent. Then she noticed something she hadn't before. A separate message that she must have sent shortly after Alice's—and it included a phrase that was severely going to impact her ability to do damage control: *I've missed you.* What the actual fuck was she thinking? She considered deleting the messages, but the attached icons meant that Chelsea had already read both of them while she and Alice were sleeping off their alcohol-induced comas.

And then her brain kicked up a gear and she saw the message that Chelsea had sent back. It was definitely too late for deletions.

"Crap."

"What?" Alice said as she pressed the coffee mug to her forehead.

"Chelsea already replied."

"Really?" Alice pried the phone from Harper's hand and took a moment to gaze at the screen. "Wow. This sounds like a great vacation. Radclyffe Hall's grave, oysters in Whitstable, princesses and—" Alice scrunched her face. "Afternoon tea with cucumber sandwiches and orange marmalade? I hate cucumbers. Why would you put that in there?"

Harper cocked her head. "Again. *You* wrote the message, remember? And those sandwiches are right out of a scene from the book. When they were at that cute little café in Windsor and—"

Alice's eyes widened. "Oh yeah," she said. "Now I remember. Ooh, that *was* a cute scene. Maybe I should rethink my dislike for cucumbers."

"Yeah, well, I wouldn't go changing your palate just yet, because we're not going to London."

"What? But you said last night we were going."

"I was drunk."

"So? And will you stop doing that."

"Doing what?"

"Making excuses to back out of commitments because you suddenly feel uncomfortable and want to retreat to your ridiculously small comfort zone. Who cares if we were drunk last night? This vacation could be awesome…and recreating that novel is a great idea. In fact, come to think of it, one of my best. Besides, Chelsea already replied, so how are you going to walk that one back? Huh?"

"Alice, I—"

"No, Harps, no excuses. Wanna know why we had such a great time with the gay guys up in Flagstaff? Because by the time we figured out our mistake, we would have looked like assholes if we backed out. So we went with the flow, had an awesome weekend, and are now honorary lady bear cubs. So, I'm not listening to any of your excuses." She pointed at the phone. "Besides, Chelsea already said she'd love to see you."

Harper couldn't stop the feeling of hope that surged through her.

"And she said we could stay with her, so right there is a huge savings. And when I'm a little more functional, I'll search for deals on flights, and the rest we'll just figure out once we get over there."

Harper opened her mouth ready to offer one or two reasons why she couldn't go from her standard *excuses list* but could tell by Alice's expression she was ready to refute them all. Damn it, she needed to make a new list. "Refill?" When all else fails, divert and regroup.

"Thought you'd never ask, and I'd have to get up and do it myself." Alice handed over her cup. "A bit more almond milk this time."

Harper shuffled into the kitchen, placed the mugs next to the coffee machine, and took a moment to lean against the counter. She let out a deep breath and massaged her temples. After all these years, the thought of possibly seeing Chelsea again was every bit as exciting as it was paralyzing. Would they still have the chemistry they once had? Thinking once again about the night they had crossed the line into something else, something that still had the power to move Harper, she couldn't help but wonder. She sighed as she pushed off the counter and grabbed the almond milk from the refrigerator, annoyed with herself. She really did read too many romances. Real life just didn't lend itself to second chances like that. And again, she reminded herself, she was just a teenager who mistook raging hormones for love. And since then, time and life had widened the gap between them. Hell, she didn't even know if they'd get along anymore. She'd been left hanging by Chelsea so many times, she even questioned if there was enough between them to make a friendship.

"Hey, how's it going in there? You milking the almonds or what?" Alice called out.

"Coming!" She refreshed their mugs and headed back into the main room as her head swarmed with doubts. Thanks to Alice, she'd put herself out there without really meaning to. But unlike her past attempts, this time Chelsea responded. Almost immediately. And it sounded as though she had a genuine desire to see her.

"Sorry about that." Harper placed the cups on the coffee table, as her eye caught the cover of the book that had sparked this whole mess. The novel really was romantic, the characters had great chemistry, and the sex was sensual and steamy. Of all the books to choose to try to recreate, that one was the best. She sat down, took a deep uneasy breath, and turned to Alice. "You're right, let's do this."

"Serious?"

"Yes."

"No backing out?"

"No…" Harper shook her head. "No backing out."

Alice leaned over, locked her in a tight bear hug, and wiggled her back and forth. "This is going to be so much fun."

"Can't…breathe," Harper choked out.

Alice released her grip, settled back into the couch, and started rambling on about everything from the clothes she wanted to pack to the sections of the book she couldn't wait to recreate. Harper nodded and mumbled her *mm-hmms* as she tuned Alice out, opened the conversation thread on her phone, tilted her neck from side to side, took in another deep breath, and typed.

Chelsea, hi. It's so nice to hear from you and thank you for your generous offer. That's very kind.

She paused. This was it. The moment she could back out and tell her it was all a terrible misunderstanding that included way too much wine. But in truth, a trip to London was a bucket list opportunity and three magical weeks in the UK recreating all the scenes in the romance novel would not only be fun but make a lifetime of memories. And who knows, maybe she really would find her Princess Charming over there. At the very least it was a chance to reconnect with an old friend who had once touched her heart like no other.

As soon as Alice and I figure out the details, I'll let you know our dates, flight number, and arrival time. It seems like a lifetime ago since we last saw each other and it'll be really nice to catch up.

She paused and let her finger hover over the send icon. She let out an unsteady breath, glanced at the novel one last time, raised her eyes to heaven, and lowered her finger to the screen. There. She did it. They were going to London. There was no backing out now.

Harper couldn't stop tapping her foot as she stood at the designated curbside spot outside the entrance to Terminal 4 at Sky Harbor Airport. "Come on, Alice," she grumbled as she anxiously checked her phone for the umpteenth time. Alice had texted her over half an hour ago letting her know that her uncle Jerry was running late picking her up, but they should be there shortly. She wiped the sweat beads forming on her forehead with the back of her hand, swatted at a fly that was on a suicide mission if it continued to invade her personal space, and craned her neck as she glanced at the constant ebb and flow of cars dropping people off. None of which contained Alice. She let out a frustrated breath. Between the early morning triple digit heat, and the fact that they were well outside her comfort zone of getting there two hours ahead of departure time, her agitation level was pinging into the red zone. She activated her screen and was halfway into a strongly worded text, when a beat-up old oxidized silver Chevy SUV squealed into the space in front of her. A moment later, Alice rolled out from the passenger side of the vehicle. She wore lime green capri shorts, flip-flops, a T-shirt with a pink flamingo sipping on a drink, and oversized sunglasses, and a travel pillow was firmly clasped around her neck.

"Alice, we need to get going."

"And you think I don't know that?" She opened the back door, pulled out a backpack and a large hard-shell suitcase, and placed them on the curb.

"Hi, Harper."

"Hey, Jerry."

Alice's uncle scurried around and opened the hatch. "Sorry about the delay. There was an accident on the 101." He apologized as he pulled out the carry-on companion suitcase to Alice's large one and an oversized and overstuffed tote.

"Holy shit, Alice, you're not seriously bringing all that with you? How about the agreement we had about packing light?"

Alice cocked a knee and rested her weight on one hip. "First of all." She held up a finger. "Don't luggage shame me. I couldn't decide what to bring. These suitcases have warmer clothes in case it's chilly there. And those have all my cute summer wear." She pointed. "And since I knew you would stick to our promise and only bring your one suitcase, you can take my backpack with you as your carry-on, to save me an extra fee."

Harper rolled her eyes, shrugged on Alice's bulging backpack, and cocked her head. "Come on, we gotta get going. Bye, Jerry."

Alice thanked her uncle with a quick hug, then scampered after Harper as they made their way into the airport, checked their bags, and found their place in the long and winding security line.

"We're never going to make our flight." Harper hunched her shoulders and let Alice's backpack drop to her feet as her stomach knotted with anxiety. She should have known this trip was too good to be true. Chelsea's offer of letting them stay at her place, Alice's successful hunt for discounted plane tickets, and an itinerary that could rival any tour company.

"I could fake having stomach cramps and tell people we need to get through the line fast so I can use a restroom." Alice grabbed her side and began to moan.

"Stop that." Harper slapped her hand. "Before you go embarrassing and scarring me for life, let's first see how fast this line moves. Okay?"

"But…"

"No, Alice, we're going to be mature about this," Harper said as she craned her neck to get a better glimpse of the length of the line and immediately began to rethink Alice's offer.

"Did you at least pack something cute to change into at the other end?"

Harper caught the up-and-down movement of Alice's head as she considered her sweatpants, faded T-shirt, and hoodie jacket slung over her shoulder.

"You know I get cold on planes. Besides, I'm comfortable in this, so why would I—"

"Damn, Harps, you haven't seen her for fifteen years, and you didn't think maybe you should make a little effort?"

"Really?" Harper gave her the eye. "Says the woman wearing a T-shirt with an image of a drunken flamingo on her chest. Besides, this trip isn't about impressing Chelsea, it's about having fun. We're invited because she's being nice, not because she's interested in me." Harper sounded defiant, but the unexpected sinking feeling was one she couldn't help. Maybe she should have made a bit of an effort?

"Honestly, Harps, for someone with a brain your size, you can be clueless sometimes." She unzipped Harper's suitcase and began riffling through her clothes. She held up a peach T-shirt before folding it and shoving it in her backpack. "It sounded to me like she's as single as we are right now." The line moved forward, and Alice shoved Harper's case a few feet with her foot before crouching down next to it again. "Here, these jeans look good on you." She rolled them up and held them out to Harper. "You have a great ass, you should take advantage of it."

"I'm going to take advantage of sitting comfortably on it for the next fifteen plus hours in my sweatpants." She sighed at the thought, wishing they could have afforded a nonstop flight.

Alice cleared her throat and shoved the jeans closer to her. Harper rolled her eyes as she put the jeans in the backpack, more to appease Alice than having any thoughts to change into them. Fashion was not a prerequisite for rekindling a friendship. Especially one that had all but died on the vine years ago.

❖

Fifty-five minutes later, Harper whined as she sat on a metal bench fumbling to retie the laces on her tennis shoes. "You'd think by now, they could figure out a more efficient way to screen people."

"Come on." Alice grabbed Harper's arm, pulling her into motion as the boarding announcement was called for their flight. The screen above their heads told her that they had twenty-eight gates to cover, and there was a sea of people between here and there to dodge. "I'm going to flag down one of those guys driving those golf carts and have 'em take us to our gate." Alice shoved two fingers in her mouth, blew out a deafening whistle, and summoned a driver.

"Gate B28!" Harper called out as they tossed their bags on board the cart and hopped in.

"And step on it…" Alice leaned over and read the nametag. "Peter. And if you get us there quickly, my friend here will grace your palm with a twenty."

"Me?" Harper huffed in protest as Peter floored the accelerator as much as possible while beeping a horn that sounded like it came off a child's tricycle.

"Seriously?" Alice said when no one seemed to heed to the cart and their urgency. She began waving her arms and used her booming voice to tell people to get out of the way, they were "Coming through, people! Move…move!"

"That's us!" Harper announced as the cart came to a stop. They jumped off and gathered their belongings

"Pay the man," Alice called over her shoulder as she jogged up to the perky-looking gate attendant, shoved the QR codes on her phone's screen in her face, and waved for Harper to catch up. "Harps, let's go!"

"I'm coming." Harper dug in her purse and extended a twenty-dollar bill toward Peter, who tipped his uniform cap and smiled. She scurried past the attendant and flanked Alice, who was already halfway down the boarding bridge. Once on board, she filed in behind her and apologized to the passengers who Alice unknowingly thumped in the head or shoulder with her tote, as they made their way to their designated seats.

"Dibs on the window seat," Alice announced as she shoved her luggage in the overhead compartment, squeezed past the woman sitting in the aisle seat, and flopped down. "Well, that was fun." She chuckled as she combed her fingers through her hair and twisted open the overhead AC nozzle.

Harper frowned as she buckled her seat belt and tried to calm her accelerated heart rate. The trip had yet to officially begin, and already she was frazzled and flustered. "Don't ever do that to me again."

"What? It wasn't my fault Uncle Jerry was…Oh my God." Alice sat up straight as she placed her hand on Harper's forearm and squeezed. "The book."

"What book?"

"*The* book. Don't you remember? The opening scene. Our heroine running through the airport to catch a flight to London that she almost missed. It's got to be a sign." She turned wide-eyed to Harper. "We're already recreating the novel."

Harper dismissed Alice with a wave of her hand as she glanced past her and out the window. Was it a sign? Nah, just a weird coincidence.

"A lot of people run through airports in a hurry to catch their flight, Alice. Not everything is a sign of something."

But as the plane pushed back from the gate, accelerated down the runway, and banked to the east, she couldn't help but wonder. The real *sign* that was tickling its way up her body had nothing to do with the coincidence at the airport. Nor was it about the thrill of making new memories in a city she had always romanticized. No, this sign was an old familiar one that she thought was long gone. She shook it away as she watched a patch of clouds engulf the plane. If this trip was going to change their lives, or even just give them one hell of a summer vacation to remember, she had to open herself up to possibilities. It wouldn't be easy, but she was going to try.

Chapter Four

Chelsea hated driving, and the journey to the airport had been a nightmare. She didn't own a car. Not only was there nowhere to park it near her apartment, but she had a Tube station less than one hundred meters from her front door. When she had offered to collect Harper and Alice, she hadn't been thinking straight. Instead of the little Zipcar she had driven here, with her hands gripping the wheel the whole way, it would have been a lot easier for them all to have taken an Uber back to hers. And her anxiety levels would be three hundred percent lower.

She couldn't entirely blame the London traffic for her stress. She had been getting more nervous as the days to Harper's visit ticked down. What had seemed like an adventure, a chance to have some fun, had turned into her examining every aspect of her life and wondering if Harper would find it as wanting as she did. Getting her apartment ready for her guests had her wondering if it would seem poky. Cleaning the mirror in the hallway had made her realize that losing her love for tennis had also meant losing that athletic shape that Harper would remember. It wouldn't feel so bad if Harper had let herself go too…but the few Facebook photos there were of Harper told Chelsea that she looked as great as ever.

She sighed, willing herself to get into a more positive mood. She'd had her hair cut that week and quite liked the shorter restyle she'd been talked into. And if her apartment was small, it didn't matter, because her neighborhood was great. Full of artists, hip coffee shops, and eccentric little stores. And if Harper was going to judge her for the weight she'd gained—or for any of it really—then she wasn't the Harper that Chelsea remembered.

The phone in her hand beeped. A message telling her Harper and Alice had cleared customs, picked up their suitcases, and were on the way to the agreed pick-up zone. Chelsea got out of the car and peered toward the terminal exit, her heart beating a little faster than she wanted at the prospect of seeing Harper again. She couldn't help but smile as a curvy red-haired woman, wearing huge shades, and with an enormous pillow around her neck, struggled to maneuver a trolley laden with bags through the revolving doors. Chelsea could hear her colorful language from the curb. And emerging from behind the woman was Harper. Chelsea was close enough to see her raise her eyes to the heavens as the other woman—who she now recognized as Alice—swiped her sideways with the trolley. It made her smile. That eye roll was something familiar to her. Something Harper had given to Chelsea every time she'd paid her a compliment. And she'd paid her a lot of compliments. She'd wanted to get closer to Harper in that way, but Harper had batted the attention away. Until she hadn't… Chelsea swallowed, the memory of the first time they made love ridiculously clear in her mind.

She stepped forward just as Harper raised a hand in her direction and smiled. And that smile, that small smile, made Chelsea feel surprisingly weak at the knees, stirring up a desire she hadn't felt in years. Harper looked great. She had on faded jeans that hugged her figure wonderfully well, and a peach-colored T-shirt that contrasted beautifully with her shoulder-length black hair and aqua blue eyes.

"Hey." Chelsea lifted a matching hand in greeting. "How was the flight?"

"Fine, thanks." Harper spoke softly and continued smiling. They were now face-to-face, just a couple of meters apart, and Chelsea had a strange urge to step forward and hug her. She didn't. It had been too long. And their college friendship, while close, had never been a hugging kind of friendship.

"Not fine actually. Long. With stops." Alice stepped from behind Harper, wrapped her arms tightly around Chelsea and leaned back, almost lifting her from the ground. "It's been like what…*forever* since I last saw you." She let go. "And Air France cut me off. Can you believe it? Gave me the 'perhaps madam has had enough wine' speech. Pfft, as though there's such a thing as *enough*. I don't think that would have happened at home."

"We were at home. I don't think we'd even cleared American airspace." Harper laughed softly and Chelsea couldn't stop staring at how beautiful she was. Harper had always been cute, but older Harper was simply stunning, even dressed in jeans and a creased T-shirt. Chelsea wondered if she was still oblivious to her beauty. "Sorry, she's never a good flyer. And drunk, she's either grouchy like this, or tons of fun. Nothing in between."

"And what kind of drunk are you?" Chelsea wanted to take back the words as soon as she'd said them. "Sorry, weird question." She tried to recover herself. "I mean, I don't remember us ever really drinking together."

Harper looked at her for a beat, her expression hard to read. "Yeah, there wasn't much drinking. Guess I was too reserved, and you were always into your fitness."

Chelsea felt like she should say something—tell Harper she had loved how buttoned up she was—but she had obviously lost her right to say such things. For a second, there was awkwardness between them. And not for the first time, Chelsea wondered if this had been a good idea.

"The clouds are nice." Alice cut through the silence, pulling her sunglasses off. "But are you kidding with this humidity?" She plucked the pillow from around her neck and used it to fan herself.

This was definitely grouchy Alice.

"Welcome to London. It's always some kind of wet here—spring, summer, winter—" Chelsea saw the mischief flash across Alice's face before she had even finished the sentence.

"Wet, you say? Well now, that might be f—"

"Alice!" Harper interrupted her, sounding embarrassed.

Chelsea suppressed a smile.

"Erm…why don't we get going, then? You must both be tired, and getting out of Heathrow is always hellish." Chelsea indicated her car.

"That car?" Alice pointed. "You're gonna put this luggage"—she waved her finger in the air between them—"and the three of us…in that teeny-weeny thing?"

"Alice, don't be rude."

"It's okay." Chelsea laughed. "It's not mine, it's a rental. It is small. But the boot is surprisingly roomy." She walked across and popped it open.

"*The boot is surprisingly roomy*." The echo came from Alice. Attempting an English accent Mary Poppins would be proud of. "Oh God, I've forgotten how much I loved your accent. If everyone here speaks like that, I'm going to fall in love every day. Princess or not."

Chelsea couldn't help but find Alice funny. "Funnily enough, everyone here does speak like that. This being England and all. I mean, not quite like THAT version of English." Chelsea kept her tone light. "But kind of. And the princesses definitely do." She winked at Alice and earned a big smile from Harper that felt as good as anything that had happened to her in months.

Chelsea picked up the first of the suitcases and Harper immediately came to her side, helping her to load the luggage.

"Sorry. As you can see, Alice hasn't changed much. She's never had much of a filter in the best of times. But with the time zones and free wine, she seems to be in rare form."

"No problem. She's always been fun. You chose a great bestie. In fact, you were always a better judge of character than me."

She was. Harper had always been able to spot the women who were going to fuck her over in college. It was a pity she hadn't been around to warn her about Jennifer. But again, she had no idea why she'd said the thought out loud. Being around Harper was making her weird.

They stood back side by side and admired the perfectly packed luggage before slamming the boot shut.

Harper turned to her.

"Thanks so much for meeting us and for letting us stay." Harper's gaze was earnest. "You didn't have to. I know it's been a really long time since we've seen each other."

"Too long. And spending time with you again is going to be a pleasure." She held Harper's gaze for an instant until she felt herself flush with embarrassment. She felt like she was back in college, trying to get Harper to notice her that way. She hadn't expected her feelings for Harper to be quite so present day. "Though I'm not so sure about Alice." She recovered herself and pointed at Alice as she climbed clumsily into the back seat of the car, complaining to herself about whether the "little car" had decent air conditioning.

Harper shook her head at Alice and then looked back at her as if she had something she wanted to say. Instead, she just nodded. "Heathrow is simply hellish. Let's get out of here." The accent was close to perfect, and Chelsea laughed as she watched Harper walk to the wrong side of the car.

❖

"I have to say, the quiet is kinda nice." Harper spoke softly and Chelsea knew she was trying not to wake Alice, who had fallen asleep before they'd even cleared the airport perimeter.

They'd chatted amiably for half an hour without saying very much at all. Talking about the journey, the in-flight movies that Harper had watched, and the scorching weather that they'd left behind in Phoenix—the one thing Chelsea had not missed when she left.

"You can say it, I wouldn't dare."

"Oh, I think you would. I remember you as being very willing to speak your mind. I was always the timid one."

Harper again went for self-deprecation. It seemed to Chelsea that her opinion of Harper was a lot higher than Harper's own view of herself. If they had been friends like before, she would have said something.

"I've changed a lot."

"So have I." Harper paused, seeming thoughtful, and Chelsea wondered if she felt the same regret about the fact that they hadn't stayed in touch. At some point, she needed to apologize, to try to explain. "But Alice, not so much." Harper smiled and the moment passed.

"It's nice you stayed besties." Chelsea had left her own school friends to go to the States and made no effort to reconnect with them when she came home. After everything that happened in the years that followed, a best friend would have been nice.

"Yeah. She's the sister I never had and always wanted. I know she didn't hang out with us all that much, but that's because she was in one of those relationships where you hardly come up for air. You know how those can be. Like you're living in a bubble and no one else exists."

Harper paused, giving Chelsea just enough time to wonder if she was speaking from experience.

"She loved going to your tennis matches, though. One of the few things she got out of Ruth's bed for. Cheered as loud as I did when you won that USTA tournament in Scottsdale."

Chelsea felt herself tense. She had expected this. Expected Harper to ask her about tennis. She had practiced explaining to people why she no longer played. But she felt that Harper would feel like she'd failed somehow, would pity her, and she didn't want that. A year ago, she could have talked about the restaurant instead, about what a success it was. It wasn't tennis superstardom, but it was something she had been very proud of. She gripped the steering wheel a little harder, staying silent, and waiting. But no question came.

"She really is the best, and she's been by my side for every accomplishment, stupid decision, or heartbreak I've had. And even though she can be infuriating at times, I can't imagine my life without her."

There was another opening there for Chelsea. She imagined it was Harper's way of giving her a chance to talk about the past, to explain, but without really asking. She had always been gentle like that. Ahead of Chelsea was a long line of cars. The GPS told her they were still an hour away from home. There was enough time to have the conversation they needed to have. But she wasn't ready.

"I'd love you to tell me about the accomplishments. If you want to, that is."

She had bottled it, bottled the chance to explain everything to Harper. When she glanced sideways, she could see Harper looking at her. Her expression was open and neutral. Was it possible that she was reading too much into everything, and Harper hadn't even cared that they'd lost touch?

"Well, let's see…" Harper laced and unlaced her fingers in her lap. There was nervousness but Chelsea wasn't sure why. "I finally got my doctorate. I even had it published—"

"You did? That's fantastic. Really! I mean, I kind of knew you'd do it. You were so smart, and so driven. I was always so in awe of that. But I hadn't picked any of that up from Facebook. Dr. Harper Fallon. That is bloody cool."

"Thanks. It was a long time coming, but I haven't really done much with it, so I'm not sure if it even counts as that much of an accomplishment. It was supposed to be my way out of teaching, but somehow, I'm still stuck in the same job I've been doing since graduation. I often wonder if the title was worth the sacrifices."

"You do that a lot." This time Chelsea let herself say it.

"What?"

"Put yourself down. Underplay how great you are. You shouldn't. Some of us are really underachieving. If you don't feel proud of what you've done, of who you are, what hope is there for the rest of us?"

Harper gave a slight chuckle. "Well, I am proud of the doctorate, just disappointed that I haven't put it to good use. Seems like the only decisions I've put in motion these days end up questionable and cringeworthy."

"So, tell me about them as well." Chelsea was taking a risk. She wasn't someone who usually came this far forward in a conversation, but Harper made her want to. The car was quiet, the atmosphere a little uncomfortable now. She regretted asking. She really had no right. There was a long pause. "Or feel free to tell me I've no right to ask."

"Ow! Ow, ow, fuck, owww!" The noises came from the seat behind Chelsea. They were accompanied by some kicks to the back of her seat and a lot of wriggling around. "I've got a cramp. Help! Owww!"

Alice stuck her leg between the front seats and Harper reached around to massage the back of Alice's calf vigorously. As Harper rotated her foot, Alice cried out even more. She was louder than Denise had been when she was giving birth.

"Alice gets these charley horse cramps when she doesn't drink enough water." Harper spoke as her fingers kneaded the calf. "I told you to hydrate when we were on the plane."

"I did."

"Water, Alice, not Merlot."

As fast as the leg had appeared, Alice withdrew it. "It's better now, thanks."

Chelsea watched in the rearview mirror as she began fanning herself again with her neck pillow.

"I don't think it's the wine, I think it's the humidity. Is your air conditioning even working? And where are we?"

"On the left is Regent's Park. We're half an hour away, less if the traffic is kind."

"Regent's Park?" Alice poked her head into the space between the front seats. "OMG!" she shouted excitedly. "They had their first misunderstanding there. Harps, do you remember? It was in Regent's Park. She stormed off and the princess went after her and they kissed at the top of some hill with amazing views over London. I can't remember the name."

"Primrose Hill?" Chelsea was confused. "It's just behind Regent's Park. The views are pretty good up—"

"Harper, tell me that isn't a sign?" Alice banged the headrest emphatically. "I woke up with a cramp just as we passed Regent's Park. Just as we passed! It has to be a sign. First almost missing our plane and now this." Alice nestled back in her seat looking satisfied. "And I loved that scene where they kissed; it was hot."

"What is a sign of what? And who kissed who in a hot way on Primrose Hill?" Chelsea had no idea what they were talking about.

"It's nothing." Harper turned to Alice as she replied to Chelsea. "Right, Alice? Just a book we read."

She was trying to close down a conversation that Chelsea was now much keener to have.

"What book?"

"Harper formed a reading group called the Romance Lovers Book Club. And we read this book…" Alice leaned forward into the space again. Still animated. "It's the reason we came, actually. Tell her, Harper, tell her about the book."

Chelsea heard the deep sigh that escaped from Harper, noticing the slight slump in her posture.

"I'm sure she's not interested, Alice."

"On the contrary, I'm very interested." Her tone was teasing. "Especially now I can see you don't want to tell me about it."

"We read a novel about an American tourist who meets a woman in London, has a whirlwind romance, and visits a lot of amazing places. So we…" Harper hesitated. "We decided to see the sights highlighted in the book for ourselves." She turned to Alice. "And that's pretty much it, and why we're here."

That clearly wasn't it. Chelsea waited. She didn't know Alice all that well, but she had a hunch that if there was more to say, Alice wouldn't let her down.

"Ha, not even close. The other character was a princess. She was English—obviously—and she gets in a car accident outside Buckingham

Palace with the American tourist. They fall in love, and after way too much angst, they kiss for the first time on that hill. Primrose Hill." She rolled her tongue around the name. "The book's called *Holiday of a Lifetime*. If you haven't read it, you should. It's a great read, and we just thought that since our own lives are so devoid of love and romance right now, we'd come to England and try to recreate the whole—"

"Alice!"

Chelsea realized that this trip was going to involve a lot of Harper scolding Alice for saying the wrong thing. She had wanted to know whether Harper had someone special in her life—hell, she'd even scrolled through Facebook in the hope of finding out—but not like this. She could tell Harper was squirming next to her. She threw her a rope.

"Well, Primrose Hill is a great place for a first kiss. But I'm not sure how realistic a car accident outside Buckingham Palace is. As you can see," she pointed out the window at the lines of traffic stretched out either side of them, "tourists should avoid going anywhere by car." She turned her head and looked at Harper directly. "And I'm sorry I didn't have the good sense to suggest the Tube. Might have made this journey a bit less hellish."

She was talking about the traffic, of course, but she was also talking about the conversation that Alice had started that Harper clearly hadn't wanted to have.

Harper nodded, looking a bit forlorn.

She pointed out the window on Harper's side of the car. "That's the British Library. A very cool place. Has a great little museum. You'd love it. Try and fit it in if you can. And the trains to Whitstable go from just around the corner. It's one of my favorite places, so I'm hoping to tag along with you if you'll have me."

"That would be great." Harper sat up a bit straighter in the seat, before peering out at the library. "And thank you."

Chelsea wasn't sure what she was being thanked for, but she replied as every British person would. "My pleasure."

CHAPTER FIVE

Harper couldn't get enough of the cozy little East End pub from the late 1800s with the endearing name. The Golden Heart was dimly lit, with dark wood walls and furnishings throughout. There was a long, narrow bar against the far wall displaying a wide range of British ales, and it was her intention to try as many of them as she could over the course of the vacation. Even though she considered herself more of a wine connoisseur, on her many Google searches for things to do in London, several mentioned how crucial it was to sample the local beer while visiting the city.

They bellied up to the bar, and as they stood waiting to order, Harper took the moment to study Chelsea. Gone was the lanky teenager with the bouncy ponytail. Instead, the person who stood next to her now was a woman who had grown beautifully into her body. She was stunning. Her auburn hair looked less blond, much shorter, and fashionably styled. The simple outfit she had chosen—a fitted black T-shirt and maroon capri pants—accentuated the curves that were also new to Harper. Her silver necklace matched her bracelet, and there was something effortless about the way Chelsea was put together that made Harper feel just as self-conscious around her as she had when they'd been in college.

"Whit ya's hevin'?" The bartender's thick Scottish accent broke into her thoughts.

"Um…" She turned to Chelsea for guidance.

"Two Young's Double Chocolate Stouts, please."

"Em, any food? The hamemade pork scratchings ur good." The

bartender emphasized with an arched brow that seemed to convey they'd be missing out on something delicious if they didn't place an order.

"No, but thank you." Chelsea waved her off.

The woman shrugged, and as she left, Harper leaned into Chelsea. "Do I even want to know what pork scratchings are?"

"No, you don't. Trust me, they're not good. Although, I will admit, this place makes some pretty amazing Scotch eggs."

"In that case…" Harper trailed off as she glanced again around the pub that was built long before Arizona was even a state. It felt rich in history and stories, and she could only imagine the conversations that had taken place within these walls over the centuries. Such a contrast to the newly constructed and nondescript bars in her neighborhood. "Next time we come to this *boozer*, I'll try some," she repeated the word that Chelsea had used to reference the place when they arrived.

"Hey, look at you sounding all English already."

Harper's attempt earned her a smile from Chelsea, which had an effect on her that was unexpected. But not unfamiliar. It had always been one of Chelsea's most charming features, and it gave her the tingles now as much as it had in college. Harper dismissively shook her head, and with it tried to shake away the desire that she had wrongly assumed had withered away with time.

"You know, I feel a little guilty leaving Alice behind. She'd love this place. But I will admit, it's nice to have some one-on-one time to catch up with you." Once Chelsea settled them into her small two-bedroom flat, fed them a delicious home-cooked meal of falafel, flatbreads, and Greek salad, Alice promptly fell asleep on the couch. After two failed attempts to wake her, they pinned a note to her T-shirt and snuck off for a beer. "I keep waiting for the jet lag to hit me too, but I feel fine."

"I'm pretty sure late afternoon drinking might have something to say about that."

Again, the smile as another pause fell between them. The ponytail and sportswear weren't the only things that were missing from her memories of Chelsea. Gone too was the person who could seemingly talk nonstop to Harper about anything and everything. Movies, food, politics, and America's love of big trucks being her favorite topics. Instead, a more reserved and withdrawn Chelsea seemed to have emerged. And it seemed like they had lost the connection that seemed to fuel the uninhibited conversations that used to easily flow between them. The battle scars of life, loss, and responsibilities seemed to have reshaped the adults they had become.

"Oh, I'm sure it will, but I kinda want to stay up. I'm afraid if I take a nap, I won't get a good night's sleep tonight."

"I hope you'll be comfortable at my place." Chelsea broke eye contact, glanced down, and fidgeted ever so slightly. "I know it's kinda small by American standards," she quietly said more to herself than Harper.

"Are you kidding, it's perfect. And not only that, you're saving us a ton of money, so thank you."

"Thir you'se go." The bartender placed two large glasses with foam snaking down the sides in front of them.

Chelsea lifted her pint. "Cheers. It's nice to see you again, Harper."

"You too, Chelsea." She touched her glass to Chelsea's and took a drink. "Wow." She coughed. "That's, uh, that's pretty chocolatey. And strong."

"You don't like it?"

"No, I do like it. It's just not what I was expecting, but in a good way."

They grabbed their beers, snagged a booth in the back corner of the pub, and sat down. As another awkward pause settled between them, Harper took a smaller, more conservative sip of the malty dark beer with the pungent taste. She searched her mind to remember the common topics they used to share and scolded herself for not making more of an effort to keep in touch. Between a full time job, working her way through her advanced degrees, and trying to maintain multiple failed attempts at relationships, time had become a scarce commodity. Wait, scratch that. She'd have found time for Chelsea, if Chelsea had given her the slightest indication that she'd had time for her.

"Remember Super Scoops? The little ice cream shop on Mill Avenue that made those huge frothy chocolate milkshakes?" Harper figured maybe the best place to begin to get to know each other in the present was to start in the past.

Chelsea's face lit up. "I loved Super Scoops. They used to sprinkle frozen bits of candy bars on the top, and I would always get—"

"Crumbled Snickers bar!" they said in unison, then laughed.

"Wow, I haven't thought about that place in a long time. Do you still go there?"

"No." Harper shook her head. "They tore it down years ago to build a high-rise apartment complex."

"What? No. Seriously?"

"Yep. Most of that area, including the campus, is now nothing but buildings, concrete, and an endless sea of people. You wouldn't recognize it. In fact, the whole city has become a mini-LA, and lately, I've actually been thinking about moving because I'm getting really tired of the traffic."

"Oh yeah, where would you go?"

"I'm not sure. Maybe head north to Flagstaff and see if I can get a job in NAU's English department and finally put my PhD to work."

"Think you could handle the winters?"

"If you ask me that when we've had back-to-back months of over a hundred degrees, my answer is always yes. But truthfully, I wouldn't know the first thing about driving in or shoveling snow, so for self-preservation, I should probably stick to the warmer parts of the state."

"Remember that day you told me you could fry an egg on the asphalt? You bet me a pizza dinner it would cook in a minute."

"I do remember that." Harper snorted. "And I also remember you winning the bet because of a technicality."

"It wasn't a technicality. A runny egg that is barely cooked around the outer edge didn't count."

"Face it, you just wanted a free pizza that night."

At the mention of the pizza, Harper felt heat and an unexpected tingle rise up her body. That night was the night they had first made love. They had waited until just before sunset to order the two-for-one Chicago-style pies from a small takeout-only place just off campus. They drove up to South Mountain, sat on the tailgate of her truck, and ate while watching the sun set over the city. When a storm kicked up, they crawled into the bed of the pickup, her camper shell shielding them from the rain, lay on a blowup mattress, and talked nonstop. The energy between them was nervous and heightened, and eventually they admitted to having feelings for each other.

Harper had really wanted Chelsea to kiss her, but when she didn't, she gathered her courage, rolled onto her side, and took Chelsea's hand. It was enough. Chelsea leaned in and kissed her, at first tentatively, and then more passionately. And they hadn't stopped kissing until they were undressed, touching, and greedily claiming each other over and over. The months of desire finally found expression in the unlikeliest of places. At midnight, exhausted and wrapped gloriously in each other's arms, they had fallen asleep. It was one of the best nights of her life.

The next day, Chelsea got the call from her parents breaking the news about Ryan's diagnosis, and three days later she was gone. It was hard saying good-bye, but it would have been a lot harder if she'd known that it was the last time she would see Chelsea for fifteen long years.

"Ever wish you could go back in time?" Harper said as Chelsea looked at her with surprise and she wondered if she should clarify the comment. "I just mean that everything seemed so much less complicated back then. I don't know if it was our age, or if life really was that much simpler. No tough decisions to make, and not yet disappointed with life."

"Maybe it was like that for you, but it wasn't for me. I'm glad I'm no longer living in those days."

"I'm sorry. I can't imagine what you went through with Ryan. I don't know why I said that. Of course you wouldn't want to relive that."

"I'm not talking about Ryan. I just mean life in general back then wasn't as easy as you're making it sound."

"I don't understand. You had it made back then. Full scholarship, popular on campus, big future in tennis. You had the world at your fingertips, and you had no idea how many times I wished I was you."

"You wished you were *me*?" Chelsea scoffed and shook her head. "I used to wish I was *you*."

"Me? Why me? I was awkward and had no social skills. My entire friendship circle consisted of you and Alice, and let's face it, I possessed nothing that would ever have qualified me as one of the *it crowd*." She repeated the phrase she and Alice dismissively used when they referred to the students who flaunted their status and popularity. "I mean, come on, you had what, like hundreds of friends."

"Not even close." Chelsea looked at her. "Most of them were just hanging around, expecting me to make it big…and look how that turned out." Her words contained a bitterness that made Harper sad. "And even if I did have more friends, it doesn't mean anything." She broke eye contact as she glanced down and fidgeted a bit in her seat. "I was struggling back then—not just trying to keep my grades up while practicing six hours a day but trying to win enough tennis matches to keep everyone happy. It wasn't easy. I mean, I was good at the game…I just wasn't good *enough*, and nobody wanted to say it. It actually made me hate tennis. But I didn't have a clue what else to do. I wasn't academic like you. I guess that's why when Ryan got sick, and they needed me at home, I was willing to walk away from everything. And watching him suffer like he did, all I wanted was to be left alone. I stopped practicing, let my coach go, I couldn't get my head back in the game. At twenty-one I was washed up. And I didn't even care."

When Chelsea flicked her eyes from the table to her, she could see the pain, and Harper felt an impulse to reach for her.

"I abandoned the few friends that tried to stay in touch—hell, I even let you go. After everything. You meant so much to me and you tried so hard for those first few years to stay in my life. But I just couldn't respond. I can't explain it, and I'm not making excuses, but everything felt so overwhelming, and I felt so empty."

This time Harper leaned across the table and took Chelsea's hand.

"Chels, I had no idea things were that bad. I just figured you had moved on. Why didn't you tell me? If I'd known I would've—"

Harper stopped herself. What would she have done? She was in Phoenix, she had her studies, her exams. And Chelsea was thousands of miles away.

"I should have." Chelsea shrugged. "I'm really sorry for not staying in touch. But I just wasn't in the best of places."

Harper gave her a knowing nod. She understood what depression felt like, and how she had felt the heavy weight of its suffocating blanket tighten around her after her parents divorced. The last thing she wanted to do was talk about it and relive the pain.

"Plus…" Chelsea continued. "I felt like such a waste of space without tennis. I kind of figured you—everyone—would do better without me around." She took a gulp of beer, then leaned forward on the table. "I held my first tennis racket when I was four. I was eight when I played my first competitive match. My summers were spent in tennis clinics and playing tournaments. By sixteen, people started talking about me going pro, and it got even crazier. I might have seemed put together on the outside, but that was an act. On the inside, I was falling apart and screaming. That's why it was so nice hanging with you. You made me feel like I had something to offer that wasn't tennis. We could go to the movies, hang out in your dorm room, or spend hours in that back booth at Super Scoops until we closed the place down, and just be…normal." Chelsea whispered the word, as though it was a distant dream in a fog.

"We did have some pretty good times back then, didn't we?"

"Yeah, we did."

Harper released Chelsea's hand and sat back in her seat. No wonder they had become fast friends. As different as they were, they were facing similar pressures. And they both needed an outlet. Where Chelsea's was athletic, hers was academic. Her dad sang her mathematics time tables instead of nursery rhymes, and her mom conducted nightly reading sessions from the time she could hold a book in her hands. Spelling bees, chess tournaments, and science clubs followed. The constant push for her to maintain high grades and pursue advanced degrees was made crystal clear from the time she was a kid. It was her parents' wish, not hers, that had pushed her all the way to the doctorate she hadn't even wanted and didn't know what to do with. A life lived trying to fulfill other people's expectations? Yeah, she knew all about that. She gazed at Chelsea with a new understanding. They'd never had the chance to have this conversation. There were so many things time and distance robbed them of. Harper tried not to let herself feel regretful in life, but sitting next to Chelsea once again made it hard not to lament the years they had spent apart.

"Well, here's to making new memories." She raised her glass and they once again toasted.

"To new ones." Chelsea agreed. "And I guess the best place to start is with your holiday. So, tell me more about this book and why you're trying to recreate it."

"Do I have to?" Harper wasn't sure that Chelsea would understand. While she had already been up front about her relationship status in a recent text exchange, Harper doubted Chelsea had ever gone without love for long. And she was pretty sure that Chelsea would be surprised by the oh-so-serious Harper Fallon's obsession with happy ever after romances.

"I could always ask Alice?" Chelsea said, and Harper knew she'd been outfoxed.

"A few years ago, Alice gave me a romance novel because she

thought I should stop reading scholarly papers and all things boring." Harper used air quotes. "I kinda got hooked. It was such a nice change from real life to escape into the enchantment of the novels, and to be guaranteed a happy ending. Soon, Alice and I were exchanging books with each other and talking about what we liked about them. Then after a couple of our friends confessed that they read romances too, I thought it would be fun if we all hung out, drank some wine, and talked about what we were reading. It turned into the Romance Lovers Book Club." Harper shrugged, hoping Chelsea wouldn't judge her for the sappiness of it all. "There's ten of us now, and we meet the first Saturday of every month at my place."

"That actually sounds like fun."

"It is, and as Alice already said, the latest novel was about an American tourist and a British princess getting together. Alice loved the book so much, she came up with the idea to plan a vacation around recreating the novel. I know it's not really the sanest of ideas to base a vacation on a book, but here we are. We can blame Alice." Harper paused, wanting to be a little more truthful than she was being. "Although I'll admit, I loved the book too. And I've always wanted to visit England. Oh, and while we're on the subject, I should also confess that Alice was the one who first reached out to you with that embarrassing message."

Chelsea threw her head back in laughter. "I was wondering about that. I had to read it twice to totally understand what you were saying."

"Well, again, it wasn't me."

"So, all the things listed in that message that you want to do—that Alice wants to do—are from that book?"

"Yep, pretty much. And please don't feel the need to chaperone us around the city while we do this. I'm sure you have a ton of other things you'd rather be doing. In fact, you've already done enough."

"No, really, it's okay. I said I'd be your tour guide, and I will. I love it here. I've been to a lot of cities around the world, but none of them compare. Showing people London is a pleasure for me too." Chelsea hesitated. "So you're actually looking for an English princess? Or was that only Alice?"

She could have easily pinned that one on Alice too. But this was a window of opportunity for Harper to be authentic. "I'm not *particularly* looking. But I have no reason to say no if I just happen to come across one, if you know what I mean?"

"I think so. I mean, I guess so."

"What about you?" Harper had to ask. "Looking or not looking?" She probably had no right to ask, but sitting in the cozy dim light of the pub, with her beer almost finished, she felt relaxed and comfortable. Right then, it felt like no time had passed between them.

"I, um…" Chelsea paused as she sipped her own beer. "No. I'm not looking. The last one was…well…let's just say I've kinda sworn off relationships."

The statement hit Harper a bit unexpectedly. Sworn off relationships? Was that even a thing? I mean, she would dramatically proclaim to Alice that she was *never dating again* after each of her failed relationships, but the pain never lasted long, and within no time she was ready to give romance another chance. She gazed at Chelsea and wanted to take a deeper dive into her declaration. To pepper her with all the usual questions friends ask when one of them makes such a bold announcement. But she could tell by Chelsea's body language the topic was closed, so for now, she let the subject lie on the table without further dissection.

"Tell you what…" Chelsea continued as she pointed a finger at her. "I'll make you an offer. I'll not only be your official tour guide, but I'll also be your wing woman while you're here."

"My wing woman?"

"Well yeah, I'll do my best to help find you a princess while we're out doing the touristy thing."

Harper laughed lightly, but Chelsea offering to help her hook up with someone was a bit of a blow. It meant that however happy Chelsea had been to welcome her to London, she was putting her squarely in the friend zone. "Well, I'm not as invested as Alice in finding a princess—so make her your priority—but if you find a spare, then it'd be rude of me to say no."

"Two of them, huh? Well, that sounds trickier, but I'll see what I can do." Chelsea tipped her glass toward Harper. "Here's to you finding romance on this holiday, or at least something that comes close." She swallowed the last of the liquid.

"That sounds wonderful." And to Harper it did. Because who

wouldn't want to fall in love with the woman of their dreams while on vacation? "Did I mention that Alice wants to have sex with her princess in a hedge maze?"

"Let me guess. A scene from the book?"

Harper nodded.

"I'm already regretting the wing woman offer. Is there more?"

"There is."

"Do we need another pint while you tell me about it?"

"We sure do. And maybe it's time for one of those Scottish egg things."

"Coming right up." Chelsea nodded and slid out of the booth, picking up their glasses before heading to the bar. Harper watched her go with a smile. Funny how fifteen years away from someone could change so many things. It numbed feelings, transformed appearances, and altered memories. Yet in a single encounter, it was equally amazing how so many of those faded things could come rushing back as though no time had passed at all.

When they left the pub the sun was setting, streetlights were on, there was a coolness in the air, and people were hanging at the various sidewalk cafes, shops, and other pubs. None of the rom-coms she watched, nor the pictures she studied online, did the setting justice. The old brick buildings, mixed with newer looking chic little shops, sat on a long cobblestone street, giving the place a magical feel. She'd read about the history of the neighborhood before coming—plagues, invasions, and even Jack the Ripper had come and gone. Different people from different cultures had settled and transformed the place over generations, and through it all, the buildings stood as a reminder of those that were here long before them. It didn't take much imagination to see why this country was the perfect backdrop for so many of the miniseries and movies she loved.

And as they walked side by side through the streets, fighting off the jet lag that was finally settling in, she wanted the magic of her first day in London to linger. "Hey." She turned to Chelsea. "This is probably a bad idea, considering we just had beer and Scotch eggs, but what do you say we go get a milkshake?"

"A milkshake?"

"Yeah. I was just thinking, today's Friday. So wouldn't it be fun to kick off the vacation, doing the same thing we did most Friday nights in college. Remember? Let's go split…"

"A cookies and cream shake," they said in unison, and as Harper glanced at Chelsea, she could see the memories dance in her eyes.

"Well, we don't have any shake shops around here," Chelsea said, "but I can take you to one of my favorite little places. They don't serve milkshakes or ice cream, but I think you'll enjoy what they do have."

"Sounds intriguing. Lead the way."

They turned in the opposite direction and rounded two short blocks, coming back—unless she was mistaken—onto Chelsea's street. The neighborhood had an artsy retro vibe with graffiti covering most walls, with vendor tents and street food stalls scattered about. Chelsea stopped in front of a tiny café nestled between another ancient-looking pub and a bagel shop with a long line of people that snaked around a corner waiting to get in. The café was marked by a small sign above an equally small green door. *The Cereal Café* was spelled out in multicolored letters.

"You've got to be kidding me." Harper spun in a circle as she entered the tiny café. "This place is awesome." Floor to ceiling shelves were stocked with cereal boxes, and jars full of different toppings lined both sides of the checkout counter where three flavors of milk and several nondairy alternatives were offered.

"Over a hundred different choices, and it's open twenty four seven, which means no matter what time of the day it is, I can always get a bowl of cereal." Chelsea sounded like the proverbial kid in a candy store.

"Hey, Chelsea." An older thin man from behind the counter tipped his chin in her direction.

"Hey, Sam. This is my friend Harper. From the States. She's here on holiday."

"Go Yankees."

"He loves baseball," Chelsea said as she leaned in.

Harper chuckled at his enthusiasm for one of her least favorite teams in the league as she turned to Sam. "Yep, go Yankees."

"Now then…" He rubbed his hands on his apron. "What can I get you?"

Harper once again scanned the boxes until she settled on the one with a friendly-looking purple monster wearing a yellow bandana around his neck. She smiled at the familiar cover. "I'll have a bowl of that one with almond milk, please." She pointed to her childhood favorite.

"You got it. Chelsea, want your usual?" Chelsea nodded and Sam grabbed two boxes, returned to the counter, and began preparing their order.

"Sometimes when I can't sleep, or I need some comfort, I come here and have a bowl. I guess you could say lately I've been a bit of a regular." Chelsea seemed to feel as though she had to explain even though Harper hadn't asked. They grabbed their trays and commandeered a sidewalk table just as a woman and her dog got up and left. As Harper dug in, she smiled at the memories the flavor invoked.

"Someone looks happy."

"I know this is basically sugar-molded squares with artificial dye and flavoring, and a ton of empty calories, but can I just say right now I don't care." It was amazing how one bite could transform her back in time. When a bowl of cereal and her mom or dad's smiling face greeted her every morning at the kitchen table.

"No calorie counting allowed while on holiday. Especially not here—in the land of the carbs. You can worry about that when you get back home. Not that you need to. I mean, you look as good as you did fifteen years ago." Chelsea held her gaze for just an instant, but it was long enough to make Harper's cheeks heat. She willed herself to get a grip. It was just an innocent compliment from an old friend.

Harper shoveled another sugary mouthful of goodness into her mouth and glanced around. "I really like your neighborhood, Chels, it's got a great vibe." She changed the subject.

"Thanks. I'd never have been able to afford the prices around here, but when my mom and dad sold the family restaurant, they gave me and my sister a chunk of the money."

"You worked at your family's restaurant?" Harper knew Chelsea's family had owned a restaurant but had no idea she had actually worked there. She was surprised, and based on Chelsea's expression, she wasn't disguising it well.

"Yeah. Not waitressing, or whatever you're imagining a deadbeat ex-jock would be doing."

"No, that's not what…I didn't mean that—" Harper flushed, feeling embarrassed.

"It's okay if you did. There's nothing wrong with that. And we both know I wasn't much of a student. But I guess I got lucky. If you can call losing the big brother I idolized lucky. When he became too sick to work at the restaurant, I stepped in to help. I practically grew up in that place, and when I wasn't on the court playing tennis, I was there, pitching in wherever I could. And most times, that meant working in the kitchen. I knew the menu well, so when Mom and Dad needed me, what choice did I have? I could never replace Ryan—he was the chef, after all, and it was his vision and passion that made the place so successful—but I didn't want him to die thinking that we weren't gonna keep the restaurant going. It was his pride and joy." Chelsea paused as she ate some cereal, fidgeted a bit in her seat. "After he was gone…the years just melted into one another, and actually, I became really good at cooking." Chelsea looked up at her and gave her a small shrug. "I began to love it actually. But the pandemic was a disaster. We lost so much money. We tried but it was impossible to keep going. We had to close…and we finally sold it last year."

Harper hated the fact that Chelsea had gone through all of that, and she didn't know any of it. A sadness washed over her. "I'm so sorry, Chelsea."

"Yeah, I was very proud of that restaurant. Of what Ryan had done. He was a great chef, worked so hard on it. And saying good-bye to that place on top of losing him was…"

As Chelsea stopped talking, Harper could see from the way she was gripping her spoon how hard it was to talk about this. She hadn't meant to make Chelsea relive what sounded like a complete nightmare. Suddenly her own stresses and worries about not doing more with her life seemed a little indulgent.

Harper watched as Chelsea swirled the milk in her bowl with her spoon before lifting her gaze to her. There was sadness in her eyes, but also a spark of something else. "I stopped cooking, but I carried on eating." She pointed at her stomach with the spoon and smiled. "Maybe you can tell?"

"I think you look great. Really great." Harper meant it and felt strangely comfortable saying it after all these years apart.

"Well, thanks." Chelsea averted her eyes for a moment and seemed to focus on nothing in particular. "You know, I started taking the whole cooking thing seriously for Ryan, and for my mom and dad. Even though I was raised in the restaurant business, it never really appealed to me. But then it turned into something I really loved. The food, the dining experience, even the interior décor. I began to love it all, and I miss it. I'm trying to find a way back to it."

"You should. I know it's cliché and all, but life's too short and so much of it is wasted on the things that don't really make you happy." Harper was talking to Chelsea, but she could have been talking to herself. She had hit a wall with teaching, and it totally felt like she was treading water.

"That's true, and I've got something in the works. It might be a crazy move on my part, and I'd have to sell my place to raise the money, but if I can pull it off, it would be a dream come true."

"Oh yeah, mind if I ask what it is?"

"I don't want to jinx my bank appointment next week, but if all goes well, you'll know soon enough. In fact, all I need to do now is make a business plan, which I've started, but you know how bad I am at writing and expressing my—"

"I can look it over," Harper interrupted her. "Writing is something I can honestly say I'm good at."

"That's very kind, Harper, and I know you were always generous at helping me with stuff like that—but I'm pretty sure with the itinerary that you guys have that you won't have time for that. I wasn't angling for you to help. I'll probably just end up paying someone to help me with it."

"Don't be ridiculous. After you let us stay with you for free, I insist on helping. When we get back to your place, I'll look it over." Harper tried to stifle a yawn. The jet lag was starting to bite.

"Just like old times," Chelsea said. "You swooping in to save my ass. Thanks for the offer, but I'm pretty sure the only thing you'll be reading tonight is the label on that pillow you're going to collapse face down onto."

"Well, the offer still stands, so hit me up if you want me to look it over, or not. And by the way, your ass never really needed saving." She leaned back, rested her head on the wall, and looked at Chelsea as long-forgotten feelings tickled their way up her spine. "I think you just wanted to make me feel useful."

Fifteen years ago, Harper had happily sat for hours on the sidelines of a tennis court helping Chelsea study—it was one of the things that had bonded them. And now, after all these years, she was about to reprise that role. They were restarting their new friendship exactly where they left off, and something about it felt both strange and wonderfully familiar. If chapter one with Chelsea was anything to go by, her book club adventure was going to be a great one.

CHAPTER SIX

"No, I don't think you're following in Princess Diana's footsteps." Chelsea smiled as she spoke. She was sitting next to Harper on a bench in Hyde Park, glad for a rest, and hot enough to envy Alice for her willingness to splash around barefoot in the fountain in front of them.

It was another sticky day in London, and they'd ended up next to the Serpentine as a rest stop on their way to Buckingham Palace, after a morning spent roaming around Highgate Cemetery looking for Radclyffe Hall. Not even the double scoop ice cream had cooled her down.

"Alice, stop, you're making a scene. You do realize you're splashing around a memorial fountain to Princess Di, and in case you haven't noticed, people are starting to stare."

"So what, let them stare. It's not like there's a sign that says I can't take a minute and cool my feet."

"I think it's implied. Besides, you don't see anyone else doing it, do you?" Harper sounded mortified.

It wasn't strictly true. At the other end of the winding structure, a small boy was playing in the water, and Chelsea watched as his mom, head bowed over her phone, completely ignored him. This was her third day with Harper and Alice, and she had come to realize that this—Alice having fun, not following the rules, and Harper scolding her—was their dynamic. It was entertaining. And despite their differences, the fondness they had for each other was obvious. Chelsea envied the easy way they got along.

Her own friendship with Harper was developing slowly. As silly as it was, she had hoped they might pick up where they had left off, but the fifteen years apart was harder to bridge than she had expected. They were having fun, but things were still a little awkward. Chelsea wished she hadn't said so much that first night. They'd only had two pints—and a bowl of milk—so she couldn't even blame what she'd had to drink for the uncharacteristic oversharing. But she hated the idea that Harper might pity her, might look at her life and see the emptiness. Emptiness was one of the reasons Jennifer had given for leaving. Except in her case, Chelsea was pretty sure it was related to the drying up of the restaurant income that Jennifer had been happy to spend so freely.

"I don't think she'd mind," Alice shouted back to them, snapping Chelsea out of her thoughts. "Princess Di seemed like a pretty laid-back person. I think she'd be happy that people are cooling off in her fountain. Hell, she'd probably join me."

It was hard to argue with Alice's logic. Diana would have done just that.

"I think we all deserve a paddle after the time we spent searching for your favorite writer's tomb." Chelsea nudged Harper. "Though you still haven't explained to me why writing a miserable book so full of self-loathing even qualifies her for a place on your romance lovers' book trip."

"Have you read *The Well of Loneliness*?" Harper arched a brow and smiled.

"I did." Chelsea turned to Harper. Her eyes looked even bluer in the sunlight, and the way she gazed so earnestly at her made her feel nineteen again. "Well, I sort of did. You loved it in college, and I wanted to read it so I could impress you by talking about it."

"*You* wanted to impress *me*?" Harper sounded even more surprised now.

"I was always trying to impress you. You just never noticed." Chelsea felt safe enough saying it now. It was obvious to her that Harper had moved on. "Didn't work the way I hoped, though. You found me very resistible for a long time."

"I don't remember us ever even talking about the book." Harper blushed ever so slightly.

"Oh, we didn't." Chelsea laughed. "I didn't get past halfway…

despite all that 'beautiful prose' you kept going on about." The way that Harper had raved about writers she admired back in college often had Chelsea feeling stupidly jealous.

"Yeah, the book's a bit of a downer," Harper said sheepishly. "But I guess I was a little pretentious back then, so I would have never admitted it. But it was groundbreaking. Look at the path Radclyffe Hall paved for all the sapphic authors that came after her." Harper covered her face, seeming embarrassed. "I can't believe I said that out loud. It's a direct quote from the book we read that brought us here. The princess takes the American tourist to the tomb and says that to her. Except her being a princess and all, she had someone let them into the cemetery at night and had the tomb decked out in romantic fairy lights. I know that sounds kinda weird, but it worked in the book."

"Aw, now you've got me feeling all inadequate. My tour guide standards are well below princess level."

"Well, I'm not sure I'd find a tomb—no matter how well it's lit—all that romantic. And anyway"—Harper pointed at Alice, now engaged in a splashing game with the small boy—"I think Alice would disagree. Thanks to your excellent tour-guiding, she's now cooling down in a princess's fountain. As embarrassing as that is."

Chelsea stood up. She hoped Harper was having as much fun as Alice. She liked Alice, but it was Harper she was trying to impress. *Just like old times.* "We should get going. It's almost one, and we said we wanted to see Buck Palace before we have lunch. We can stop by Marble Arch for an Instagram moment on the way."

"I don't do Instagram," Harper said as she stood.

Chelsea wasn't surprised. She'd tried to find Harper's account and come up blank. "Me neither. But I bet Alice does."

"Like her life depends on it." Harper snorted, and Chelsea couldn't help but smile as she watched Harper cross the few yards between the bench and the fountain to hand Alice her sandals. Alice had on the brightest pair of bright pink shorts she had ever seen, and the sandals were a perfect color match.

Spending time with them both was a lot of fun. But sometimes the way Harper had her feeling was a lot like old times. She shook away the feeling. Harper was back in her life—a person she had loved, and someone who had never once let her down—but she was only here for a holiday. Chelsea was determined to show her the good time she wanted, and to let their friendship develop in whatever way it was meant to. She hadn't yet regretted inviting them, and that had to be a good sign.

❖

Okay, so maybe Harper overdid the hundred or so pictures that she took of the palace, but the place was postcard perfect. And besides, she knew everyone in the book club would love to see them. She swiped her screen and relived the photos she took of the ornate palace railings from various distances, selfies with Chelsea and Alice, and the three of them huddled together taken by several random tourists who seemed as awestruck with the palace as she was. She zoomed in on one particular photo and admired the craftmanship of the palace's balconies, windows, and its beautiful royal crest. It was all such a stark contrast to the architecture of the Southwest, and none of the photos did justice to the sheer all-encompassing majesty of the place.

The sound of a woman's voice made her look up from her phone. An impossibly gorgeous woman standing next to her was narrating something into a camera mounted on a hi-tech handheld tripod. Influencers, she thought as she scoffed, they were everywhere. She had no respect for them, but to be fair, it was probably more out of envy that someone could babble to a camera for minutes on end and not only have thousands of people care about what they had to say, but also get paid for it. Hell, she couldn't even get a classful of eleven-year-olds to listen to her.

"He's home, you know, and I haven't once seen you curtsey." Chelsea's voice at her shoulder brought her out of her reverie.

"What?"

"The King. See the flag? It's the Royal Standard. And they only raise it when he's at home. Otherwise, it's a plain old Union Jack. I've been teaching Alice to curtsey, and I gotta say, she's a natural. Now it's your turn." Chelsea smiled as Alice, on demand, curtsied like she was a member of the royal household, then put her own spin on it by cocking a knee and lifting her back leg.

Damn, Chelsea's smile could make her weak at the knees, and it made Harper feel things she was pretty sure she shouldn't. They were old friends, lives colliding for a moment in time, and she'd be a fool to get all misty-eyed about what that smile might mean.

"You're serious? You want me to do that?" Harper pointed at Alice as she obliged with a rerun of her new curtsey.

"It's tradition," Chelsea said with a hint of a dare.

"O-kay." Harper overemphasized the last syllable. "But stand back, I've never been known for my coordination skills," she said as the beginnings of a desire to curtsey crept in.

"Trust me, everyone can curtsey."

"Says the woman who decided to teach me how to play tennis to pay me back for all my tutoring, and fifteen minutes later took the racket out of my hand and said she'd take me out for a burger instead."

The slight lowering of Chelsea's gaze was a guilty acknowledgment. "I don't remember that at all—"

"Yeah, right." Harper cut off the denial, shyly smiled, then quickly dipped her knees a few inches before bouncing back up.

"What…" Chelsea laughed. "What was that?"

"It's my curtsey, and it's all you're gonna get. Be grateful I didn't trip over anything." Chelsea held up her hands in surrender as Harper turned to take in the sights once more. "You know"—Harper indicated the completely carless road behind them, closed off at both ends—"you were right about the impossibility of a princess getting into any kind of car crash this close to the palace. I feel kinda cheated by that scene in the book."

"Yeah, it's almost as if those romance novels aren't real life," Chelsea teased her with a lifted eyebrow.

"I'll give you that one. But because of that book," Harper stepped backward, "I'm here, in this beautiful palace." She finally gave Chelsea a slow, deeper curtsey, both arms outstretched extravagantly. "And I love it. I love London, the beautiful green parks, the hard-to-find tombs, the breakfast cereal cafés, the wooden paneled pubs, and the river boat trips that go right past Big Ben." Her curtsey had turned into a spin. She lifted her face to the clear blue sky and let herself enjoy the feeling of a cooler sun on her face. As the happiness and joy coursed through her body, she spun, wheeling her arms around like a happy child. God, it was nice to be here.

"Harper!"

She registered Chelsea's shout a split second before she registered her arm colliding with something hard and metallic, a crashing sound followed, and her body ended its spinning with a solid bump against what she guessed was another person.

"Sorry! I—"

"Oh, for heaven's sake! Are you bloody well serious? That camera cost me eight hundred pounds."

Harper saw the woman at the same time she registered Chelsea's arm around her waist, in what she assumed was an attempt to steady her. She looked from Chelsea to the woman and back again, getting her bearings but still feeling a bit disoriented. She watched the woman pick her camera off the ground, straighten herself, and scowl at her.

"It would have cost you eight hundred pounds if you'd paid for it, but since you got it free, and can replace it by simply asking for another one, you really should stop being such a drama queen. We both know that that's my job." The man who was speaking emerged from behind the rather rude, but still gorgeous, woman who Harper recognized as the same person she had seen a few minutes ago filming herself. The man was dressed in a canary yellow polo shirt and bright pink shorts, topped off with a rainbow bandana. "Nice spinning, old girl. Maximum points for artistic impression, but let's not focus too much on the technical score."

Although Harper hadn't hit her head, she couldn't help feeling like there was something weirdly dreamlike about what was happening. Only the feeling of Chelsea at her side seemed real.

"I, um..." She stammered, finding her voice. "I'm so sorry about the camera. I didn't mean to...I mean...I just got a bit carried away and all." She waved a hand. "It's my first time in London." She took a deep breath, steadying her embarrassment. "I'll pay for the damage, of course."

For the first time, Harper really studied the woman holding the broken camera, who was staring at her with a curious expression. She was beautifully put together, in a way that Harper had once envied but was now just intimidated by. Her blond hair looked like it was made by the sun itself and her pale face was the kind that often stared back at her from the covers of *Vogue* or *Vanity Fair*—flawless skin, full lips, wide eyes, long lashes. She was stunning—if perfect, poised, and pouting was your thing.

"You're American. Of course you are." The woman looked her up and down in a way that made Harper feel self-conscious about her appearance. "From…don't tell me…somewhere West Coast." Her tone made it clear she wasn't asking a question. "This is the best friend." She indicated Alice with a perfectly manicured hand. "And this is the girlfriend." She pointed at Chelsea.

"Also a friend actually." Harper felt Chelsea drop her arm as she responded and took a step away from her. *Wow, is the idea of being my girlfriend that terrible?* Harper had clearly misread some of the vibes she thought she'd been getting from Chelsea the past few days. "And not at all American," Chelsea clarified in a flat tone.

Harper watched as a small smile tugged at the corner of the woman's mouth. "The Londoner showing her friends London. First stop, Buckingham Palace." She paused. "Of course." Her amusement was obvious.

Beautiful but a bit sarcastic. It felt as if she was mocking them. "Well, not that it's any of your business, but it's not our first stop. We've been here for days. And we've seen a lot of other great places." Harper made her annoyance clear.

"I'm Alice." Alice extended her hand. For a second, Harper thought the woman wasn't going to respond, but she took Alice's hand and offered a perfunctory shake. "And this klutz is Harper. The one standing next to her is our friend Chelsea." She stressed the word "our" and Harper felt herself react in an oddly possessive way.

This time the woman smiled widely at Harper. "Klutzy but kind of spunky. I like it." She held Harper's gaze as her edge and expression softened. "I'm Laney."

Did she just…did she just wink at me? Was this gorgeous, arrogant woman now flirting with her? Harper glanced around to confirm there wasn't anyone behind her.

"And I'm Oliver." The guy whose shorts matched Alice's reached around Laney and extended his hand to Harper.

"Holy shit, I recognize you." Alice jabbed a finger in his direction. "You're the guy who has that makeover channel."

"Guilty as charged." Oliver placed his hand over his chest and bowed.

Harper glanced at Chelsea, who shrugged, then turned to Alice with a clueless shake of her head.

"You two really are unbelievable." Alice scoffed as she whipped out her phone, let her fingers fly over the screen, and shoved it in their faces. "From frogs to princesses."

Harper squinted at a YouTube video of Oliver talking to the camera while a makeup artist beside him applied eyeshadow to a woman's face.

"I still don't get it?" Harper leaned away from Alice's phone.

"He takes plain-Jane-looking women—frogs—and transforms them into walking beauties. So they end up looking like princesses..."

"I'd rather refer to them as hidden Cinderellas."

"Ha. That's a good one." Alice glanced around. "So, are you out here filming for your channel?"

"No, Laney and I were just...wait a tick." Oliver tapped the tip of his chin as he circled Alice. "How would you like to be my next Cinderella?"

Alice snorted. "You're kidding, right?"

Oliver shook his head. "Trust me, sweetie, I'm not."

Harper took a protective step toward Oliver. She wanted to tell him to get lost, that Alice was beautiful just as she was, and how dare he insinuate that she needed a makeover.

Alice held out a hand blocking Harper from advancing. "So, like, what are we talking about here? Tons of free stuff like those women get on your channel?"

Oliver nodded. "A spa day, treatments, bags of clothes, free makeup, and most definitely a new hairdo. But you have to agree to put yourself *completely* in my hands."

"Look, Oliver—" Harper had had enough of him insulting Alice.

"I'm in," Alice chimed in.

"Will you excuse us for a second?" Harper grabbed Alice's forearm and pulled her aside. "What are you doing? We don't even know these people."

Alice wiggled out of Harper's grip. "Harps, the guy's famous. I've been subscribed to his channel for years."

"Well, *I've* never heard of him," Harper bit back.

"That's because you live under a rock." She squared off with Harper. "Look, I really want to do this, okay?"

"Excuse me..." Oliver interrupted them. "I couldn't help overhearing your rather loud whispering. If it would help to persuade you, why don't we head over to the Ritz for a spot of afternoon tea and get to know each other a little better. Laney and I were actually planning on popping in anyway. Why not join us?"

He waited a beat for Laney to respond. It was obvious to Harper that between the two, she was the one in charge. She looked at Harper coolly before turning to Oliver with a small nod.

"I think that's one of your better ideas, Ollie." Laney nodded. "What do you say?" She addressed the question directly to Harper.

Harper didn't know what to say and was aware that all eyes were now on her, waiting for a response. "Oh, I, um…" She'd read about afternoon tea at the Ritz, and how *iconic and timeless* it was. In fact, one of their guides yesterday had described it as an "absolute must" for anyone visiting London. Surely an hour or two detour in their plans wouldn't hurt. She glanced across at Chelsea for guidance.

"I don't think so…thank you for the offer," Chelsea cut in. "Turning up without a booking at the height of the season obviously isn't going to work." Chelsea hesitated. "Besides, we were planning to go somewhere a lot less touristy." Chelsea's annoyance was as clear to Harper as she was sure it was to everyone else.

"You're turning down the chance of afternoon tea at the Ritz?" Laney arched a brow. "You're seriously going to deprive these lovely American friends of yours the chance to eat unlimited Victoria sponge and lemon drizzle cakes? That's not very hospitable."

"You won't get a table, so I'm not really depriving them of anything." Chelsea shrugged. "And we're not stupid enough to waste fifty quid on a few overpriced cakes."

"I can get us a table. And please don't worry about the costs. You'll be my guests, after all." Laney's challenge to Chelsea was clear. "And if we're turned away—"

"As if." Oliver laughed and Laney shushed him.

"You're very sure of yourself," Chelsea said, sounding full of challenge.

"Sweetie, people don't say no to Laney." Oliver smirked.

"But if they did, I'd take it as something of a challenge." Laney still hadn't taken her eyes off Harper. She couldn't help feeling that she was being sized up for something. "And I'm pretty sure this isn't something you'd let your friends say no to—if you're serious about them enjoying their trip. We both know that afternoon tea at the Ritz is one of those experiences not to miss."

Harper glanced over at Chelsea, who was now wearing a dejected expression. "She's right, Harper, this is what you came here for."

"Well, yeah, I mean, it is, but—"

"No buts, Harps," Alice cut in. "We came here to take it all in and to be open to meeting new people." She gave Harper a meaningful stare. "I say we all go have lunch and get to know each other." As she spoke, Alice approached Oliver and hooked her arm around his. "We can always visit the lunch place you had in mind tomorrow, right, Chelsea?"

After a pause, Chelsea simply shrugged, and despite the awkwardness, Harper was happy to have it resolved.

"Thank you." She meant the comment for Chelsea, but Laney appeared at her side and responded with a cheery *you're very welcome.* Ahead of them, Alice and Oliver walked side by side chatting and laughing like they were old friends. The more Harper watched them interact, the more they seemed to exhibit the same overexaggerated mannerisms. It was uncanny.

Harper walked in silence between Chelsea and Laney, feeling like she had done something wrong but not really understanding what. All she really understood was that she was getting hungry, and tea, baked goods, and finger sandwiches at the Ritz sounded delicious. And Alice was right, they had come to London to meet people. To find romance. And it was pretty incredible that she was strolling through a sunny park side by side with a gorgeous woman she had just—quite literally—bumped into outside Buckingham Palace. And if she had wanted Chelsea to object a bit more forcefully, then she was being ridiculous. They were now nothing but friends. Chelsea had made that clear. She made herself focus on the here and now. On the simple, uncomplicated chance to have a new experience, with a woman who seemed inexplicably interested in taking her to lunch.

❖

Chelsea had been wrong about the fifty-quid cakes. The standard afternoon tea—pretty much the only thing on the menu—was on offer for seventy bloody pounds. She had been determined not to join in, as hungry as she was, but Harper had pleaded with her. If this was the kind of thing Harper wanted from her holiday, Chelsea didn't want to be the party pooper. That didn't mean she had to enjoy it, though, and she was well aware that her mood since sitting down was wavering midway between grumpy and grouchy.

She had felt foolish when their little group had not only been welcomed into the busy dining room, but—thanks to Laney—had been seated at a great table right next to one of many ornate mirrored partition windows. As well as her own face, the mirror showed her the reflections of several opulent chandeliers, an enormous golden statue—ostentatiously filling a recess across the room—and more potted ferns and marble columns than seemed strictly necessary. And the animated way that Harper and Alice were chatting with their new friends and cooing over the tiny sandwiches and finger cakes was not helping her mood. She wanted them to enjoy themselves—they were tourists, and this place was as English an experience as it was possible to have—but Laney's all-too-obvious pursuit of Harper left a bitter taste in Chelsea's mouth. And when she had accidentally dripped one of the fourteen types of tea she'd been offered onto the tablecloth, Chelsea felt a grim sort of satisfaction. Even the pristine whiteness of the tablecloth was annoying her.

"At least you got your tiny cucumber sandwiches." Chelsea addressed Harper quietly, determined to buck up and stop moping. She could handle one afternoon tea with Laney and Oliver, say a warm good-bye, and concentrate on making the rest of the trip special for Harper.

"We did. Something else we can check off our list. And this place is every bit as amazing as I hoped." Harper put down her napkin and picked up her phone. "Am I allowed to take photos in here?"

Chelsea shrugged. She doubted it, but she'd been wrong about everything so far.

"They don't normally like it, but they won't say no to Laney. We even filmed a video in here last month."

Chelsea had tried to be interested when Oliver explained the work he did. She didn't live under a rock, and she knew what an influencer was—but that didn't mean she'd ever given it much thought. It sounded very simple from the way they talked about it—he got stuff for free as long as he was willing to say nice things about it on social media. And Alice was already under his spell. Had been ever since he'd promised her a luxury shopping trip and a facial. Harper hadn't expressed a desire to go with them, and Chelsea had to hope that would mean that the two of them could maybe hang out together for the evening.

"We did a catwalk show right in the middle of this dining room—when it was closed, of course." Oliver leaned in. "We got Pierre there to do some of the modeling." He pointed at one of the handsome suited waiters. "He got very excited. I don't kiss and tell, but be reassured that the downstairs kitchen here is every bit as spotless as you'd expect." He tapped the side of his nose.

"Wait, I don't understand what you're saying." Harper turned to Alice, who shrugged, then to Chelsea.

"He fucked Pierre in the kitchen." Chelsea regretted being so crude when she saw how much Harper blushed.

"Ohhh! I get it now. Sorry."

"You really are adorable." Laney said it under her breath, but it was loud enough for everyone to hear, and Chelsea felt herself tense as the table fell silent. She looked across at Harper, a look on her face that was hard to read. Her cheeks now an even darker shade of red.

"Your Royal Highness!" A tall, well-dressed man appeared at their table. "How lovely to see you again." He bowed at the waist as he spoke. "Was everything to your satisfaction?" He snapped his fingers in the direction of one of the waiters. "Get the princess and her guests some champagne. Roederer—the Cristal."

"It's okay, we're heading out. Next time, Christopher. Thank you. We'll just have the bill." Laney dismissed the waiter with a faint nod of her head.

"Princess?" Harper and Alice said the word in unison.

"You're a highness? A royal highness?" Alice clapped her hands. "No fucking way."

Chelsea couldn't say for sure, but Laney looked uncomfortable. Heads had turned in their direction, and a couple of people had taken out their phones and were now recording their table. Chelsea watched Christopher cross the floor and make them stop.

"You didn't know?" Again, Laney addressed only Harper. "You came with us without even knowing who I was." The last part wasn't a question. It was like Laney couldn't quite believe it.

"No. How could I? Are you *really* a princess?"

"Sweetie, of course she's a princess," Oliver spoke as he took out his phone and displayed pictures of Laney and a Wikipedia page confirming the title. He passed the phone around proudly. "Youngest daughter of the youngest son of the King's brother."

Chelsea had never heard of her, but that didn't mean anything. She rarely followed anything about the royal family, apart from a few episodes of *The Crown* Denise had made her watch one weekend when Mike was away.

"Holy fuck, Harper, you know what this means?" Alice sounded breathless as she grabbed Harper's forearm. "You totally just bumped into a princess in front of Buckingham Palace. It's destiny." She nodded seriously at Harper. "And you know it is."

"What are you babbling on about?" Laney asked.

"We read this book..." Alice rushed out the explanation. "It's about an American tourist and a British princess who get together. It's why we decided to come on vacation to—"

"Alice!" Harper interrupted her. "We don't need to be telling every person we meet our story."

"I'm just saying, how crazy is this? Even you have to admit it's spooky as hell how much is coming true."

Their waiter appeared just in time to save Harper from replying. Chelsea could see from the look on her face that she was stunned. She felt the same.

"Why didn't you tell us?" Harper asked the question uncertainly.

"I don't use the title. It's tiresome." The waiter came and dropped the bill onto the table. Laney opened the embossed leather folder and closed it again. "Besides, it's hard to tell the difference between the people who like hanging out with princesses and the people who like hanging out with me." She extended her hand and closed it over Harper's. It was hard for Chelsea to stomach. "But you, you sweet naive thing, just passed the test."

The Harper she knew at college wouldn't have been impressed at all by Laney—not by her title, her confident swagger, or her ability to get a table at the Ritz. In fact, Chelsea was pretty sure Laney wasn't at all Harper's type. But then old Harper hadn't been looking for a princess. And she hadn't been a fan of romance books back then either. They had been Chelsea's guilty pleasure, one she'd always imagined her super-intellectual friend wouldn't approve of.

"Maybe it's time to go." Chelsea rushed out the response, hating to see Harper letting Laney hold her hand. She stood, wanting to somehow break the strange spell that had descended over the table. "We need to get going, go home, get changed and all that." They hadn't made any concrete plans for the evening, but she thought of taking Harper to that cocktail bar that Denise had told her about. The one with the upstairs balcony that had wonderful views of St. Paul's Cathedral. Since it sounded like Alice was going to spend the evening with her new BFF Oliver, she could finally spend some time alone with Harper.

"I thought we were going shopping?" Oliver addressed Alice.

"If you're buying, then you bet your ass we are. Right?" Alice was either asking her or asking Harper. Chelsea couldn't tell.

"You surely don't have to ask permission?" Laney teased Alice with an easy wide smile.

Chelsea had to acknowledge Laney was attractive—if you liked that kind of high maintenance, super-put-together look—but she knew it. And that was off-putting. She was about as opposite to Harper's unstudied beauty, a beauty that Harper still seemed completely oblivious to, as it was possible to be. Much closer to the person Jennifer had wanted to be. Chelsea knew it was a factor in her dislike of Laney. The other factor was how much, despite how opposite they were, Harper seemed to like her.

"I'm not really asking. I'm just making sure Harper and Chelsea don't mind, and that I'm not screwing up any of their plans."

"Yeah, no, it's totally fine. We haven't made any yet." Harper spoke before Chelsea could.

"Actually, I had thought we could go to—"

"In a foreign city with no plans…" Laney interrupted Chelsea confidently. "We can't allow that. Why don't you give your tour guide the night off and let me take you out to dinner. For some proper food. I know a great place in Mayfair, just off Berkeley Square. I can't promise nightingales, but it's a lovely place to sit in as the sun sets."

Chelsea badly wanted Harper to say no. But the look on her face said she wasn't going to.

"She's my friend, not our tour guide." Harper's defense of her did nothing to untie the knot in her stomach. She was Harper's friend. She had no claim on her, no right to be jealous and absolutely no intention of preventing her from doing whatever she wanted with this ridiculously beautiful princess. The princess she had come to London to meet. Chelsea sighed. Harper was a catch. She didn't know it herself, but Chelsea couldn't expect others not to see the qualities that she had always been able to see.

"Sounds great, Harps." She took in a small breath. "Go for it. Mayfair is quite the experience. Most expensive square on our Monopoly board, for one." She looked everywhere but at Harper. "That alone should get it on your list."

"Are you sure?"

"Sure. I have a lot of stuff I need to get done anyway." She kept her tone light.

It was true, but it wasn't how Chelsea would have chosen to spend the evening, if Harper wasn't so obviously blowing her off.

Laney and Oliver both stood, neither of them making a move to pay the bill. Chelsea frowned. She couldn't cover a check as massive as the one she knew was sitting in that leather folder. And Laney had promised to pay.

"Should we…erm…split the bill or something?" She flipped open the folder and picked it up.

"Sure thing, divide it by five and we can all pay our share." Laney seemed unconcerned about breaking the promise she had made to treat them to the overpriced meal.

Chelsea looked at the bill and saw that it had been comped. Not for the first time since meeting Laney, she felt kind of stupid.

"Okay, so I wasn't paying attention when you said you get things for free."

"Paying attention is a good thing. For lots of reasons. I make it my business to do so. To know what it is that people want…and need."

Chelsea could have gotten mad. Asked Laney why she thought she needed her advice. But that would spoil things for Harper. And that she didn't want to do.

"I have somewhere to be now, but if you give Oliver your address, I'll send a car for you. Seven thirty. Make sure to wear something formal. Something a little more fitted. You definitely have the shape for it."

Chelsea should have told her to fuck off for speaking to Harper that way, but Laney had already turned her back on them all and was heading for the exit.

"Maybe you do need to come shopping with us after all, Harps? Did you even pack a dress? The place sounds pretty swanky. Pants probably aren't the preferred attire."

Now, even Alice seemed determined to tell Harper what to wear. Chelsea couldn't stand it.

"I'm heading home. Shopping's not really my thing." She kept her voice even. "I'll see you back there later with all your bags of swag."

She turned to leave but felt a hand on her arm. When she turned back, Harper was gazing at her.

"Thank you."

"What for?"

"For…everything."

"No problem."

"See you later." Harper said it like it wasn't at all in doubt, but who knew? Laney was pretty good at "knowing what people needed," and Harper obviously liked her enough to say yes to a romantic dinner.

Chelsea nodded at Harper and continued on her way out of the dining room, wanting to be away from all of them. She had spent the weeks since she knew Harper was coming to London telling herself things would be different, that the yearning she'd felt for her at college would be nonexistent after their time apart. Right then, the unmistakable feelings of jealousy knotting her stomach told her that was something else she was wrong about.

Chapter Seven

Harper had felt more than a twinge of disappointment as she had watched Chelsea walk out of the dining room, but she had made it very clear she had things to do, and Harper interpreted that statement as Chelsea needing some space. She couldn't really blame her. Since their arrival, she and Alice had been monopolizing her time and encroaching on her life and daily routine. A free evening was probably a good thing, and besides, she knew Chelsea hated shopping almost as much as she did.

She hummed more from contentment than a specific tune in her head as she strolled behind Oliver and Alice. She had unexpectedly enjoyed the afternoon with Laney and was looking forward to dinner. Laney was such a surprise, and not really what she expected from a princess. One minute she seemed completely pompous and at home with all the princessy trappings, and the next she acted like she hated it. She was a walking contradiction, that was for sure, but one thing that was clear from her not-so-subtle hints was that, for whatever reason, she was interested in her. A slight chill tingled its way up Harper's body at the thought. In the course of her dating life, she had never once been the one who was pursued, so having a princess come on to her was a bit of a mind fuck. Very foreign, yet very nice.

A thought tickled at the edges of her mind. Chelsea said she had pursued her. But even then, she had been the one to make the first move with Chelsea when they were in her truck. She smiled at the distant memory and remembered how deep the desire had been, and how much she had wanted to touch her.

"Are you keeping up, Harper?" Oliver called over his shoulder.

"Yep, sorry, I'm right behind you." She scurried up closer to him. She needed to pay more attention to where they were going, and not get so distracted by the beautiful architecture that surrounded her. And of course, the thoughts of Laney, and of Chelsea, that were swirling in her head. "So, where did you say we were going?"

"To the arcade." Oliver turned and walked backward. "If you're going to find something befitting for tonight's dinner, that's where we need to go. And…" He checked his watch. "We have just over an hour to make that happen, so no more stops."

At Oliver's urging, they'd taken a couple of hours indulging at a little champagne bar, and for the second time that day, the bill had once again been comped. *How the other half lives*. Harper shook her head a little, taking in a breath in the hope of it clearing her mind. The couple of glasses Oliver had insisted they have before shopping were already making things a little fuzzy.

Harper liked Oliver. He was kind of loud and obnoxious and seemed unapologetic if it offended or put anyone off. But he seemed authentic. He held a confidence about him that suggested he was secure in who he was, and he was the only other person she had met, besides Alice, who snorted when they laughed. In fact, if Alice had a long-lost twin brother, Oliver would be it. They had been babbling and giggling like schoolgirls nonstop since they met.

"Okay, for the sake of the uninformed American, can you clarify what an arcade is, because I'm pretty sure you don't mean it the way we do back home."

Oliver paused and unfolded his arms in display. "This, my dear, is an arcade."

Harper turned and glanced down a long, ornately tiled corridor, enclosed with a canopied glass roof, and flanked by little boutique-looking stores on both sides. Unlike the shopping malls in Phoenix, this was neither spacious nor sprawling, but just as equally, it wasn't anywhere near as sterile. Well-placed planters full of spring flowers accented the interior space, and clusters of well-dressed people were chatting and seemed happy as they milled around, drifting from store to store.

Harper had never found the full-on retail mall shopping experience appealing but performed her best friend duties and tagged along when Alice asked her to go. Unless there was a killer sale, and an item marked down to a rock bottom price, she never purchased anything, and more times than not became an extra set of hands if Alice decided to add more debt to her credit cards and needed help carrying bags. Thrift stores were Harper's go-to place to buy her mandatory professional attire, with shorts or jeans and tees and sweatshirts rounding out her preferred choice of casual clothing.

As she strolled behind Alice and Oliver, glancing into windows displaying elegant jewelry, crystal glassware, designer purses, Belgian chocolates, and collections of artistically arranged clothing, a knot formed in her stomach. Surely Oliver wasn't assuming she could afford to buy anything in any one of these stores? She had to hope his passion for a free makeover would extend beyond Alice, or this was going to be an exercise in embarrassing futility. She felt a rising panic. She hadn't come on the trip expecting an evening of formal dining, so the best she had in her suitcase was a little black skirt that had seen better days.

"Ah," Oliver announced as he stopped in front of a store and opened the door for them. "We have arrived."

As they filed in, Alice let out a whistle and Harper spun in a three sixty. The place felt as luxurious as the Ritz. Marble tiled floor throughout, a huge vase of flowers sat on a center stone table, several mannequins displayed outfits that were probably from designers she never heard of, and every salesperson was dressed as though they were waiting to go to a cocktail party instead of waiting on customers. A collection of hats was off to one corner, perfumes in another, and shoes and accessories delegated to yet another. Harper quickly took note that there was more empty space than displayed merchandise, a clue that the variety of the designer items they sold must have a price tag that more than compensated for the space given to show them off.

"Oliver, I can't afford anything here," she whispered, but the acoustics carried her voice further than she intended.

"Sweetheart, trust me, we're going to have you looking the part without spending a single penny," he replied as a tall, thin woman in a tight-fitting black dress sauntered over to them, swinging her hips in a perfect cadence as she precisely placed one high-heeled foot in front of the other.

"Oliver." The woman leaned in.

"Jess." Oliver gave the salesclerk two quick pecks, one on each cheek. "You look stunning as always."

The woman bowed her head at the approval of his words, then flicked her eyes at them. "Another Cinderella makeover?" Jess mused as she circled Harper, clearly sizing her up.

"No, Alice here is my next Cinderella." With a flop of his wrist, Oliver singled out Alice, who sloppily curtsied. "Harper is a new friend of Laney's, and she needs an outfit worthy of Mayfair dining with a princess." He rested his hands on Harper's shoulders.

Jess gave a knowing nod. "Laney? I see. Well then, in that case, I think I might have the perfect dress for the occasion. Give me a moment."

Oliver turned. "Jess comes on my show from time to time as a fashion consultant. She's a little wooden, but very popular. I'm trying to talk her into coming on more frequently, and oh my God…" His gaze refocused to one corner of the room. "Is that a St. James's fedora?" He scampered over, gently removed a dark brown hat from a display, gingerly placed it on his head, and gave the rim a quick brush with his hand.

Harper gave him a thumbs-up, then turned. "Hey, Alice, what do you…Alice?" She scanned the store until she located her in another corner spritzing herself with an assortment of colognes. Harper approached, coughed, and waved her hand in front of her face as the overpowering scent of perfumed air assaulted her nose. "Alice, I'm feeling a bit uncomfortable about this whole thing."

"What? Why? This is fun."

"I can't afford anything in here."

"Pfft. And you think I can? The only thing that'll fit my budget is one of those chocolates they have at the checkout."

Harper glanced at a silver platter of chocolate balls wrapped in gold foil that sat to the side of the register. "I think those are free to customers."

Alice's eyes widened "Really? Then I'll be right back."

"Paying customers."

"Oh." Alice paused, then turned back to her. "Well, that's a buzzkill." She softened her tone. "Look, Harps, I have no idea what either of us have done to deserve this. But can't you just go with it? For once just accept—"

"Alice, I'm freaking out a little bit right now, okay?"

"Okay, yeah, sorry, I just mean, we wanted the vacation of a lifetime. Right? We joked about romance and princesses, and if you think about it, it's kinda sorta all coming true. You're going on a date with a real fucking princess, and if the way she looked at you over those cucumber sandwiches was a sign of anything, I'd say she's pretty into you."

"It's not a date, it's just dinner." Or so she kept telling herself to calm her nerves. Normally, she liked to get to know someone for a few days, weeks actually, before declaring time spent with them constituted an actual date.

"Whatever. Look, Oliver has made it clear this shopping spree is all paid for through his channel, so can't you just relax and enjoy it?"

It was a simple enough question. But the answer was probably no. Harper wasn't sure she was comfortable enough in her own skin to enjoy it in the way Alice was. She let out a sigh. If only she were that carefree.

"Okay." Jess returned holding a dark blue silk dress. "This is the perfect mix between cocktail and formal length, and the color…" She held the dress close to Harper, who jerked back a bit at the intrusion into her personal space. "Will accent your eyes beautifully."

Oliver approached, glanced at the outfit, and gave a nodding approval. "You, my love"—he turned to Jess—"are a master. Laney will be so pleased."

Jess flushed and then frowned deeply. The reaction was at odds with how put together she seemed.

"Oh, and are you available for a few hours later this week? I'm going to start filming my next episode tomorrow with Alice, and I'm definitely going to need your expert help with this one."

Jess paused as she glanced in Alice's direction, looking her up and down as she tapped a finger against her chin. "I am, and I accept your challenge."

Harper cringed at the word. They were talking as though Alice was a building that needed to be fixed up in some way. She let out a breath and calmed the distaste that was building toward Jess and the idea of Alice participating in the makeover. Why in the world did Alice agree to be made a *before and after* example?

"And, you, follow me." Jess broke Harper's thoughts as she spun and strolled toward a large dressing room.

"Go on." Oliver encouraged her as he gave her a nudge. "Let's see how it fits."

"Oliver, I..." Harper held her position. This whole being dressed and scrutinized thing was beginning to make her feel very uncomfortable. Fashion was never her thing. Taking the time to pair colors, figure out styles, and accessorize was something she always deemed a waste of time and brainpower. Jeans never went out of style, the denim color always went well with any top, they were affordable and lasted for years. She owned that one customary black dress for weddings, funerals, and everything in between, and a rotation of five business pants and three skirts completed her professional attire. Simple. Comfortable. Easy. *That* was her style.

"Trust me, you might be surprised at what awaits you."

"Yeah, Harps." Alice approached, bringing with her a cloud of perfume, causing Oliver to scrunch his face and hold his hand in front of his nose. "Go try it on."

Harper leaned in. "Alice, that dress isn't me, and this whole thing"—she waved an arm, referencing the room—"isn't us."

"I know it's not. But don't you see, that's the whole point. It's why we read romance novels, and why we came here. Everything about this trip is meant to take us away from the routine and reality of our normal lives. You think I don't know that Oliver thinks I'm a plus-size frog and his whole schtick is about how hard it will be to turn someone like me into a princess? Of course I do. But I still said yes. I agreed to it because for a few days, I'm going to experience something I'll probably never again have the opportunity to. I will have hundreds of thousands, maybe even millions of people watching me, and for a brief moment in my life, *I'll* feel like a princess. Plus..." Alice winked. "A shitload of free stuff...so, um, yeah."

Harper couldn't help but chuckle.

"And it's why you need to get ready to have dinner with Laney—a goddamn royal highness of a princess. None of this is who we are, or who we'll be once we go back home, but for this brief moment, it's our time to shine."

Harper let out a sigh as she glanced over her shoulder at Jess, who seemed to be impatiently waiting. "Yeah, okay. You're right."

As Harper closed herself into the dressing room, she took a moment to stare at the dress hanging on the hook. She ran her fingers over the material and admired how silky and light the fabric felt in her hand. It really was gorgeous. She slowly undressed, and carefully—as though the garment was made of fine crystal—removed the dress from the hanger and slid it over her head. The best way to describe the sensation of the material gliding down her skin was that of feathers brushing down her flesh as they gently floated and came to rest just above her ankles. She turned and looked in the full-length mirror. She cocked her head from side to side as she glanced at the elegant stranger that she didn't fully recognize, because the reflection staring back at her looked so…stunning.

"Well, how do I look?" She stepped out of the dressing room as Oliver shifted his focus away from his phone and stared at her, wide-eyed. Alice, once again, let out a loud whistle.

"Holy shit, Harps, you look fantastic…incredible…" Alice gushed, then swung her arm backhanded into Oliver's chest with a thud. "You're going to make me look like that, right?"

"Oh, honey, don't you worry. I have the works planned for you." Oliver smiled.

"You don't think it's too over-the-top?" Harper glanced down and smoothed her hands over the fabric as a bashfulness flushed through her.

"Trust me, there's no such thing." Oliver approached, reaching one hand into the messenger bag slung across his chest. He pulled out a clip and began gathering Harper's hair. "I think if you wear your hair up, instead of down…like this." He clipped her hair on top of her head and pulled some strands down to frame her face. He stepped back and gazed at her. "That looks so much better," Oliver said as he once again dug into his satchel and pulled out a makeup kit.

"Oh no." Harper waved him off. "I don't wear makeup."

"Honey, trust me, everyone can use polishing. Now, I usually have a professional do this, but I can do the basics of what's needed…" He went to work on her face as though he were a painter working on a canvas. "Look up, look down, turn this way, turn that way, part your lips…now pucker." The demands came one after the other until he paused, tilted his head, and with a smirk that signaled he was pleased with his work, stepped back.

Harper turned to Alice, who gave an enthusiastic thumbs-up.

"Wow," Jess said as she returned holding a matching-colored clutch purse. "You look like a different person." Jess handed her the bag and frowned as Harper noticed her attention was focused on the gray suede Birkenstocks still gracing her feet. "Those"—Jess pointed—"have got to go."

"No heels, please. I'm not good with balance." Whoever thought women should tiptoe-walk on a three-inch spike while squishing round-shaped toes into a point was clearly deranged.

"We have some stylish flats that might work. What's your size?"

"Nine."

"That's a seven in the UK. Be right back." Jess shuffled off as Alice jumped into Harper's face and started snapping photos.

"Stop that." Harper held her hand in front of Alice's cell phone.

"What?" Alice lowered her phone. "You really look beautiful, Harper. Just wait until Laney sees you."

"Yeah, you think I look good enough to be out with a princess?"

"Look around." Harper did as she was told and noticed several patrons staring at her. "They ain't looking at me, girlfriend."

It felt odd, standing there. She felt on display, and she averted her eyes as she squirmed a bit in her dress. A part of her wanted to take it off and say to hell with all of this. Yet there was something tickling its way up her body. A feeling she had never acknowledged or embraced before. Chelsea had often told her she was beautiful, but it was a compliment she dismissed because she never thought of herself that way. Not in college, and not since. She'd had girlfriends who said she was cute, but never beautiful. But as she turned and glanced back to the dressing room mirror, she felt the true essence of that word, and for the first time in her life, it seemed to fit.

It took three tries, but eventually Jess found the perfect shoes that had the right combination of comfort and style.

"Our work here is done." Oliver draped an arm around Jess. "Now let me text Manny your location."

"Manny?"

"Laney's driver."

"Oh, I don't think that's necessary. You said the restaurant wasn't that far from here, so just give me the address and I can walk. It's beautiful out, and I definitely need some air."

It was obvious from the look on Oliver's face that suggesting she walk was akin to blasphemy. He cocked a hip. "Those are Jimmy Choo shoes, designed for fashion, not walking." He returned his focus to his phone. "There." He glanced up. "Manny said he'll be here in fifteen minutes."

"Oliver..." Harper huffed.

"Nope, not another word. Now then, let me go finish up with Jess and see if I can't persuade her to let me keep that hat that makes me look so fabulous. I'll be right back."

Alice handed Harper her backpack. She tried to pull out the few essential items she needed to transfer over to the clutch purse but fumbled them to the floor. Her nerves were already frayed. How on earth was she going to get through dinner?

"Don't worry about your clothes. I'll hang on to them and take them back to Chelsea's for you."

"Thanks, Alice. What are you two going to do the rest of the evening?"

"We're going to some rooftop pub because he joked that I was too perfumed up to go anywhere that had walls." Alice pinched her T-shirt and pulled the fabric to her nose for a sniff. "Which is weird because I kinda like the way I smell. Oh well..." She released her shirt and dismissively shrugged. "I'm just hoping there's food, because it's dawning on me that he drinks a lot more than he eats. Anyway, he said he wants to talk about everything I should expect for the makeover."

Oliver returned wearing the hat, and with a snap of his fingers, had them out the door and curbside as a sleek black sedan pulled up. A tall thin man with gray hair got out, rounded the vehicle, and opened a door.

"Well." Harper turned and faced them. "Guess this is my ride. Have a nice evening and, Alice, I'll see you back at Chelsea's."

Alice stepped forward. "You really look great, Harps. Enjoy your evening and don't forget to take lots of pictures."

Harper nodded as she folded herself, and her nerves, into the car and gave them a final wave through a heavily tinted window as they pulled away.

Twenty minutes later, she was being escorted across a low-lit dining room that was not only spacious, but one of the most opulent rooms she had ever seen. Music drifted from a grand piano and huge paintings of Picasso-style art graced the walls. A Chihuly sculpture hung like a chandelier, its hundreds of multicolored blown glass tentacles wrapping around each other, and full vases of white roses were scattered throughout.

She concentrated on seeming as graceful as she could as she approached the table, aware of Laney tracking her with an intense stare.

"Here you are, madam." The maître d' extended his hand as he pulled out the overstuffed chair opposite Laney. As Harper took a seat, a white linen napkin was draped on her lap.

"Wow, you look absolutely breathtaking." Laney rolled a not-too-subtle gaze over her body. "Better than I even imagined."

"Thanks to Jess and Oliver." Harper tucked a strand of hair behind her ear as a slight heat flushed her cheeks at yet another word that was never before used to describe her.

"Yes, those two are marvels, aren't they? But with your natural beauty, they had so much to work with, it just needed a bit of help to blossom."

Uncomfortable with Laney's praise, Harper moved the subject away from herself. "Jess agreed to help Oliver with Alice for the makeover. I hope she finds Alice something as amazing as this to wear." Harper smoothed a hand down her dress.

Laney raised a brow. "I'm sure she will. She's very talented. In some ways."

"Do you know Jess well?" Harper said as she began scanning the menu and did a double take at the prices of some of the items. Holy shit, she could eat a week on what one main dish cost.

"We were lovers, but only briefly. She wasn't my type." Laney locked eyes with Harper. "Too keen."

She couldn't help the goose bumps and the shiver as Laney's eyes conveyed so much more than the words she was speaking.

"So…" Laney sat back and folded her arms across her chest and Harper felt released from the tractor beam of Laney's stare. "Are you enjoying your stay so far?"

"I am. I've never traveled out of the States before now, so it's a pleasure to be here."

"Never been out of America? At all?" Harper didn't know if that was a look of confusion or disgust on Laney's face.

"Yeah. My parents never had much disposable income, and since graduating from college, most of my own money has gone to living expenses and paying off student loans. And even though I always run away with Alice for three weeks every summer, those trips mostly consist of camping around the cooler parts of Northern Arizona or surrounding western states."

"How charming," Laney said in a curious tone. "Well, you simply must expand your horizons. You're missing out on so much of what the world has to offer."

A twinge of inadequacy flashed through Harper as she forced a smile and returned her attention to the menu. It wasn't as though she didn't like traveling, she just didn't have the means to do anything extensive. And yes, her trips with Alice were probably low-rent compared to where Laney had been and the accommodations a princess would be accustomed to, but Harper could honestly say that she wouldn't have swapped them for anything. And especially not for the awkward feeling that this restaurant was giving her. Right now, a grilled cheese sandwich cooked on a camp stove while overlooking a lake wearing a pair of her scruffiest jeans sounded wonderful.

A server approached. "Princess Laney, how nice of you to join us this evening."

"Charlie, so nice to see you again, and please, just call me Laney."

"But of course." He placed a basket of dark brown bread on the table. "And who might your beautiful companion be?"

"This is Harper. She's visiting us from America."

"How lovely. I hope you are enjoying your stay?"

"I am, thank you."

"Now then." Laney pointed to the menu. "How's the lobster thermidor this evening?"

"Exquisite. I highly recommend it."

"Excellent, we'll have that, the Cornish crab salad, a side of the market vegetables bouquetière, and what do you recommend for a pairing wine?"

"The Bonneau du Martray Corton-Charlemagne. We have a 2008."

"We'll take a bottle of that as well."

"Right away."

Charlie gathered the menus and Harper had to pause a moment. While it was nice of Laney to take the lead and order for them both, she was actually eyeing the Scottish salmon more than the lobster. But maybe Laney knew something she didn't. Still, it would have been nice if she was given the opportunity to talk to Charlie about the menu options instead of Laney just assuming.

"So why don't you want to be addressed as princess?"

Laney grabbed a slice of bread, tore a piece in two, and smeared butter over it. "Because I can't stand all the expectations that come with being a royal. It's such a bore. There's always someone telling me what I can and can't do. I hate it. I just want to be my own person. Do my own thing. Is that so hard to ask?"

Harper shook her head as she dug into the breadbasket. "Have you ever thought about breaking away from your family? Leaving it all behind? It's been done before."

"And give up my trust fund? And all this? How do you think meals like this get paid for?"

"Oh, um…sorry." Okay, there seemed to be a bit of hypocrisy there, but since Harper had never been gifted with money, she had no reference to the pull it would have when considering a choice between wealth or being true to herself. "I was just…" She waved a dismissive hand. "Never mind. Are they at least okay with you being gay?"

A cloud passed across Laney's face. "They hate it. When I first told Father, he thought it was a phase, something that I would grow out of. When he realized this is who I am, he threatened to cut me off if I continued my *indecencies* with women. Can't have a tarnish on the family name."

"What'd you do?"

"I went into the closet like a good girl and continued being with women more discreetly." Laney shrugged and Harper tried to fill in the blanks. Maybe that was why after googling her, she had not found one single article tying Laney to anyone, male or female.

Harper nodded. Both of her parents were fine with her being with whomever she chose. As long as she was happy, they didn't seem to care. But as she sat back, chewing on her bread listening as Laney comfortably talked about herself, she wondered what life would look like being with a closeted princess. Always being in the shadows, watching a lover fake her way through a lifestyle of pretense and posturing. The thought was unappealing to her, but then again, every relationship she'd had seemed to come with a price. At least Laney was being honest about what the cost of maintaining her title was.

"What if you met someone you fell in love with?" Ever the diehard romantic, Harper couldn't help but ask. "Wouldn't you want…I mean, wouldn't you want to live together, or to marry, or even just to go walking hand in hand through a park?" The princess in the novel they'd read had given up her title for love and told everyone why. It was an epic ending.

"Everywhere I go there are photographers. So I've learned to do without that kind of thing." Laney seemed annoyed now. "I've worked very hard to cultivate a private life, to find places where I can go, where I can entertain the women I like. I know you aren't very worldly, Harper…" Laney leaned in, holding her gaze. "In fact, it's one of the many things that attracts me to you. But believe it or not, there are plenty of women out there who would happily hide away with me as long as it means they get to spend my money."

"I'm not like that," Harper protested.

"I'm not saying you are, my sweet thing." She sat back in her seat as the waiter arrived with their wine. "If you were, we'd have skipped this amazing dinner we're about to have and gone straight to my flat. And where would be the fun in that?" She lifted an eyebrow.

Harper didn't like the feeling Laney's words created in her body. It was an odd mixture of arousal and discomfort.

"You're a bit sure of yourself." Harper wasn't going to let herself be intimidated. "Who's to say that if not for this amazing dinner, I would've even come?"

Laney's laugh was long and genuine. "I don't believe in fate—or in your romance books—but finding you has been a wonderful surprise."

Harper was glad for the pause created by the waiter asking Laney to try the wine. The compliments, the attention, it was all a bit overwhelming, but maybe it was something she needed to try to get used to. Despite everything she and Alice had talked about, Harper hadn't come to England looking for a princess—every time she had thought about the trip in the weeks before arriving, her thoughts had been full of Chelsea. But the fact was that Chelsea wasn't interested in her, and Laney was. She took a huge gulp of the wine, barely tasting how delicious it was, and turned her attention fully back to Laney, determined to let herself enjoy the evening.

CHAPTER EIGHT

Chelsea was sitting at her kitchen table, half-empty glass of wine in hand, and staring out the window. The twinkle of her neighborhood lights was a blur as she held a distant gaze at nothing in particular. She tilted the glass until the last drop of wine swirled in her mouth, swallowed it in one gulp, and greeted the beginning stage of numbness with welcome relief. She hoped it would take the edge off the irritation that had been building since she left Harper at the Ritz. She activated her watch. One minute had ticked away since the last time she checked. She rolled her eyes and scolded herself for caring as she grabbed the bottle off the table and refilled her glass. So Harper was out on a date with a princess, having a wonderful time, at some fancy restaurant. So what? That was the deal, wasn't it? She would show her around and help her "find a princess" while they were reconnecting as old friends. She was even the one who said she'd be a bloody wing woman. But never in her wildest dreams did she think Harper would actually happen upon royalty, or that her royal highness would make quite such a play for her. Bloody fucking hell. She took another sip. Those things were only supposed to happen in fairy tales.

The knock on the door brought her jumping to her feet. She'd been terrified that Harper wouldn't come home at all. She was pretty sure Laney could find a hundred ways to make her want to stay.

"We brought donuts!" Denise announced as Chelsea swung open the door and her niece and nephew burst in.

"Aunt Chelsea!"

Chelsea blinked away her thoughts as she bent with outstretched arms. "Invaded by my favorite people." She wrapped them in a tight hug as they giggled. Denise approached, sat, and placed two donut boxes on the pile of papers scattered on the table.

"One of these is for Mike." She opened the top box and then set it aside. "And one's for you." She pushed the second box in front of Chelsea. "They were out of the Baileys and chocolate, so I got you an extra strawberry one." Denise handed one of the donuts to Millie as Nick clambered up onto Chelsea's lap.

"Thanks, Denise, what do I owe you?" Chelsea tousled Nick's hair as she kissed him on the cheek.

Denise waved her off. "Nothing, we were passing through and the kids wanted a donut." She commandeered Chelsea's wine glass and took a sip. "Besides, you sounded a bit down when I called, so I thought you needed them. What's going on, Chels?"

"Nothing."

Denise sat back and gave her the look. The one that says *I'm your sister and I can smell your bullshit a mile away*. Chelsea knew resistance was futile, so she surrendered with a sigh. "Harper's out having dinner with Princess Laney."

"Princess who?"

"Prince Daniel's youngest daughter."

"Are you fucking joking?"

"Mum! You said a bad word." Millie placed her hands over her ears.

"Oops, yes, I did, sweetie. It just kinda slipped out, and what did I say you were supposed to do if you heard me swear?"

"Not tell Dad."

"That's my girl." Denise kissed Millie on the forehead and handed her a second donut, as Chelsea averted her eyes and tried to refrain from laughing.

Denise leaned in. "How the hell did Harper meet Princess Laney?"

Chelsea grabbed a donut and walked Denise through the day. By the time she finished the sticky bun, her sister was caught up. "Wow." Denise pushed herself deep into the chair. "She actually bumped into a real princess? That's ridiculous. I've lived here my whole life and I've never seen, let alone met, *any* member of the royal family."

"I know. I'm kind of gutted. We were getting on well. It's been really nice reconnecting. I thought she was feeling the same way, but…" Chelsea shrugged.

"No wonder you sounded down."

Chelsea gave a repeat shrug. What else could she do? Tell Harper that after reconnecting with her she also reconnected with the feelings she had for her fifteen years ago? That Harper was the first person she had loved and that everyone who had come since couldn't hold a candle to her? No. She needed to manage her feelings toward Harper and be happy for her. It's what friends did for one another, right?

"Look, if I were you," Denise said as she finished Chelsea's glass of wine in three quick gulps and poured another, "I would tell her how you feel about her before Princess Laney gets her royal little hands on her."

"Denise, eww, no visuals, please." But that's precisely why she had been checking her watch all evening. She knew the longer the night progressed without Harper returning to her flat, the better the chance of her and Laney hooking up. She sighed. "I can't do that, I don't...I mean, it's been ages. It's kind of pathetic to still have feelings for her. And you should have seen how excited she was."

"Well, I think you should say something...anything. Your strong, silent pining thing might be sexy but it's kind of ineffective, I'm surprised you haven't realized that yet—" A text notification interrupted Denise as she glanced at her phone. "That's Mike wanting to know how much longer I'll be. God help me keeping that man from his sugar addiction." She grabbed the extra box. A piece of paper stuck to the bottom, and as she dislodged it, Denise brought it closer. "Is this—"

"Yeah," Chelsea confirmed. "The estate agents called again and said the space is still available. Apparently, the other person's loan application fell through, so it's back on the market." Last year, on the anniversary date of Ryan's death, Chelsea decided she wanted to open a restaurant in Whitstable in his honor. When she ran it by Jennifer, instead of supporting the idea, she scoffed at it. She claimed Whitstable was not the kind of town she wanted to live in, and it wouldn't make anywhere near as much money as the place her family had already sold in the Docklands. In fact, Jennifer revealed bitterly, she was sick of Chelsea being in the restaurant business at all. Although she didn't seem to mind the long hours when Chelsea was making plenty of money. But rather than following through on her instincts, Chelsea scrapped the idea of the restaurant, and instead bought her flat in Shoreditch. Hoping somehow that a good job would follow, and the artsy neighborhood would make Jennifer happy. She was trying to salvage a relationship that was already submerged and sinking. And it didn't work. So now, she was going to do what she had wanted to do in the first place and follow her passion rather than focusing on the money.

"You going through with it this time?"

"Yeah, I think I am."

"Do you have enough money?"

"I already crunched the numbers. If the bank approves my business plan and gives me the loan, I'll be good. Then I'll sell this flat and buy a smaller place in Whitstable. I think I can make it work."

Denise extended her arm and squeezed Chelsea's hand. "Mum and Dad are really going to be proud of you." She paused. "And so am I."

"I was thinking of calling it Ryan's." Chelsea saw his smiling face in her mind, and the way he always laughed when she cracked a joke, no matter how bad. And how in the end, he was so emaciated he could barely talk, much less laugh. And she remembered the cold and rainy afternoon when they were all huddled around him, the monitors announcing what she already intuitively knew. As the nurses rushed to his side, and the heartbreaking words tumbled out of the doctor's mouth, the walls closed in around her so tight she felt like she was going to suffocate.

"Feels like it's something I could do to remember him. Keep his dream alive." Chelsea wasn't being completely truthful. "And I need it too. I'm drifting. I'm not happy. It'll give me a focus. And hopefully, an income."

Denise placed her hand over her heart. "Oh, Chels, I love it."

Chelsea fetched a piece of paper from the bottom of the pile to the top. "I still had the plans, so I've been sketching an idea of how I'd like the layout to be. I thought I could put the tables here, the kitchen would be back here, and the bar there." She tapped the drawing. "The menu wouldn't be extensive, I'd focus on seafood obviously, and showcase all of Ryan's favorite dishes." She sailed another piece of paper in front of Denise.

"This looks fantastic," Denise said without taking her eyes off the paper.

"I'll be in Whitstable tomorrow with Harper and Alice, so I'm going by there to get a better feel for the space. Then I'll crunch more numbers, and if the bank says yes, I'll make an offer." It wasn't as easy as she was making it sound. The one thing she kept getting stuck on was the business plan. Harper had offered to help, but that was before Laney. She wasn't sure how much she was going to see of Harper. And she had considered already that Harper might not even want to go to Whitstable now.

Denise's phone chimed again, and she rolled her eyes. "I need to get going before my impatient husband has a coronary." She stood, called Millie and Nick away from the TV, and headed for the door. "But I want to talk to you more about this. Call me tomorrow after you see the place—"

She opened the door to Harper, who stood frozen, hand outstretched, about to ring the doorbell. "Oh my God. Denise?"

"Harper?" Denise stepped back as she gushed. "My, my, you have definitely improved with age. You look fantastic."

"Thanks." Harper blushed as she averted her eyes. "And who is this?"

"My tearaways. Millie and Nick. Ten and three."

"Hello, Millie and Nick." Harper's voice slurred ever so slightly.

"You're very pretty," Millie said.

"Well, thank you," Harper said, then addressed Denise. "Please tell me you're not leaving. I would love to sit with you and catch up."

"Another time. I have a husband chomping at the bit for his donuts." She jiggled the box.

"Ah, I see. Well, we have to make plans for lunch or dinner before I leave."

"We will, I promise." Denise mouthed a silent "wow" in Chelsea's direction as she pointed at Harper before herding the kids out of the door and down the stairs.

Chelsea stood silent as she stared at Harper. Wow wasn't even halfway to how great she looked. The loose-fitting casual clothes she had always associated with her were now replaced by a formal gown so tight it was as though it were sculpted to her shape. Her hair was up with wispy strands drawing attention to a face with hints of colors and sheen she had never seen on her before. She had always thought Harper was beautiful, but the goddess of a woman standing before her was next-level gorgeous. So when the words "you really look *nice*" came out of her mouth, she all but rolled her eyes. Nice? Really? That word didn't even begin to do Harper justice.

Harper smiled shyly as she tucked a strand of hair behind her ear. "Thank you, but truthfully, I'm dying to get out of this dress and put something more comfortable on." She stared at Chelsea for a beat before clumsily kicking off her shoes and gathering them on her way to the bedroom. "Is Alice back?" she called out.

"No, she's not." Chelsea tracked Harper as she crossed the room in front of her, an unwanted pulse of arousal low down in her belly confirming just how good she looked in that dress. There was a slight sway to her walk, which confirmed that Harper was a little drunk. She wanted to be jealous about it, but she needed to just be glad Harper had come home.

She returned to the table and her own wine, determined to stop acting so possessive. She had no claim on Harper, none at all. And it was her fault they hadn't even stayed in touch. She rolled the tension out of her shoulders, picked up a highlighter, and went back to her floor plans.

"She must be having a nice evening with Oliver," Harper shouted to her from the bedroom, the door ajar. "I swear they're like two peas in a pod those two. I find him a bit much, but Alice finds him hilarious." Harper emerged from her room wearing a faded ASU T-shirt and boxer shorts. "Ah, that feels so much better," she said as she headed into the bathroom. Chelsea heard the water and wished she could stand under a cold shower herself. Feeling like this about Harper, a completely disinterested Harper, felt wrong somehow. She took a few calming breaths while waiting for Harper, who came into the kitchen, grabbed the box of cereal off the counter, and poured some in a big bowl. "Want some cereal?"

"No thanks, I just had a donut…but didn't you just have dinner?" Chelsea focused on Harper's every move. Her face was now scrubbed of the makeup, her hair was down, and she was barefoot. As beautiful as Harper was when she walked in, she had to admit, this was the Harper that Chelsea found the most attractive.

"I did. Laney took me to this really upscale restaurant, but their food portions were ridiculously small. I had lobster thermidor. I thought it would be a whole big lobster, but it wasn't. Instead, all I got was this little baby lobster the size of a crayfish, and my dessert was no bigger than a postage stamp, so I'm still hungry." Harper poured almond milk into the bowl as she spoke. "Oh, and here's a fun fact, I learned the difference between lobster thermidor and lobster Newburg. But also a fun fact, I already forgot. Sorry." The words kept tumbling out. Chelsea smiled. Tipsy Harper was kind of funny. She joined Chelsea at the table, leaning back in the chair, bowl in hand as she shoveled cereal into her mouth.

"So you had a good time?" Chelsea couldn't help but ask.

"I did. The restaurant was so fancy, it made the Ritz look shabby. We tried some great wines too." Harper gushed as she chewed. "And Laney's kinda interesting—she's well-traveled, like you'd expect a princess to be, she knows three languages, has a stable of horses, her own helicopter, and oh…" She pointed the spoon at Chelsea. "She said she has a tennis court. I told her how good you are at tennis, and I asked her if you two could play sometime and she said yes."

Chelsea took a gulp of wine, hoping to tamp down the negative feelings caused by Harper's casual admission of how much she liked Laney. It wasn't just that she liked her, it seemed like she liked the lifestyle too, and that was not something that Chelsea had expected. She again reminded herself that not only did she not really know *this* Harper but Harper's trip here was never about her. She took a breath and forced a smile.

"I'm a bit out of practice, but yeah, maybe." Chelsea was pretty sure she could outplay Laney as rusty as she was, but she had no intention of spending any more time with her.

"She also knows a ton about the history of England. In fact, she wanted to take me on a trip to Oxford tomorrow—which sounds amazing—but I told her we were all going to Whitstable. She even said she could get us all some tickets to that Monet exhibition I really wanted to see, the one that's sold out. She's a trustee there or something like that."

"Sounds like you had a nice evening." Chelsea tried to sound pleased about it.

"I did. She's nothing like I envisioned a princess to be. I mean, yeah, you know, she has that edge of pompous royalty about her, and she leads a ridiculously exotic lifestyle, but she's also really easy to talk to and even kind of gritty around the edges. The juxtaposition is kinda interesting." Harper scooped another spoonful of cereal in her mouth as she shrugged. "Anyway, she had just ordered brandy for us when she had to leave. Her family sent her driver for her, and it sounded like something serious was up. I took an Uber back here and it cost a small fortune. But there's no way I could have managed the subway in those shoes. They were really starting to pinch my feet."

Chelsea couldn't tell how Harper felt about the evening being cut short, but it sounded like she would have stayed if Laney had let her. She felt the sinking feeling in her stomach. "If you'd rather go with Laney to Oxford tomorrow instead of Whitstable, you should. Oxford is amazing, very historical." This wasn't exactly what Denise had in mind when she suggested Chelsea fight for Harper. It sounded like the date had gone exactly the way she had dreaded, and the idea of Harper in Laney's arms was surprisingly hurtful.

"I'm sure it is, but I'm really looking forward to going to Whitstable." She paused in thought. "It was an entire chapter in the romance novel, and it's been on my bucket list since I read *Tipping the Velvet*, so I'm dying to see it."

Another feeling of disappointment hit Chelsea when she realized the reason Harper wanted to go to Whitstable had more to do with the book than her. "I think you should go to Oxford." The sickly feeling in her stomach made her want to withdraw. It was what she did. "Because when a princess invites you to go out, you should definitely—"

Harper reached across the table and placed a hand on her arm. "Chels, I really want to go to Whitstable with you, okay?" A jolt shot through Chelsea's body as Harper began to caress her arm softly. "I'm really enjoying spending time with you."

Chelsea took in a breath, confused at the sudden attention. Her body wasn't confused. The goose bumps caused by Harper's touch confirmed what her body had been telling her since the moment they had reconnected. That although they had been separated in time and distance, something deep within her remembered the way Harper could make her body react. When she lifted her gaze to Harper, her eyes—the beautiful blue color shining, the pupils unmistakably dilated—were completely focused on Chelsea. The connection was intense and completely unexpected—not least because she'd been gushing about Laney just moments before. They stayed like that until Harper broke the trance by retracting her hand and averting her eyes. She fidgeted with the bowl and spoon in front of her, and for a moment, an awkward silence fell between them.

"What's all this?" Harper cleared her throat as Chelsea quickly shuffled the papers in a pile and placed them at the far side of the table.

"Oh, um, it's nothing, really."

"Wait a sec." Harper pinched back the top piece of paper. "Did you draw this?"

Chelsea nodded.

"Is this a restaurant?"

Again, Chelsea nodded. "Remember the other night, when I told you I was trying to find a way back into the business?"

"Yeah."

"Well, there's an empty space for lease in Whitstable, overlooking the sea. I've decided I want to open a restaurant of my own and make the menu a kind of tribute to the dishes Ryan used to make."

"Chels, that's amazing! Is that why you needed the business plan for the bank?"

"It is. I have to get a loan. My ex spent most of—" Chelsea stopped herself. Harper had just been out for a fancy meal with a fucking princess. The last thing Chelsea needed was to tell her how Jennifer had burned through what was left of the proceeds from the sale of her parents' restaurant and then walked out, leaving her with nothing. "I just mean she—Jennifer—spent most of her time in London and would never have been happy in Whitstable. So I couldn't really do it while we were together. But now I'm ready to give it a shot."

"Is this the menu?" Harper pointed to another sheet of paper as Chelsea nodded. "Wow, this all sounds absolutely delicious. I'd eat here in a heartbeat."

"Thanks, Harper. Hopefully, it'll be successful. I mean, everything's pretty much back to normal as far as the pandemic is concerned. And in the end, I was running my parents' place, so I know what I'm doing. I've got everything that Ryan left behind. He kept such detailed records, it was almost like he knew." Chelsea couldn't keep the emotion out of her voice. She swallowed down her feelings. "Plus, I know I can count on Mum and Dad for guidance and advice when needed, so hopefully it won't be another one of my screwups."

Harper pushed her bowl to one side and leaned closer. "Hey, the Chelsea I know can do *anything* once she sets her mind to it. She's amazing, talented, and just all-around fucking incredible. You've got this, Chels." She pulled Chelsea toward her in a sideways hug, and every nerve in Chelsea's body vibrated at her closeness. After a few beats, Harper let go.

"I need to do a walk-through tomorrow, and I'd really like to show you and Alice the space and get your opinion." Her voice sounded thicker than usual, Harper's closeness was making her body react.

"Alice can't make it. Oliver wants to start filming tomorrow, and for day one, she's going to some luxury spa in the country for a massage, a facial, and a mani-pedi." Harper again closed her hand over Chelsea's. "But I wouldn't miss a day in Whitstable with you for the world."

"Yeah?" Chelsea felt a heat flush her face as her heartbeat sped up and time slowed as she held eye contact with Harper.

"Yeah."

Chelsea studied Harper's eyes and noticed for the first time the slight gray specks that blended with the aqua blue. The way Harper was gazing at her made her feel like she was held in a trance. She slowly moved closer, until their breathing seemed to become one, and as she parted her lips in anticipation, she could feel the warmth of Harper's breath tickle across her skin.

The front door swung open, startling Chelsea, as Alice waltzed in. "Oh man, what a great day. This makeover's going to be so much fun." Alice paused as she glanced at them. "Okay, what's going on with you two?" She pointed at them accusingly. "Because there's a weird vibe in here telling me I just interrupted something."

Harper cleared her throat. "Nothing's going on. Chelsea was just, um, she was just showing me the plans for the restaurant she's going to open in Whitstable." Harper haphazardly grabbed at the papers.

"You're opening a restaurant? Hot damn, girl, that's awesome." Alice joined them at the table. "Congratulations." She slapped Chelsea on the back. "And not to take away from that awesomeness, but is that a box of donuts?"

"It is." Chelsea slid the box over to Alice as she caught Harper's eye. Harper offered her a shy smile. "Help yourself."

"Thanks. I had fish and chips with Oliver. They were delicious and all, but my stomach's been feeling a bit wonky ever since. I'm thinking I need some carbs to help settle it down." Alice grabbed a donut and took a bite.

"Perhaps a cup of tea and some crackers would be better?" Chelsea stood.

"Nah," Alice said as she waved her off. "Donuts will work. Oh, and if there's extra wine, I'd love a glass." Alice nodded to the bottle as she took a seat at the table. She finished the donut in three quick bites, licked a drizzle of jam from her fingers, then dipped into the box again.

"So, Harps, I'm dying to know how your date with Her Royal Highness, the magical Princess Laney was?" Alice mumbled as she chewed.

And there it was. The word "date" was like a needle scratching across a vinyl record. Chelsea's body stiffened as Harper filled Alice in on all the details. She didn't want another recap of how wonderful dinner with Laney was. She faked a yawn, and through half-hearted protests, she waved Alice and Harper off and dismissed herself. As she crawled into bed and slid under the covers, she clasped her arms behind her head and stared at the ceiling. Her brain was spinning with thoughts of Harper and Laney, the restaurant, the business plan she needed to write and the plans she needed to make for them in Whitstable to make sure Harper had a day to remember. But in truth, her brain wasn't the thing that was going to keep her awake. Her body was thrumming with tension, with unexpressed feelings and desire. She had been about to kiss Harper when Alice barreled in. And if she wasn't wrong, Harper was about to kiss her back. Yes, she was a little drunk, and yes, she was sitting outside Chelsea's door telling Alice how great Laney was…but Chelsea was the one she'd come home to, and Chelsea was the one she had been about to kiss. Maybe, just maybe, the romance that Harper had come to London to look for didn't involve a princess after all.

CHAPTER NINE

Harper sat with her knees tucked to her chest at the edge of a long, shingled beach, with the sea stretched out to the sides as far as her eyes could see. The almost cloudless sky with its wispy clouds offered a little shade from the afternoon sun, but the constant wind blowing across the water brought with it a bit of a chill. Seagulls squawked overhead, and as she took a few meditative breaths, she welcomed the briny salty air that reminded her of the few seaside visits she'd made to Southern California. She missed the ocean and the calming sound of the waves lapping against the shore. No wonder Chelsea had raved about this little seaside community, with its rows of brightly painted beach huts, weathered fishing boats lining the harbor, quaint shops and restaurants bookending its main street, and the overall laid-back vibe. Whitstable was a town full of charm, and she could easily see herself living here.

"Okay, I know I've been rambling all morning about *Tipping the Velvet*." She glanced to Chelsea, who sat next to her with eyes closed and head tilted to the sky. "But I have to confess that I have goose bumps knowing we're sitting here enjoying the same view as Nan and Kitty. And even though they were doomed in their love and all that, it's still kind of romantic." She sighed.

"Doomed but entirely fictional, right? I mean, I feel like I know them now that you've told me ALL about the book…and about exactly what 'tipping the velvet' means…" Chelsea lifted an eyebrow, and the teasing smile she gave Harper had her heart beating a little fast. "But I don't think we have to worry too much about them. Not least because

Nan gets her happy ever after, with—" Chelsea scrunched her face in concentration. "Florence?"

"Yes!" Harper laughed and offered Chelsea her hand for a high five. "And I know you think my romance reading obsession is a bit dumb, but I don't care."

"No, not at all. I think it's lovely. It's just…" Chelsea hesitated.

"What?"

"I dunno. Those happy ever afters can feel like a bit of pressure when your track record is like mine. I used to read those books myself… before…at college." She picked at a few pebbles on the bench. "When I was all hopeful and pining for you." Chelsea held her gaze as she spoke, and Harper felt like there might have been an invitation there, a chance for them to finally break the thick ice and talk about what had happened between them. But when Chelsea playfully nudged her, then turned and began tossing stones into the water, she dismissed it as nothing more than lighthearted banter.

"You were a closeted romance reader? Why didn't you say so?"

"Because it's been way too much fun to tease you about it." Again, Chelsea gave her a shy smile. It was *lovely*. She settled on the adjective she would never think to use had it not been for the fact that Chelsea had said it repeatedly throughout the day. But the single word held the perfect description of not only Chelsea's dimpled smile, but their day so far. A day spent eating seafood snacks, chasing them down with local brews, milling around a craft fair, and slowly peeling back the layers of time that had accumulated between them.

In the past few hours, Harper learned more about Chelsea than she'd known in the past fifteen years. Her passion for cooking and food, her love of London—and Whitstable—and now even the fact that, despite that air of cynicism, she used to read romances. Although they had been inseparable the latter part of their freshman year, it seemed they were both guilty of holding feelings close to their chest and not always tipping their hand. If both knew back then what little time they had, would either of them have waited so long to make the first move? Probably not. But between Chelsea's quiet and reserved demeanor, and Harper's chronic lack of confidence—it was amazing they crossed the line at all.

"Well, I think being hopeful and open to the possibility of

happiness brings its own rewards." Harper sounded like Alice giving one of her pep talks. She was talking to Chelsea, but also to herself. This vacation had been a risk, but so far it was working out better than she could have ever hoped for. "I mean, look at me—"

"You met a princess. Yeah, we know." Chelsea sounded a little snarky.

"I didn't mean it like that." She really didn't, and it dawned on her that she hadn't thought about Laney all day. In fact, despite her annoyance at the way Laney had been called away at the end of dinner—cutting short their evening and leaving her stranded in Mayfair—as soon as she arrived back to Chelsea's apartment, none of it had mattered. The little time she'd spent with Laney was enjoyable, but having Chelsea waiting up for her, in her cute pj's and with a glass of wine in hand, had felt like coming home to something she could get used to. She shook her head. Who was she kidding. She was being ridiculous, even by the standards of the books she read. Chelsea hadn't been waiting up for her. She had been enjoying an evening with her sister. And Harper had barreled in, and with liquid courage from the wine she had at dinner, let her feelings get the better of her and almost kissed Chelsea. Only Alice had saved her from making a total fool of herself. She sighed. In ten days, she was headed back to Phoenix, and the thought of leaving, of not knowing when she and Chelsea would see each other again, caused a sadness to wash over her.

"I'm not talking about Laney. I just mean that I'm sitting here with you, after all these years of us not being in touch. I'm having the best time, and if I hadn't taken the chance to come, I wouldn't..." She trailed off. Funny how after fifteen years, the feelings she had for Chelsea could still make her tongue-tied. But if she were being truthful, it wasn't just that. The woman sitting next to her, the one she had come close to kissing last night, was also the one who had not responded to any of her messages when she had tried to get back in touch. And that reminder hurt.

A beat passed and neither of them spoke as they both fixed their gaze at the sea. The high-pitched barking of a dog interrupted Harper's thoughts. She shaded her eyes until she focused on a bouncing black bundle of joy stubbornly refusing to leave the water as a woman stood shore-bound repeatedly calling his name.

"Well, I'm very glad you took the chance to come. I've missed you. And I'm sorry for, y'know, being a rubbish friend over the years. I feel like I've wasted a lot of time."

Chelsea spoke so softly that Harper almost lost her words in the breeze. But she felt the power of them in the fluttering in her stomach. When Chelsea turned to her with a sorrowful expression on her face, her eyes watery and a darker shade than usual despite the sun, Harper wanted to reach for her, but instead, comforted her with words.

"It's okay, you don't need to apologize."

"No, let me say it. I should have said it before now. After I returned from that trip to Phoenix, I finally gave in and let Jennifer move in with me. She was always jealous, but living together took it to a new level. She started becoming paranoid about me having exes, friends—anyone that wasn't her actually. It really drove her crazy. I made the mistake of telling her you'd got in touch, and she made me promise not to respond or be in contact. She was already mad as hell that I'd tried to see you in Phoenix. She said that it was like cheating on her." Chelsea turned to Harper. "But I want you to know that I wanted to respond, I wanted to be back in touch. I was just in this weird space with Jen." She averted her eyes as she openly struggled with her words. "And I gave in, I didn't treat you like I should have, like I wanted to…" She trailed off.

"I'm sorry I couldn't see you when you were in Phoenix. I thought you understood, but when you ghosted me when I reached out to you afterward, I figured you were pissed, and punishing me because I went on that ski trip rather than stay in town to see you. But I couldn't. I mean, I would have stayed if I could, but we had planned that trip for over a year. Besides, I had my own relationship stuff going on."

"I wasn't mad at you. How could I be? Attending that conference was a last-minute decision. I didn't expect you to change your plans. And ghosting you was all on me. I let myself become controlled by an unhealthy person and it got the better of me. I'm so sorry, Harper."

The sting had worn off long ago, but it still bothered Harper that Chelsea didn't send just one simple explanation text to put her mind at ease. Anything to soften the hurt of her getting back in touch only to drop out of sight again. But there was no point rehashing it now. The answer to the question about why had finally been answered. And besides, it wasn't like she had never been negatively influenced by a lover. Of course she had. She shrugged. "It's okay. It's in the past." Harper hoped her words didn't come across in a dismissive tone, but the painful expression on Chelsea's face made her wonder. "I just mean, we're here now…and we can't change anything that happened back then. And maybe the Universe had a reason for us not reconnecting, so…" Harper lightheartedly nudged her. "Maybe we should just sit and enjoy the view together until we have to meet with your real estate agent." She held Chelsea's gaze until she offered a small nod, seemingly satisfied with where they had got to, and then Harper turned back to face the sea as a gust of wind made her shiver.

"You can't possibly be cold?"

"You forget, I'm a desert rat. I'm used to hot temps."

"Move closer. I'm actually kinda warm. Plenty of body heat to share."

Harper closed the distance between them, slipped her hand under Chelsea's arm, and snuggled in slightly. Chelsea tensed and Harper almost pulled away, wondering if she had crossed a boundary. But after a few seconds, Harper felt her relax into the contact. They sat there for a while, the breeze from the sea no longer chilling her. Every nerve in her body vibrated with being this close to Chelsea. When Chelsea began to graze her thumb softly across the hand that held her arm, Harper felt the touch like an electric current, the soft pulsing between her legs making her arousal undeniable. She shifted position, wanting to press her side more fully against Chelsea. Chelsea adjusted her posture to lay an arm across her shoulders, pulling Harper closer to her. She could feel Chelsea's breathing, her chest rising and falling against her.

"I never meant for things to turn out the way they did." Chelsea said the words quietly. "Even though I know it was my fault." Harper felt her take in a breath. "And the last week has told me how stupid I was not to stay in touch. I know I can't compete with Laney on any level and I'm not trying to, I just…you know…wanted to tell you and do everything I can to make sure you have a good time."

Compete? Did Chelsea actually think she had to compete with Laney financially to make her trip here more enjoyable? Or was there more meaning in her vague statement? "I don't understand. The high tea and fancy dinner were wonderful and all, but I'm loving days like this, just relaxing, and chilling out with you."

"Okay." Chelsea turned her body slightly, breaking some of the physical connection between them. "I'm really glad about that."

Wow, that clarified nothing. Damn Chelsea and her English reserve. At that moment, she wanted nothing more than for Chelsea to pull her into her arms and kiss her. And for Chelsea to know that was what she wanted too. But the trouble was, Chelsea had been clear with her from the start that she was not in the market for another relationship, and after what Chelsea just shared about her ex, Harper couldn't really blame her. Still, there was something unspoken that she was convinced was stirring between them. Maybe there was a chapter for them that had yet to be written. Or was that just wishful thinking on her part?

"We should get going. I said we'd be at the restaurant around six and it's about twenty minutes from here, out west past that pub." Chelsea pointed at the quaint little building sitting on the esplanade a hundred yards away, before pulling away from Harper and standing up.

Harper nodded, and just like that the moment was gone. She stood as her phone chimed. She fished it out of her back pocket. It was Alice. She opened the photo attached to the message and smiled. She turned the screen to Chelsea. "Looks like someone else is having a great day." Alice was resplendent in a fluffy white bathrobe, her face completely covered in a thick green mud mask. She was lying on a covered white massage table, with Oliver on a matching table to her right.

"I'm glad she's having fun."

"Me too, and I hope this doesn't make me sound like a shitty friend, but I'm also glad she's having fun *there* while we're *here*."

"I'm not sure if that's all that shitty, but maybe that's because I'm glad too."

Harper's phone chimed a second time. This message was from Laney asking her to call her. It sounded casual, but Harper wasn't sure. Laney was obviously annoyed when Harper said no to the trip to Oxford, which was kind of odd. It was still mystifying to her that Laney had such an interest in spending time with her. She was beautiful, sophisticated—and a goddamn princess. And Harper was…well… Harper. She pushed the phone back into her pocket, determined not to think about Laney. She hooked her hand into the crook of Chelsea's arm, the intimate gesture hopefully conveying to Chelsea that whatever had happened in the past, in the here and now, Harper wanted to keep her close. "Now then, let's go see your new restaurant space."

❖

"What do you think, Harper?" Chelsea was happy when the estate agent had stepped outside to take a call. She hadn't wanted to talk in front of him, but she really wanted to know what Harper thought of the place.

The previous owners had left a few large stainless-steel items scattered haphazardly around the room, so it didn't look or feel much like a restaurant. But on the train to Whitstable, they had not only finished off her business plan, but Harper had listened intently as she talked her through the sketches she had made for the restaurant, and now she felt more hopeful about the place than she ever had.

"So, this will be the main dining area." Harper walked to the back of the room. "And along that wall will be the oyster bar?" She pointed to one side.

"Yes, exactly." Chelsea loved the fact that Harper had remembered everything she'd seen in the plans. "People can just come in for a glass of sparkling wine and a few oysters, or they can have a proper sit-down meal. Only the freshest fish and seafood, straight off the boats, with the sauces that Ryan created being what makes it all so special." She walked to the window. "And out front, a seating area…with a sea view. The previous owners used the space for parking, but not only do the cars ruin the view down to the sea from that huge window, but most people that come want to be able to drink with their dinner, so it's a complete waste of the space. It won't always be warm enough to use, but when it is, it'll be a glorious spot to eat at." In her mind, Chelsea could see it all. The interior, the full tables out front, even the sunset.

"I love how passionate you are about it all." Harper joined her at the window. "I know you're doing this for Ryan, but I can also see how much it means to you too." She turned to Chelsea. "I can imagine you here, greeting the customers, and making sure the food is perfect. In fact, every single thing you've cooked for Alice and me has been perfect. I probably haven't thanked you enough."

"I haven't cooked for you, not in the way I'd like to. Eggs Florentine and French toast doesn't count as cooking."

"It does to me." Harper laughed. "I'm a terrible cook."

"I'd like to cook for you properly. One of Ryan's dishes, one of the dishes we'll serve here—" Chelsea stopped herself. She didn't want to tempt fate. The loan application was in and she was pretty sure the estate agents would accept her offer. But Whitstable—despite Jennifer's dismissal of the place—was a popular weekend haunt for Londoners with plenty of money, and if it wasn't for the pandemic scaring people out of the restaurant business, the price of the lease on this place would be beyond her. She felt a tight feeling in her chest. If she didn't land the lease on this place, she had no Plan B. She made herself take a few breaths. *All is okay.* She used the phrase Ryan had used with her when she was nervous before a tournament.

"You know, I don't even know if you like seafood. Seemed as though we survived on pizza, burgers, and shakes at ASU. I don't want to kill you with my homemade shrimp pâté if you have an allergy or something." Chelsea tried to keep her tone light, but she realized she would hate it if Harper didn't like seafood.

"Oh my God, I can't believe how much junk we ate back then. But to answer your question, I love seafood and no, I don't have an allergy. In fact, lately I've been into ono fish tacos from this little restaurant not far from my house. They're so good. In fact, I can honestly say that I enjoy them more than the lobster thermidor Laney ordered for us last night."

"I'm not going to serve that kind of pretentious stuff. It's rich people's food, and all about style over taste." Chelsea couldn't help but react. She stopped herself and took in a small breath. "I'm sorry. I shouldn't be so rude. I'm sure it was really nice. I just mean the menu here will be simpler, more accessible." She hated herself for her jealousy about Laney. She couldn't compete with her. It would be stupid to even try.

Harper looked at her with an expression Chelsea couldn't read. A beat passed. "Well, I would love to let you cook a seafood dish for me." Harper put a hand on her arm, her gaze sincere. "Name the day and I promise to send Alice out somewhere with Oliver." Harper smiled warmly.

"Deal." The idea excited Chelsea.

"Have you ladies finished having your look-see?" Billy, the far too youthful looking estate agent, bustled back inside the restaurant.

"We have. Thanks, Billy."

"Gonna make an offer?" He looked down at his phone. "I'm

supposed to tell you that we've got loads of interest and you should get in quick, but I think we both know that's not true. It's yours if you can meet the asking price."

Chelsea again felt her chest constrict with nervousness. "I hope to. Might take a couple of days, but I'll be in touch." The bank had said decisions on loans were made within forty-eight hours.

Outside the restaurant, Chelsea and Harper watched Billy lock the doors and pull down the shutters before sauntering off toward the town center, clipboard under his arm. The sun sat low in the sky not quite ready to settle itself down for the night.

"All that talk of food has made me hungry again." Harper had again tucked her hand into the crook of Chelsea's arm. It was a new thing. She'd never done it before today, and every time she did, it felt kinda nice. Like Harper was laying claim to her somehow. They'd never had that at college. By the time they'd decided they wanted to be lovers, Chelsea had been called away. She couldn't remember them ever even holding hands. Sometimes, the simplest things were the things that she missed.

"Me too. How about for old time's sake, we get some pizza and eat it on the beach while the sun sets—" Chelsea stopped, worrying she was coming on a bit strong.

"Sounds fantastic." Harper's quick response cut right across her doubts. "And maybe we could try another local brew. The last time we had pizza and watched the sun set, we definitely had beer." Harper held her gaze for a beat.

So Harper was thinking about the same night she was. The idea of it made Chelsea feel happy and warm—and nervous as hell. It didn't matter how much she regretted losing Harper, there was no denying that fifteen years had gone by, and they were both very different people. She knew no amount of nostalgia-infused pizza and beer was going to change that, but it was hard not to hope.

❖

"Okay, my turn." Chelsea tapped a finger against her chin as if she were thinking. "Who's your favorite *L Word* character? Past show, not present."

"My favorite *L Word* character?" Harper echoed as her head

danced with fond memories of her and Alice curled up on her couch bingeing the box sets. "Ohhh, don't ask me that."

"Why? I remember you had all the DVDs. You were such a fan. You have to have had a favorite. Mine was Alice. All that kooky vulnerability was hard to resist." Chelsea nudged her. "C'mon."

"I guess if I had to choose," Harper steeled herself, "it would be Dana."

"Dana? The tennis player?" Chelsea lifted an eyebrow. "Really?"

"Too obvious?" She covered her eyes.

"I mean, if sweaty athletes are your thing, I'm not gonna judge you. Hurts a little to know that I was a Dana-substitute for you, though." Chelsea gave her a mischievous smile and Harper felt herself blush.

"Your turn to ask." Chelsea pointed at Harper with her beer bottle. The shining in her eyes suggested she was at least as tipsy as Harper was.

"Hmm, okay." Harper thought hard. The questions had only started because Chelsea couldn't believe she didn't know that Harper was allergic to cherries. They'd gone through favorite foods, favorite movies, and now even favorite TV characters. They were sitting side by side, leaning against one of the breakers on the beach. Their legs outstretched, beer bottles wedged in the shingles as if they were ice, and she was sporting a blue hooded sweatshirt with Whitstable written across the chest, that Chelsea had bought for her. They'd finished the pizza a long time ago, and now that the sun was close to setting, Harper realized they would soon need to head home. She wanted to make the most of this chance to get to know Chelsea better, to fill in some of the gaps from the time they'd been apart. "But let's make a rule. We can skip any question that feels uncomfortable to answer." Even with the numbing effects of the alcohol, she couldn't help her cautiousness.

"Sure. I think I'd refuse to answer if I didn't like the question anyway."

"I'm serious. You…we…can absolutely do that."

"I know. But since you seem to think we need an actual rule, I'd better agree to it. Though the fact we need one is making me anxious."

"Okay, okay, let me think." Harper wanted to ask Chelsea about her past relationships, if she missed Phoenix, if she missed her. But she didn't want things to get too heavy. They'd had a wonderful day and it always felt to her that every time she dipped too deep with personal questions, Chelsea retreated. Her brain searched for a general topic that floated safely on the surface. "Okay, what's the—" Harper's phone chimed. She ignored the interruption. "What's the thing about yourself you'd most like to change?"

"Physically or emotionally?" Chelsea held her gaze while taking a long swallow of her beer. Every time she looked at her like that, it was harder for Harper to focus.

"Both." Harper maintained eye contact.

"That's technically two questions…but since I'm going to ask you the very same questions after I answer, I'll let it go." She shifted position and turned to Harper. "Physically is easy. I'd like to lose some of the weight I've put on over the last few years. Working with food, not enough exercise, all that pandemic comfort-eating—"

"Don't say that. I think you look amazing." Harper really hadn't meant to blurt it out, but the smile Chelsea gave her was its own reward.

"No commentary, remember?"

"Yeah, sorry. Go on." Harper made a zipping motion across her mouth.

"Emotionally…I guess I'd like to be more *available*." Chelsea wrapped the word in an air quote. "I mean I had reasons not to be for a long time, but there comes a point when you realize it's really not good for you. That you can lose things. Lose opportunities. Lose people." She hesitated. "Out of some stupid sense that you don't deserve anything better. Jennifer was…"

Harper took a sip of beer, staring and waiting. She had not anticipated the answer to go in this direction. She thought Chelsea would keep it light but welcomed another opportunity to know her better.

"Jennifer had a good life with me. Lots of holidays, nice car, plenty of money to go around, the restaurant was booming. But when all that stopped, she left. Kind of made it clear I wasn't enough, that the travel and the money was what she had stayed for, not me. It was a bit of a knock to my confidence." She smiled uncertainly. "And that, right there, is a great example of our famous British understatement."

Harper knew that feeling. At the end of every one of her failed relationships, she had been left feeling like she wasn't good enough, but it surprised her that Chelsea felt some of that same lack of confidence in her own appeal. She had always been the one people wanted. The captivating one. And Harper, like many, couldn't resist her.

"And you?"

"Me what?" Harper was lost in her thoughts once again.

"If you could change anything about your life, what would you change?"

"Ohhh. That's a tougher question when you put it that way." Harper let out a sigh as her phone chimed again. This time she fished it out of her pocket and saw with surprise that she had several missed messages and voice mails from Laney. "Huh, that's weird."

"What?"

"I have a bunch of missed calls, but I never heard my phone ring." She took a moment to make sure she had not mistakenly placed her phone on silent.

"From Alice?"

"No, Laney." She looked up to see Chelsea narrow her eyes.

"If you need to…" Chelsea waved a hand at the phone, her tone flat.

"No…erm…no, I don't. Sorry." She shoved the phone back in her pocket without listening to the messages. She wanted to stay present, with Chelsea, in this moment. She closed her eyes and gathered her thoughts.

"I didn't…I mean, I don't…trust myself to take risks." Harper paused. "Maybe risk isn't the right word. I'll rephrase that to say I don't really trust myself enough to take chances. I get…" She searched for the word. "Stuck. I mean, look at me, doing the same job for ten years, a job I'm really sick of. Oh, and let's not forget the fact that I'm single, and choose to spend my time reading about other people's romantic adventures rather than make a single attempt to make any of my own," Harper said as she lifted her eyes to Chelsea's.

"You don't trust yourself, or you don't trust other people?"

Harper finished off her beer. She was buying time.

"That's a great follow-up question." It really was. And answering it would mean laying bare to Chelsea all the times she had taken chances with people, given them her heart, and had it blow up in her face. And whether it was fair or not, that list included Chelsea. The way she dropped out of contact after Ryan died had hurt her badly.

But when she reappeared out of the blue, with the text to say she was in town, before vanishing again, that felt just as bad. A fresh rejection. "Let me consult the rule book about difficult-to-answer supplementary questions and whether they're allowed." She pretended to open a book and leaf through it. "Nope, sorry." It was a cop-out, but it was sensible. The beer and her closeness to Chelsea meant she might say something about how much of her heart she had trusted Chelsea with that night in the back of her truck. They had said how much they loved each other. She had meant it, but she had no idea if Chelsea had.

"Okay." Chelsea lifted her hands. "I'm not gonna push. But from where I'm sitting, next to you, on a beach in Whitstable watching the sun set, it looks to me like you're putting yourself down. You took a chance to come to England for the first time, took a chance to look me up—"

Harper's phone chimed. She glanced at it, then back to Chelsea. "Carry on, please."

"Laney again?"

Harper nodded, and Chelsea moved imperceptibly away from her. Harper hated it.

"See, that's another chance you took. Meeting Laney, going on a date with her. This trip is full of chances it looks like you're happy to take."

Chelsea didn't seem like she was meaning to be unkind, but Harper had felt the mood shift. Her phone rang, this time from a number she didn't recognize. Again, she ignored it.

"I didn't come here for Laney. And I didn't come because of the book either if I'm being totally honest. I mean, it's a fun idea, and I'm loving all of the experiences it's bringing, but I came mostly because it gave me an excuse to try to connect with you again."

"You mean, gave Alice an excuse—" Chelsea was looking at her intently.

"I would have sent that message," Harper said, but was that really true? She had her doubts. "At least, I like to think I would have contacted you. Alice just beat me to it. In a way, that proves my point. She messaged you because she thought I might not take the chance. But she knew…she knew that losing touch with you was…" She hesitated.

"Go on."

"Was really painful." Harper took a breath and took a chance.

"That it had been hard to lose you." Harper's chest tightened and her mouth turned uncomfortably dry as she felt anxiety build over how her words would be perceived. She took a long swallow of her beer.

"It was hard for me too." Chelsea reached down and took her hand. "If I could have done things differently, I would have come back—"

The ringing of Harper's phone startled them both. Chelsea dropped her hand and pushed herself back against the breaker. "Laney again?"

"Don't…wait…hold on." There was nothing Harper could say to get them back to where they were. She glanced at her phone. *What the fuck?* She rejected Laney's call. "Chelsea, I…" Another call interrupted her, and at this point, she felt like chucking the phone in the sea.

"She obviously wants to talk to you." Chelsea picked up the pizza box and shoved it roughly into a plastic bag before starting to gather the empty beer bottles. Harper wanted to shout at her to stop, and to sit back down. But her phone kept ringing.

"Something must be wrong. Let me take it really quick. Please sit back down. I'd like to finish this conversation…and…" *Fuck*. Who was she kidding, she'd like a lot more than that. "Just give me a minute. I want to make sure everything's okay." Chelsea turned away as Harper accepted the call and walked a few yards down the beach.

"Where are you, Harper, and why on earth aren't you answering your phone? Manny told me he doesn't know where to pick you up."

"I'm sorry, what are you talking about—"

"You should be sorry. It's probably going to take you an hour to get here and they're saying they can only keep the place open till ten. Do you have any idea how difficult it is to get the Royal Academy to agree to open late? And how stupid I'll look with half the staff here gawping at me, wondering why I even made them do it, if you don't show."

Harper held the phone away from her ear as Laney practically shouted at her. And while it was true that Harper had been drinking, she wasn't *that* tipsy—and she had absolutely no idea what Laney was talking about.

"Laney, slow down. What the hell is going on? I'm in Whitstable."

"I know you're in Whitstable," Laney slowed down, "but you said you wanted to see that Monet exhibition at the Royal Academy. The one that was all sold out. I told you I'm on the board here and I could get you tickets. I sent Manny to drive you to—"

"Wait, what? We didn't arrange anything…I don't remember agreeing to…" Harper racked her brain to see if she had perhaps mistakenly agreed to go. She was sure she hadn't. This was crazy. She turned and saw Chelsea standing rooted to one spot, watching her with narrowed eyes. Harper walked back in her direction.

"Harper, are you serious? I have used every ounce of influence I have here to get them to reopen the gallery for you tonight so you could see the exhibition. The one you mentioned twice over dinner about wanting to see. They are opening the Royal Academy just for us, until ten, and you're telling me you don't want to see the exhibition?"

"I'm not saying I don't want to see the exhibition. I'm just saying that I'm still in Whitstable and I wasn't expecting to come back to London until late tonight." She glanced at her screen for the time. "I don't even think I could get there before ten anyway." She tried to do the math. "It took us over two hours to get here."

"That's why I sent Manny." The irritation in Laney's voice was biting. "He's going to drive you to the chopper, it'll take about twenty minutes once you're airborne. Another fifteen minutes by car once you land. If you leave now, you can be here well before ten. And if you'd answered any of my calls before now, you wouldn't have had to rush. You'd already be here." She sounded exasperated rather than unkind—and it was true that Harper had ignored all her texts and calls. A tiny amount of guilt seeped in. Not over her decision to disregard the calls, more over the fact that Laney had inconvenienced other people on her account.

"I'm with Chelsea."

"I know."

"I'm not going to leave her in Whitstable." Harper could feel her heart sink. In any other situation she would have been elated. A helicopter ride and a private tour of a world-renowned art gallery were things that only happened in fairy tales. But moments ago, she had been sitting next to Chelsea holding hands, talking about missing each other, and she wanted them to keep talking. To keep connecting. And she definitely wasn't going to leave her stranded like Laney did to her last night.

"I'm not asking you to leave her in Whitstable, silly. Bring her along."

"Seriously?"

"Look, Harper, I'm not going to ask you to abandon your friend in some godforsaken corner of Kent. But I am asking you to please hurry yourself along here by telling me where you are so I can send Manny to take you to the chopper."

"Hold on. I just need a minute." Harper put the phone on mute, took in a breath, and stepped closer to Chelsea. "So it appears as though there's been a bit of a misunderstanding and Laney has arranged…" How could she explain without it sounding as insane as it was? "She arranged for the Royal Academy to open late tonight for me to see that exhibition. The one I mentioned that I wanted to go to, the one that was sold out. She took it upon herself to pull some favors. I haven't agreed to go. I told her I wanted to stay here."

"So stay here." Chelsea held her gaze.

"I really want to." Harper swallowed and took in a breath. The urgency in Laney's voice and the guilt was starting to get the better of her. "But she said a bunch of employees are staying overtime to accommodate me. And she sent a helicopter, and her driver, who's apparently waiting for directions on where to pick us up. And I'm feeling responsible because I didn't answer any of the messages so I could stop and correct this mess before it got to this point." Harper paused. "She said you can come too."

Chelsea took an actual step backward. Harper felt it like a slap.

"I don't want to see whatever exhibition that is. I want…wanted… to stay here a bit longer and…" She shrugged. "I don't know what comes after *and*. I've just had a really nice day and I wasn't expecting it to end like this."

"I wasn't expecting this either, and the night doesn't have to end. It could continue with a helicopter ride back to London. I've never even been in a helicopter, have you?"

"Harper, don't."

"What?"

"Go and see your exhibition. But don't try and make the best out of this, okay?"

"What do you want me to do, Chelsea? Huh? People are bending over backwards to make something happen because of something I said I wanted to see. And as much as I wish I had stopped this whole thing from ever happening, the fact is, I didn't. So I'm really not sure what it is I'm supposed to do at this point." Harper waited. Not sure what else to say or do. The truth was she didn't owe Laney a damn thing. She seemed interesting, her life was exciting, and she had been very sweet to Harper, but none of it compared to the way Chelsea made her feel. But Harper didn't know whether what she and Chelsea were doing was revisiting the past to agree they'd lost something or doing it to agree they wanted something from each other. The signals were mixed and confusing.

She heard her name being called. Laney's voice was muffled by the phone's speaker, but it was loud enough for them to both hear her.

"Sounds like the princess is getting impatient." Chelsea leaned down to pick up the last of the beer. "You'd better get going. You can tell her to pick you up in front of the Hotel Continental on Beach Walk."

"Only if you come too." Harper put a hand on Chelsea's arm. "Please. I'm sorry for fucking up our evening, but I don't want to say good-bye to you here, like this."

Chelsea looked at her for a long time. In the golden light of the fading day, she looked as beautiful as she ever had. The small frown and creases in her forehead made her look like she had things to say. Instead of words, she simply nodded, before turning back toward the path behind them.

Harper watched her walk away with a heavy heart. She unmuted her phone, gave the location to Laney so she could relay it to Manny, and scurried after Chelsea.

❖

Chelsea had been standing in front of the same painting for several minutes. It wasn't because she particularly liked it, she just wanted to stand still, to take a moment and clear her head. She'd had a glorious day but was now having an evening worse than she could have imagined. Across the room, Laney was loudly exclaiming the virtues of a painting of a woman with a big blue parasol sitting on a beach, while Harper seemed to be hanging on to her every word. She felt a little nauseous, not sure if it was the after-effects of the helicopter ride, the beer, or the feelings stirred by seeing Harper together with Laney like that.

"It's honestly a masterpiece." Laney's voice rang out. "Most people love the water lilies, of course, but this one—*The Beach at Trouville*—is my favorite. It's less recognizable but a much better example of his brilliance. I had painting lessons as a child, and we went there, to Trouville, to paint, so we could see exactly what he had seen."

Somehow Chelsea doubted that it would have been exactly the same, but what did she know. She made herself stare at the little boat on the mud-colored water on the canvas in front of her and tried to tune out their voices. She had no idea why she had agreed to come with Harper instead of simply going home—it was like she hadn't wanted to stay but she couldn't bring herself to leave Harper with Laney either. Even for a princess, the act of opening up a gallery like the Royal Academy was a gesture that suggested Laney's interest in Harper was pretty intense.

"Do you like it?" This time the voice was Harper's.

She waited for Laney to reply.

"Chelsea, I said, do you like it?" She turned and saw both Harper and Laney looking in her direction.

When they'd first arrived, Harper had tried to include her with questions like that, but Laney had done her best to gradually peel Harper away from her.

"I guess so." She shrugged. What could she say? She didn't know a thing about art.

"I think a big print of it would look great on the main wall of your new restaurant." Harper looked at her with wide eyes. "Don't you think? I mean, you said you wanted to incorporate the beach theme into your place."

"You have a restaurant?" Laney sounded surprised. "Harper had said you weren't working."

Chelsea blinked. The idea of Harper discussing her with Laney was not a nice one.

"I'm not. I'm..." She had no interest in explaining herself to Laney.

"She's about to open one. In Whitstable. It's an amazing spot, right on the beach, near the harbor. Beautiful doesn't even begin to describe the location."

Chelsea wasn't superstitious, but hearing Harper talk about the restaurant with such certainty made her feel panicky.

"Not about to open it, just considering it." It really was time for her to go home. Hanging around like a third wheel was making her feel ridiculous. She pointed at the door. "I'm actually going to head out now if that's okay. I have a lot to do tomorrow." She didn't have a lot to do.

As Harper had felt the need to point out to Laney, she was currently unemployed. Her only plan for tomorrow was to find something to do that would keep her away from Harper until she got her feelings under control.

"Sure thing. I'll have someone drive you." Laney waved a hand at someone standing by the door.

"It's okay, I can get myself home." Chelsea's reply was terse, but she didn't care.

Harper was staring at her uncertainly in much the way she had done on the beach, when she was telling her that she was about to ruin their perfect day by flying off to London to see Laney.

"I think I'll head out too." Harper turned away from her to look at Laney. "I'm pretty tired, it was a long day. I really appreciate this, Laney, I've had an amazing time, but—"

"Are you kidding?" Laney's tone made her annoyance clear. "You're leaving already? After I sent a bloody chopper halfway across England for you?"

"Here you all are!" The voice that rang out from across the room was Oliver's. He strode across the room with a breathless Alice in tow, the two of them dressed up to the nines. "We didn't think we were going to make it. Might have taken less time if Alice here was able to walk a bit quicker. I know you Americans never get out of your cars, but honestly, a fifteen-minute walk shouldn't take thirty."

"Too many people to dodge on the sidewalks." Alice huffed the words. "What did we miss?"

"Actually, we were just about to leave." Harper smiled as she spoke, seeming to Chelsea a lot more relaxed than a minute ago. "I was just about to thank Laney for the helicopter ride here and the amazing tour of this place from such a knowledgeable and charming guide." Harper tilted her head in Laney's direction. Laney's face was still fixed in a scowl.

"You rode in a helicopter? Damn, girl, how awesome is that?"

"It was pretty awesome."

"Well, I can't compete with that, but I will say my day was pretty awesome too. After the spa, Oliver took me to this place at the top of the Shard and we taped a segment of me trying out some of the food and being waited on like a princess. We had this private little room and our own personal waiters. One for wine and one for food, which, by the way, was incredible. Although all the cutlery choices were a bit confusing."

"Wait, back up, did you say you were leaving?" Oliver looked from Harper to Laney and back again. "Leaving as in going home, or leaving as in going somewhere else?"

"Going home, we're tired. It's been a long day. And if I'm honest, I had a little too much beer in Whitstable and it's given me a bit of a headache."

"So you're blowing off Laney because you…" Oliver laughed loudly, his expression gleeful. "Because you have a headache? Oh, that is priceless."

Chelsea watched as he threw an arm around Laney's shoulders. "Losing your touch, old girl?"

"Fuck off, Ollie." Laney said it like she meant it.

To Chelsea, the meaning was clear. Laney had expected to persuade Harper to go somewhere else with her—the helicopter, the gallery, all of it was meant to make it impossible for her to resist. But she had. Chelsea felt her mood lift. Maybe Harper wasn't as interested in Laney as Laney was in Harper?

"Well, I wanna stay and look at some of the paintings. Stay with me a bit." Alice linked arms with Harper and pulled her across the room before standing, head tilted ostentatiously, in front of what might have been a canvas full of irises…or lilies. Chelsea had looked at it earlier and found it impossible to tell.

"I'm heading out." Chelsea made a move toward the door. Harper turned in her direction briefly before Alice dragged her along to look at another painting. "Thanks for this, Laney." She swept her arm out. "Really appreciate it." She could have happily missed the whole thing, but she had been raised to be polite.

Harper pulled away from Alice and joined her at the door. It felt to Chelsea like the whole room was watching them.

"I'll be home in a bit."

Chelsea didn't move, didn't say a word. She didn't really know what Harper expected from her. She never had.

"It's up to you."

Harper held her gaze.

"Thanks for coming." She lowered her voice. "And thanks for today." She reached out her hand and squeezed Chelsea's arm. It was similar to the way she had squeezed her hand when they had been in the helicopter, and it was no more welcome than it had been when they were airborne. It felt like a consolation, and she hated it. And she especially hated the fact that they were being watched.

Chelsea nodded at Harper before turning and leaving. She didn't look back. Harper was confusing her. One minute hot, one minute cold. The best thing she could do for both of them was let Harper have a bit of space and let her decide if her holiday romance was supposed to involve a princess.

CHAPTER TEN

Happy birthday, Alice." Harper sat upright on the side of their bed as she presented a small, wrapped package and envelope from behind her back.

"Aw, thanks, Harps, you shouldn't have." In one motion, Alice had the paper ripped off and the dainty box opened.

"Ha! I love them." Alice placed the dangling pink flamingo earrings in her ears. "How do I look?" She flipped her head from side to side.

"You look fabulous."

"I feel fabulous." She giggled as she pinched a card out of the envelope. The cover design was of a hot air balloon and the inside was blank—except for Harper's signature—giving no hint to the meaning behind the design. Alice cocked her head.

"For your birthday I'm taking you on a hot air balloon ride in Sedona."

Alice squealed as she pulled Harper into a tight hug. "When we get back home," Harper said as she wiggled out of Alice's constricting grip. "We'll book a time and head on up." Two months ago, one of the women from their book club talked endlessly about the balloon ride she and her girlfriend took over the red rocks of Sedona. Since then, Alice had mentioned more than once that she had put that adventure high on her bucket list.

"Breakfast in five minutes," Chelsea announced from behind the door.

"Be right out," Alice called back before slumping back onto her bed. "Harper, Chelsea's awesome. She cooks, keeps her place tidier than I ever could, is sexy as hell, and she smolders enough to start a fire. Why you aren't falling over yourself to make something happen with her is a mystery to me." Alice poked at Harper with her toe. "Hell, if I didn't think you'd stab me in my sleep, I'd make a pass at her myself."

"Don't, Alice." Harper had heard this from Alice more than once over the past few days. Even though they hadn't seen much of each other because Alice had been living the high life with Oliver, when they had, lounging in bed before heading off to their respective days, Alice had been relentlessly cheerleading for Chelsea. It was especially weird since only a few days ago, she had been just as persistent in pushing Harper toward Laney. "I told you, it's not like that. We're friends."

"It's not like that, but it could be. I've seen how you look at her, and how she looks at you. And watching you two dance around each other is like reading a slow burn romance novel. And you know how much those books drive me nuts. If something sexy hasn't happened between the main characters by page twenty, I'm yawning."

"This isn't a romance novel." Harper ran a frustrated hand through her hair. "Besides, we've barely seen each other since Whitstable. I told you it kind of ended badly that night, and I think she thinks I'll be better off with Laney. And anyway, this was never going to work. We live on different continents, and we're different people. Maybe we always were."

"I'm not convinced. You and Chelsea got together in college despite neither of you being willing to say how much you wanted it. And here you are fifteen years later, still interested in each other and *still* not able to say it. And don't even try to deny it, I can read you like a book." Alice huffed. "And if you want to talk about different people, let's talk about you and Laney. You two are wildly different people. And don't get me wrong, I'm not saying you're not a good catch, but you gotta admit her relentless pursuit of you is a little weird."

Harper had told Alice that despite Laney being away at a wedding, she had been messaging often. So much so that it became a bit annoying. Lots of photos of banquets, and of famous people she had never heard of, and a flirty drunken two a.m. call that had woken them and wasn't at all welcome.

Alice was staring at her with an expression that was uncertain, even a little worried. It was like she wasn't sure how Harper was going to react to what she'd said. As if Harper didn't already know that being pursued by a beautiful princess—her, Harper, the geek of all geeks—was ridiculous.

"You say weird. I prefer to think she's just being nice. British people seem very hospitable. Look at the way Chelsea has bent over backwards to accommodate us. And now she's cooking you a birthday breakfast, which is probably getting cold while you waste time intruding into my love life." Harper made an effort to change the subject.

"What love life?" Alice scoffed. "Seems like you're avoiding the possibility of one like always. And that wasn't the point of coming here. We promised each other that if the chance came up, we'd take it."

"Well, if the chance comes up, I will take it. So far I've not had anything—or anyone—to say no to." Harper wasn't being entirely truthful. She hadn't told Alice that she'd said no to Chelsea when she'd asked her to stay in Whitstable and not go to London. And she certainly wasn't going to prove Alice right by admitting she had regretted it every day since.

Harper extended her hand and helped Alice peel herself off the bed. As they shuffled out of the bedroom, she tripped over one of several shopping bags stuffed with the clothes Alice had worn during the makeover, now scattered in piles on the floor. "Think you have enough free stuff?"

"Ha. As if there's such a thing." Alice chuckled as they headed into the kitchen.

"Mmm, the coffee smells good." In one movement, Harper grabbed the pot, filled two mugs, and handed one off to Alice. They headed toward the table as Chelsea flipped the last pancake on a platter and followed close behind.

"Morning, birthday girl." Chelsea placed the stack of pancakes on the table with a flourish. "A little bird told me banana walnut is your favorite. I hope you don't mind, but I took the liberty of tarting them up a bit by adding some yogurt, nutmeg, vanilla, and even a dash of local honey to the batter. Maple syrup is in that bottle, and whipped cream is in the bowl."

"Wow, this all looks amazing. Thanks, Chelsea." Alice slid the top three pancakes onto her plate, scooped a huge spoonful of whipped cream on top, drizzled some syrup, and dug in. "Oh my God, these are delicious." She moaned.

Harper sat opposite Chelsea and mouthed "thank you" to her as she forked two pancakes to her plate. Chelsea simply nodded. Not only had they not had time to finish the conversation they had started in Whitstable, but a depressing awkwardness had settled between them after the night at the art gallery and it had left Harper feeling completely out of sorts.

For the past three days, Harper had only seen Chelsea at breakfast, and Alice had always been present. She had seemed too busy with paperwork, lawyers, and trips to Whitstable for Harper to bother her, and since Alice was in the middle of her taping, Harper had tried to make the most of her spare time and distract herself from her confused feelings for Chelsea by getting out and about while she still had days left in the trip. She signed up for two tours. One to Hampton Court, and the other a long and exhausting day trip to Windsor Castle and Stonehenge. Both were informative, magical, and inspirational. And for the first time in years, she felt the grip of the writer's block—that prevented her from making progress with her own romance novel—loosen.

"So, how does it feel to be finishing up with the makeover?" Harper mumbled as she chewed. Alice was right. These were the best pancakes she had ever tasted.

"Actually, kinda sad. I was enjoying all the pampering."

"I bet." Chelsea reached across the table, scooped a dollop of whipped cream out of the bowl, then spread it evenly across the top of her pancake.

"Oliver said we'll be finished in a day or two and then they'll need half a day to edit, so it should be uploaded to his channel before we leave. And I can't wait to see it."

"It's going to be wonderful, Alice. And I'm proud of you for doing it. Plus, you made a nice friend in the process." Harper nudged her.

"Yeah, I—" The chime from her phone interrupted her. "Speaking of. That's Oliver. Huh, looks like there's a slight change of plan. We're to meet him at nine instead of eight outside a club called Indigo Blue."

"Never heard of it." Chelsea grabbed her phone, and a few taps later scrunched her face as she read from the screen. "This place is a high-end members-only club. In Mayfair." She glanced at Harper. "I thought you said Laney wasn't coming tonight?"

"She's not, at least I don't think so. She said she's away until tomorrow."

"It's probably an Oliver thing." Alice waved them off. "He doesn't need Laney's pull to get us into swanky places. That guy has so many connections around this town it's crazy." She pointed her fork at the two remaining pancakes on the platter. "So, you guys going to eat those, or what?"

Chelsea slid the plate over. "They're all yours. In fact, I was just thinking about making some more." As Chelsea rose from her chair, her phone rang. She pointed at it. "Excuse me, it's Billy, from the estate agents."

Chelsea sank back into her chair and Harper tried to read the expression on her face, which seemed to morph from concern to elation.

"Good news?"

"Yes. Looks like all my paperwork is in order, the bank confirmed the money is ready to transfer, and barring any hiccups, I should be able to go down and sign the contract tomorrow." Chelsea's smile lit up the room.

"That's freakin' awesome, Chels," Alice murmured through a mouth full of food.

"Yeah, it really is. Congratulations, Chelsea." In any other circumstance, Harper would have pulled her in for a hug.

"Well, I won't be happy till I've got the keys in my hand, but it's looking pretty good."

Harper raised her cup. "Well, here's to Alice's birthday and to Chelsea's new restaurant."

They clinked their coffee mugs.

"Okay, round two of pancakes, and another pot of fresh coffee coming up." Chelsea headed to the kitchen.

"What time do we need to get going?" Alice asked.

"We should probably get going in about an hour so we still have plenty of time to relax and have more pancakes. Chelsea said from here, it's only an hour by train."

The birthday plan for Alice consisted of an afternoon in Brighton for a fun-filled day of fairground-style amusement rides, arcade games, and plenty of junk food and drinks. It was a nod to a scene in the romance novel where the princess went undercover to spend a "normal" day with her love interest. Afterward, they would return to Chelsea's to shower and change, then meet up with Oliver, Jess, and the video crew members that Alice had charmed into coming along for a night of drinking and dancing.

"You sure we can't persuade you to come to Brighton?" Harper asked, suddenly bothered that another day was going to go by without her having a chance to talk to Chelsea.

Chelsea paused before she replied. "I have too much to do here." She spoke from over her shoulder as she whisked eggs in a bowl. "And I promised Denise that I'd go bowling with her and Millie. Sorry." When Chelsea finally turned to her, Harper was glad to see that her expression conveyed she was as sorry as her words suggested.

Harper quashed her feelings of disappointment. She had no right to expect Chelsea to put her life on hold for them, and maybe for Chelsea the countdown clock to the end of her visit wasn't beating quite as loudly as it was for Harper. She sipped her coffee and settled deeper into her chair and thoughts. She felt at home here—in London, in this cozy little apartment, having breakfast with Chelsea. And for the first time in a long time, she began to feel herself wanting not only a different job, but a different *life*. One that was richer in all the things her present life seemed to be lacking. And yes, one with Chelsea in it. She hadn't meant to get so attached, and she couldn't quite believe that in a few short days, she was going to lose her all over again.

Chelsea took a few steps forward and offered both her palms to Millie for a high five. For a ten-year-old, Millie was very good. That was her second strike in five frames, and she was already comfortably ahead.

"If I miss again, I'm going to go and ask them to put the rails up for me." Denise picked up a bright orange ball, took a few tentative steps forward, and sent it skittering down the gutter once again. She let out a soft curse as she turned back to the table.

"Too much beer?" Chelsea said.

"Nah, not enough beer probably. My sporting prowess is improved a hundred percent by alcohol."

"Doesn't look like it, Mom. Maybe you should be drinking water like Aunt Chelsea. She knows the right thing to do because of her tennis training…and she's bowling loads better than you."

Behind Millie's back, Denise showed Chelsea the middle finger. "Yeah, what's with that? Water? It's my day off, I need a drinking buddy. Are you on the wagon or something?"

Denise wearily headed back to the lane to take her second try. This time she rolled the ball so slowly that it took an age to make contact, but at least it didn't gutter, and the gentle nudge actually knocked over two of the pins. She returned to the table with more of a spring in her step.

"Go and get us some snacks, love." Denise rummaged in her bag before handing Millie a twenty-pound note. "Something to soak up the beer. Maybe grab me a bottle of water as well. Just in case it works."

Millie skipped off in the direction of the food counter.

"Well? Are you on the wagon or just hungover? I'm guessing the latter as you're so grouchy."

"Neither actually. And I'm not grouchy, I'm just not as much of a day drinker as you." She nudged Denise not wanting her to take offense. "Actually I'm going out later to some birthday party thing, so I don't want to drink this afternoon. I don't have the stamina for both."

"With Harper?" Denise raised an eyebrow.

"With Harper, yes, and with Alice and a few of the people Alice has been hanging out with. It's Alice's birthday, and we're celebrating at some swanky club in the West End. Some VIP place in Mayfair." She took a swallow of her water, suddenly wishing it was beer. "I'm dreading it actually. Maybe a few beers would make it feel more bearable."

"Sounds like fun. Why would you be dreading it? Are you and Harper still being weird?"

"We're not being weird." Chelsea grouched at her sister. "We're giving each other space. It's different."

"You're giving each other space? Of course you are. Even though she traveled halfway across the world to visit you, you're giving her space. Oh, Chelsea, come on. Honestly, I despair. I thought you guys were getting on well. You said—"

"We were…we are. As friends. It's been great seeing her again."

"Chels!"

"What?"

"You're insufferable. A few days ago, you were telling me you had all these feelings for her. Feelings that hadn't ever gone away. Not even over the passage of a long and dusty fifteen years of never really loving anyone else blah-blah-blah."

Chelsea blanched. Denise was blunt, but even for her, this was a bit much.

"I was drunk when I made that call."

"Yeah, well maybe you should get drunk more often if it puts you in touch with your feelings. You're such a stereotype. All that holding back and pining is straight out of a Jane Austen novel. Sometimes she who dares wins."

"And sometimes she who has a helicopter and unlimited fun times at her fingertips wins." Chelsea couldn't help sounding bitter. "Look, sis, I know you mean well, but I don't need a pep talk. Harper came here looking for a fairy-tale romance, and she's found one. With me, she just wanted closure. And now she's got that too. It's been great having them around." Chelsea was lying. It had been great before she caught feelings and realized Harper didn't feel the same way. "But soon they'll go back to their lives, and I'll go back to mine. I'll have the restaurant to focus on. And it's not just that…" Chelsea made herself say out loud the thing that had been bugging her the most. "The Harper I fell in love with all those years ago wouldn't have been interested in Laney. She was loyal to her friends and never impressed by money."

"I know this is just about protecting yourself, but I think you're being very harsh."

"Why?"

"Maybe she likes Laney. Did you ever think about that? Maybe she's still loyal and unimpressed by money. Maybe she likes Laney despite her being a princess, not because of it."

Chelsea had tormented herself with the same thought. It was worse than the idea of Harper being attracted to the fairy tale.

"Is that supposed to make me feel better, because it doesn't."

"No, I'm just saying that if Harper is as great as you claim, then it makes more sense. Or even more likely is that she's just enjoying someone paying her some proper attention and giving her new experiences. And if you weren't so stubborn and risk averse, it could be you making her feel special like that. And all that space you're giving her might be the opposite of what she actually wants. You told me that she said she missed you. Fuck, you even said that she almost kissed you. You said you were having fun reconnecting. But then you let Laney throw you off and backed away. You didn't even try to fight for her, so don't be sitting here all moody and feeling hard done by. You gave up too easy."

"That's not true." The denial was automatic, but Chelsea knew Denise was right. She had been quick to assume what it was that Harper wanted. And quick to assume it wasn't her.

"You know I'm right. I think you sporty, water-drinking people call that game, set, and match. I might be crap at bowling but I'm better at relationships." Denise softened her tone. "And I want you to have someone who makes you happy."

"So do I." Chelsea blinked, determined not to cry. She wanted that person to be Harper. She had to find a way to let her know. And if it ended in humiliation, Harper would soon be an ocean away. *An ocean away.* Chelsea let the realization sink in. She had four more days to avoid losing Harper all over again.

CHAPTER ELEVEN

Chelsea glanced at the unassuming black door marked with a gold "IB" crest. It was the only thing designating the members-only entrance, and it held no hint as to what lay beyond its threshold. A large man of Middle Eastern descent stood in front of the door wearing a dark suit that looked uncomfortably small for his muscular physique. She assumed he was there to reinforce the members-only part of the club, and he had been eyeing them suspiciously as they stood a few yards away from the entrance waiting for Oliver, who was now twenty minutes late and counting.

Harper was standing to one side of her. She had dressed up more than Chelsea had expected, in the same tight-fitting blue dress she had worn to dinner with Laney. The one that showed off her glorious curves, but this time, Chelsea noticed, her hair was styled more simply to hang in soft open curls across her shoulders. She looked stunning and Chelsea had found it hard to take her eyes off her since she had first emerged in the outfit from the bedroom in her flat. Chelsea had opted for something a little more casual, refusing to be intimidated by the swanky choice of venue, but she had definitely made more effort than usual—Denise's words about not giving in as far as Harper was concerned ringing in her ears.

"I keep forgetting how chilly your evenings can be." Harper folded her arms across her chest and shook off a shiver as she addressed Chelsea. "I didn't think we'd be hanging around outside for this long and I'm wishing I'd brought a jacket."

Chelsea took hers off and offered it to Harper without missing a beat.

"Oh, I wasn't hinting…I mean, I didn't mean for you to do that."

"Take it, desert girl. For a Brit, these temperatures are tropical." She draped the jacket around Harper's shoulders as she spoke and was happy to see Harper pull it together across her chest.

"Thank you. That's the second time you've saved me from these 'summer' temperatures." Harper emphasized the word with raised eyebrows.

"I'm sure when we get inside it'll be much warmer with all those sweaty dancing bodies," Chelsea said.

"I'm banking on it." Alice waggled her eyebrows. "I came as much for the sweaty bodies as I did the champagne. And I'm planning to drag both of you onto the dance floor with me. It's my birthday, so no wallflowers allowed."

"Understood." Chelsea offered a mock salute.

"And since you're both looking so damn gorgeous, I absolutely insist that you dance together," Alice added.

Chelsea felt heat at the idea of Harper in her arms, but Harper was staring at her with a curious expression on her face, and she had no idea if Harper was thinking the same thing.

"Understood." This time it was Harper who offered Alice a lighthearted salute. She turned to Chelsea with a smile. "Looks like the birthday girl is dictating the evening's dance activities."

"Yep, it's gonna be a long night." Chelsea laughed.

"Alice!" Oliver shimmied up to them, with Jess and a couple of other people not far behind him. "Happy birthday, Cinderella." He planted a kiss into the ether an inch or two away from Alice's face.

Alice curtsied. "Why, thank you."

"Okay, everyone." Oliver raised his hand like a tour guide. "Introductions. This is Seth," he said as he pointed. "Cameraman extraordinaire. Mary is my makeup goddess, and Jess, as you already know, is my fashion guru. Sorry we're a smidge late, Seth's fault. He got delayed at the studio. More footage than we realized."

"And this is Harper and Chelsea." Alice rounded out the introductions as "nice to meet yous" and nods were exchanged. "Okay, now, who's ready for a drink?"

"Hold that thought." Oliver held up a finger as he glanced at his phone. "We're just waiting on one more."

And as if on cue, a black sedan Chelsea recognized pulled up in front of them and Manny appeared, hustling around to open the back door. *You've got to be fucking kidding me.* Chelsea completed the thought as Laney stepped out looking like a million dollars in a shimmering backless dress that looked like it had been painted onto her perfect figure.

"Laney?" Harper stepped forward, sounding as surprised as Chelsea was. "I thought you were in Scotland until tomorrow."

"What, and miss this magnificent birthday party?" Laney leaned in to air kiss Alice half-heartedly. She took Harper's hands. "And miss you looking as divine as this?" She bent and planted a lingering kiss on Harper's cheek before slowly pulling back.

Although the sun was setting, it was light enough for Chelsea to see Harper blush, and her mood nose-dived instantly.

"Everyone accounted for?" Laney turned to Oliver, who nodded. "Great, then what are we doing outside?" She took the lead and nodded to the hulk of a man, who opened the door. As Laney passed beside him, Chelsea saw her place a hand on his bulky shoulder and squeeze. It was an oddly intimate gesture, one that seemed to suggest that in some way everything about this place, including the bouncer, was hers.

Electronic music assaulted Chelsea's ears and vibrated within her chest as she followed behind the group as they walked through the dimly lit venue. An impressive neon-lit bar and DJ booth were off to the side, and the decor had that unfinished and industrial style look that seemed at odds with where they were. The dance floor was center stage, and red fabric booths outlined the perimeter, giving the place an intimate feel. Chelsea hadn't been out clubbing in a long time, and never in Mayfair with such an elitist VIP crowd. She shook off the urge to be at her neighborhood cereal shop, sitting on their patio, in a more relaxed and quiet setting. This was for Alice—and for Harper. Their time together was short, and she had promised herself she would have a good time tonight. And that she would try to find a way of letting Harper know she was every bit as interested in her as Laney was. Okay, she hadn't expected Laney to put in an appearance, but that didn't mean the evening was ruined. Harper and Alice were her friends, and they had agreed to drink and dance together until, as Alice put it, they either got so shit-faced drunk they collapsed or got thrown out. As she glanced at Alice—and saw the ear to ear smile she was sporting—Chelsea had to admit this seemed the perfect way to top off her birthday celebrations.

They ventured to the back of the club, where five large semicircular booths were designated by a golden VIP placard outside each bricked-in room, making them feel a bit separate yet connected to the club. The music was quieter once they entered the space, and she welcomed the relief from the pulsing beat.

A woman in a tight indigo blue cocktail dress approached, and before she had even parted her lips in greeting, Oliver confidently ordered two bottles of Boërl champagne and told her to keep a tab open. The waitress nodded and disappeared. Chelsea guessed that since it wasn't a champagne she'd ever heard of—and she had looked at plenty in researching menus at the restaurant—it would be stupidly expensive.

"So, Laney," Oliver raised his voice over the music. "How was Scotland?"

"Boring and dreary. It rained the entire time. Including during the wedding. But at least there were benefits to staying indoors. The staff were as attentive as ever."

Chelsea might not have caught the exact meaning behind the words, but she did catch the smug smile that Laney and Oliver exchanged.

As the waitress returned with the requested champagne, glasses were filled and distributed until a toast was made to Alice's birthday and another to Oliver's soon-to-be completed thirty-eighth video episode.

The chat drifted from Oliver's plans for the channel to the ways in which he was making money from all the subscriber milestones he had passed during the pandemic. It seemed that the world staying home in pj's had at least been good for him. Chelsea was happy to let them all talk. Harper was positioned next to her, and her proximity would have been even more of a pleasure if Laney hadn't been sitting on Harper's other side. Every time Chelsea tried to engage Harper in conversation, Laney interrupted, cutting rudely across them, determined to be at the center of Harper's attention.

"I'd kill for a pint of chocolate stout right now." Harper said the words so softly that Chelsea wasn't sure she'd heard them right. "This is probably very good—and very expensive—champagne, but it's not really my thing. Hope that doesn't sound too ungrateful." She pulled a comical face.

Chelsea felt her heart smile. She'd been thinking exactly the same thing.

"It doesn't. And anyway, look at Alice, she's died and gone to heaven." Oliver and his friends were hanging on to Alice's every word as she guzzled the champagne while telling them an unlikely tale about hypnotizing a bear while out camping with hairy gay men. "This is all for her."

"And for us." Harper nudged her thigh. "We're still young enough to enjoy a wild night out. And don't think I've forgotten that Alice made you promise to dance with me."

"She did."

"Dancing together was something we never got the chance to do back in college." Harper's gaze was intense, and despite the champagne, Chelsea felt her mouth go dry.

"There were a lot of things we missed out on. I'm sorry."

"Stop apologizing. It wasn't your fault. I'd just like to think it bothered you just as much as me that we missed out on those things..." There was a question there. A need for reassurance.

"Of course it did. Are you serious?" Chelsea reached down and took Harper's hand. She needed—wanted—to say something more. To reassure, yes, but also to stake a claim somehow. She had known since they met at the airport that she still wanted something from Harper, that they had something unfinished and important between them, but she couldn't say it. She wasn't sure she had the words. Or that Harper wanted to hear them.

"Do you want that dance?" If Chelsea couldn't find the words she needed, she hoped being physically closer to Harper would help unlock something. As she spoke, a loud burst of laughter from across the table signaled the end of Alice's story, drowning out her offer.

"Harper, tell them it's true. You were there. You can confirm my bear dancing skills."

Harper switched her gaze from Chelsea to Alice and back again, seeming confused, and not responding to either of them, but not letting go of her hand either.

"Harps?"

"Yeah, sorry. Absolutely. If you're talking about getting the bear cubs of Flagstaff to teach you the choreography to 'Single Ladies,' then that totally happened. I still have nightmares about it."

Chelsea laughed, appreciating the snark. As the waitress arrived with a couple of fancy platters of food that she unloaded with much ceremony onto their table, she waited not very patiently to ask Harper again for that dance they'd waited so long for.

"I'm so tired of sitting, what do you say we go out and have a spin on the dance floor?" Laney spoke to Harper before Chelsea could.

Chelsea noticed Harper hesitate as she glanced between the dance floor and Laney. "Oh, I, um, I'm not the most graceful dancer."

"Well, I can assure you," Laney scooted out of the booth and extended her hand, "you'll do just fine, and if you stumble a bit, you can always lean on me. I might quite like that." Laney said it loudly enough for them all to hear.

Harper hesitated for a moment and Chelsea willed her to find a way to refuse—Laney was so cocksure of herself, and Chelsea hated it—but then Harper released her hand, followed Laney out of the booth, and allowed herself to be escorted to the dance floor. Watching them, the taste of bile filled Chelsea's mouth. She finished her glass, refilled it, and chased it down with another.

"I'd go easy on that stuff." Jess arched a brow. "It has a nasty way of sneaking up on you."

Chelsea shrugged. This wasn't her first experience with champagne, and right now, she welcomed anything that would take the edge off the brewing feelings of jealousy. Fuck Laney and her ability to ask Harper for what she wanted. And fuck Harper for always going along with it.

"So, are you American as well?" Jess spoke a little louder than she needed to.

Chelsea shook her head. "No, I'm local. I know Harper and Alice from when I was at uni in the States."

Jess leaned back. "And you stayed in touch all this time? That's pretty cool."

"Not quite. This trip is a reunion…" Chelsea forced a smile and tipped her glass toward Jess. "Of sorts." She tried to keep her tone polite. It wasn't Jess's fault that Harper was dancing with Laney. She made herself focus on the conversation and not on whatever was happening on the dance floor.

"And you work with Oliver?" Chelsea remembered Harper mentioning Jess when she retold the story of shopping with Oliver and Alice.

"Yes. But this will be the last time I work with him."

"Why? Trouble in influencer paradise?" Chelsea felt as bitter as she sounded.

Jess shrugged. "The show is harmless enough. Although, every now and then, Oliver's mean spirit rears its head, and I'm getting a little tired being an accomplice to it."

"I don't understand."

"He tells Seth to keep the camera rolling, even when 'the Cinderella' thinks it's off, in hope of catching some embarrassingly cringeworthy moments that he can edit into the show. I've told him more than once that I don't agree with it, but he says his followers love it, and he swears it generates more subscribers. And in his business, that's all that matters, so it becomes easier and easier to make unethical choices."

Chelsea glanced at Alice and hoped Oliver didn't have it in mind to do that to her. She liked Alice, always had. Her over-the-top personality was loveable. And she knew how much Harper loved her. She hoped Alice wouldn't be betrayed for the sake of a few more subscribers.

"You don't think he'd do that to Alice, do you? I mean, he seems fond of her."

"Friendships take second seat to subscribers. And I've kind of grown fond of Alice myself, in the few days I've worked with her. She's rather..." Jess paused seemingly searching for a word. "Endearing. Loud, and absolutely without class, but probably the nicest, most genuine person I've met in a long time."

"That she is." Chelsea couldn't stop herself glancing again at the dance floor. This time Laney and Harper were in view, shuffling to the music, standing far too close together, Laney's arm around Harper's waist. She felt sick at the sight of it.

"You like her, but you're not together?"

"I'm sorry?" Chelsea responded without taking her eyes off Harper. Was she really too late? Had Harper already chosen Laney?

"Harper. You like her but you're not together." This time it was a statement, not a question. "I only say that because you keep looking to the dance floor like it's killing you to see her and Laney out there together. But if you were together, I'm guessing you wouldn't be letting her dance with Laney like that. Obviously, no sane person would."

Chelsea turned her attention to Jess. "Not sure what you think you're seeing, but Harper and I are just friends. She can dance with whoever she wants." The truth of the statement landed like a thud on her chest.

"Okay, so that means you can dance with whoever you want?" Jess tilted her head as she spoke. "Including me."

"Yes, but…"

"But what?"

"I'm not much of a dancer. And my mood is a little off tonight, I'm sorry."

It really was. And that was before Jess seemed to have seen something in the way she was acting that gave away her feelings for Harper. She was mad at herself, and yes, she was hurting, but she didn't want anyone to notice.

"That's a real shame." Jess shrugged, tipping her glass in Chelsea's direction. "But you can't fault a girl for trying."

Chelsea looked past Jess, looking for Laney and Harper again, but not seeing them now through the mass of bodies. She couldn't help but wonder how close they would be getting amongst that crowd. *Fuck.* This was ridiculous. She should have spoken up sooner, and not given way to Laney. That was her problem, she wasn't being bold enough. She ran a frustrated hand through her hair. But Harper wasn't exactly helping.

"Hey, Chelsea!" Alice shouted her name across the table. "Our turn to give it a whirl." She stood and beckoned Chelsea toward her. It was the last thing she wanted, but Alice was impossible to say no to even on days when it wasn't her birthday. "Come on…it's my birthday, you can't say no." Alice was now reading her mind.

"I wasn't going to say no. How could I?" Chelsea got up from the table, swallowed in one gulp one of the indigo-colored shots that sat on a round tray in the middle of their table, and held out a hand for Alice. "Come on then, birthday girl." The orangey bitterness of the curacao hit the back of her throat. How could something that blue taste so orange?

As she reached Chelsea, Alice placed a hand on Jess's shoulder. "You too, wardrobe girl. Let's go and have a sapphic shimmy together. Just us lesbians!" She blew a kiss over her shoulder at the rest of the table.

"Thought you'd never ask." Jess looked up at her with a smile, before standing quickly.

As Chelsea headed to the dance floor with Alice and Jess, they crossed paths with Harper and Laney heading back to the booth. Harper didn't look very happy and Chelsea couldn't help but be glad about that. Maybe Laney, despite all her talents, had two left feet.

"You too!" Alice grabbed Harper's arm. "We need you. We can double dance. Four is so much better than three." Harper looked at Laney, who looked as if she was going to object, or worse, try to join in. "Not you. Sorry. Five is an odd number. Next time, Princess." Alice waved Laney away and Chelsea offered a silent prayer of thanks for Alice's lack of manners.

They threaded their way into the center of the dance floor and began dancing as the foursome Alice wanted, but it was impossible to stay together. The swaying, jostling sea of bodies nudged them apart as fast as they came together again. And it was impossible to talk. Unless you were Alice, who was shouting at Harper, animatedly telling her a story with arm gestures that seemed a danger for everyone dancing nearby. If Chelsea had hoped for a meaningful conversation with Harper, it was going to have to wait till they were off the dance floor.

The lively thronging of the crowd served to carry Harper and Alice a few yards away, and at the same time, pushed Chelsea and Jess closer together. They were still swaying in time to the music, but the closeness felt awkwardly intimate.

"It's okay, I won't bite."

Chelsea saw Jess's mouth move but didn't catch the words. She leaned down and placed her ear closer to Jess's mouth.

"I said, loosen up, I know you're not into me." Chelsea felt Jess's hot breath in her ear. "I just want to dance." Jess—the same height as Chelsea in her heels—rested her arms lightly on her shoulders as if to underline the statement. Chelsea leaned in.

"I know, I'm sorry. I'm just…I told you, my mood is off. And I hadn't expected it to be so busy. I'm not much of a dancer—"

"Shush." Jess placed a finger on Chelsea's lips. "Let's just dance." She moved closer and Chelsea stiffened, but when she looked at Jess she could see that her eyes were closed as if all she was doing was getting into the music. Chelsea tried to relax. She could handle a dance with someone who seemed both pretty cool, and not at all into her.

She scanned the dance floor and found Alice, dancing not with Harper but with a petite brunette in a diamond-encrusted vest. Alice's gyrating was enthusiastic, and the woman seemed into it. She turned slowly—taking the chance to pull away from Jess as they moved—until she was facing the front of the club. And there, a few yards away, off to the side of the dance floor, she saw Harper. Staring in her direction with a look on her face that was blank. Chelsea lifted a hand, still hoping for a dance, still hoping to find a way to let Harper know the way she was feeling. But instead of responding, Harper turned and walked away, in the direction of the bar.

"I have to go, sorry." Chelsea pulled away from Jess and followed Harper to the bar, pushing her way through the crowd. She lost sight of Harper for a second, but nearer to the bar, the crowd thinned out and Chelsea saw her. She was standing at one end of the bar, seeming lost in thought, and she looked so beautiful that Chelsea felt a rush of feelings rise up in her chest.

"Hi."

Harper blinked at her.

"Are you okay?"

"I just needed some water." Harper sounded flat.

"Good idea." Chelsea hesitated. "I kind of lost you on the dance floor. I hoped…I thought we could, you know, have a dance. Like Alice suggested."

"You didn't seem lost to me. In fact, you seemed kind of *found*." Harper held her gaze for an instant before looking away. "Not that it's any of my business."

Chelsea took a second to understand.

"You're talking about Jess?"

"I'm not talking about anything. I'm just saying you guys looked pretty close for two people who just met. I forgot you had that power. To make people fall for you. Well, I didn't exactly forget, that would be a lie." Harper stopped talking and took a deep breath. Chelsea waited. "I suppose I hadn't realized you were interested. All that talk about not being ready for a relationship and wanting to concentrate on the restaurant. I believed you. I didn't expect to see you all over Jess at the first opportunity. I thought you hated all these *posh privileged people*."

Harper attempted an English accent but fluffed it. Chelsea had seen her taking shots with Alice but was surprised Harper had gotten so tipsy so early. And then the penny dropped. She wasn't drunk, she was angry.

"You're jealous of Jess?"

Harper turned away from her in silence. Her body taut with tension. When she returned her gaze to Chelsea, she had composed herself.

"No, I'm not jealous. I'm just surprised." The words came out clipped.

"Well, good. Because you being jealous given everything else wouldn't be very fair." Chelsea had wanted them to talk, but not like this. "You and Laney. You've done a lot more than dance. You've been dating." Even saying the word was hard. But that was exactly what Harper had been doing.

"I'm not dating Laney."

"Dinner, art galleries, dancing. Dancing a lot closer than we were. You think I didn't see you? How is my dancing with Jess what we're talking about here when you're choosing to spend what little time we have together with your romance book princess?" Chelsea let out an exasperated sigh. This was crazy. She tried to slow down her thinking. If Harper was jealous that meant she had feelings for her. But if she had feelings for her, why was she dancing with Laney and choosing her every single time.

"I'm not choosing Laney over you. You're not giving me a fucking choice. You come close, then you back away. You come close and you back away again. And then when I turn my back for a minute, you're whispering into the ear of Jess, who by the way, you just met. It's as if I don't matter. At least Laney makes me feel like I matter. She chooses me."

"And you abandoning our evening in Whitstable for a helicopter ride is you coming close and me backing away? Just so I'm clear. Is that what that was?" Chelsea felt anger rise from within her chest.

"I explained about that. I didn't want to leave—"

"But you did."

"Stop punishing me for that. I wanted to stay."

"But you didn't. It was a chance for us to get close, I wanted to spend that evening with you. You were the one that backed away, not me."

"And is that why you've been sulking for the past three days? You've wasted what little time we have, and you've shown me that you don't want what I want, that you'll always back away, like you always have done."

"That's not true. I won't. I thought you wanted the space. That you wanted Laney, that you wanted…I don't know actually. I don't know what you want."

"And what do *you* want, Chelsea? One minute you're holding my hand and I think we're reconnecting on a level that's more than a friendship, and the next, you back away and act like all we'll ever be is friends. It's like you don't want me, but don't want anyone else to want me either. And if I'm wrong, then you have a funny way of—"

"You're wrong." Chelsea stepped into the space between them, taking hold of both of Harper's hands. She stared at them for an instant, willing herself to find the words to tell Harper just how much she wanted her, how much she had always wanted her. She lifted her gaze to Harper's face, her eyes wide and a shade of dark blue that in any other situation she would have described as indigo. The desire to kiss her came with passionate force. Their history had been all about her waiting, wanting to be sure that Harper felt the same way she did.

This time she didn't wait, didn't ask, she reached one hand to the back of Harper's neck and the other to the small of her back, pulling her closer and capturing her mouth in a hard, possessive kiss. The soft warmth of Harper's lips caused her to take a breath. Harper moved a hand to her chest and Chelsea waited for her to push her away. Instead she placed it flat on Chelsea's chest and kissed her back, just as passionately, parting her lips and moaning softly. Chelsea pulled Harper closer, heat coursing through her body at the taste of Harper's lips, the urgency of their kisses. She moved her hand into Harper's hair and deepened the kiss, hungry for her taste, the passion igniting her center, making her swollen and aroused. They were both breathing heavily, the kisses all that mattered. Harper's mouth was so soft, her kisses so certain, Chelsea couldn't stop. She could only hope the kisses communicated to Harper all the feelings she hadn't been able to express over the years. She had no clue how long they kissed. Kisses like Chelsea had never experienced before. Kisses that felt like coming home.

When she finally pulled away, they stood still, staring at each other while Chelsea waited for a reply to a question she had not really asked. She scanned Harper's face. In those beautiful blue eyes, Chelsea wanted to believe she saw acknowledgment of everything they had meant to each other in the past and all that they could still be. But Harper was staring back at her blankly, as if deep in thought. Her tousled hair, her swollen lips, the only things that were giving away that seconds ago they had been kissing passionately.

"I'm sorry, I…" Harper stepped back a half step and Chelsea wanted to reach for her again. She moved closer. They were inches apart. Something heavy between them.

"Say something, Harper. Please. Did I do the wrong thing?"

"No, no, I…I just. I wasn't expecting to…" She flicked her eyes to the ceiling and then refocused them on Chelsea. "Look, I know we've both had a bit to drink, but please tell me you're not drunk. I need to know this was real, that you feel—"

"There you both are." Laney's words were like nails on a chalkboard. "I've been looking for you. They've just delivered Alice's cake to the table and are getting ready to cut it. We need you."

Chelsea remained silently frozen as she willed Harper to say something more. And she wanted to reassure her that the kisses meant something important.

"Harper, did you hear me?" Laney sounded impatient. "You need to come back to the table." She gave Chelsea a cold, hard look. "Both of you."

As Harper glanced between her and Laney with uncertainty in her eyes, an awkwardness fell between them. Chelsea wanted to tell Laney to fuck off, to tell her that she and Harper had a history—and a future—that they meant more to each other than she would ever know. And she had so much to say to Harper. But this wasn't the time…or the place. She reached down and took Harper's hand.

"Let's talk about this later."

Harper nodded at her.

"Alice needs her cake."

Another nod. Harper seemed lost for words. And Chelsea couldn't shake the feeling that despite Harper kissing her back, she had done something wrong.

"Exactly that." Laney took Harper by the arm, spun her around, and practically frog-marched her back toward the booth before Chelsea had even a moment to react. She followed behind them determined not to let the moment go. Harper had kissed her like it meant something. She was going to tell her she wanted this, wanted her, wanted them to try. She should have said it days ago, but tonight would have to do. She loved Harper. She had been stupid to think she had ever really stopped.

As they reached the table, Alice was standing waiting for them. She waved them impatiently forward, pulling Harper to her side, before giving a speech about taking chances, being brave and pursuing joy. She blew out the candles, basked in a chorus of happy birthdays, and cut herself a big slice of cake. When they resumed their seats, Laney positioned Harper so she was sandwiched between her and Alice, giving Chelsea no hope of talking to her.

And Harper seems content to let her. The unwelcome truth hit home. She pushed it away. She was behaving like Jennifer. Harper was there for Alice. It was fine that they were sitting together. And Harper wasn't responsible for Laney's attempt to monopolize her.

Chelsea was seated at the edge of the booth with Jess at her side. She would let the evening play out, dance with Harper as soon as she could, and then later, at home, they would talk, she would make her feelings clear…and hopefully Harper would admit she felt the same way. They had time. Not a lot of time. But enough time to find themselves again. She let out a deep, slow breath, aware of the tension still thrumming through her body. Jess gave her a look.

"Are you okay?"

"Yeah, sorry. Just a bit tense."

"This might help." She accepted a slice of birthday cake from Jess, picked up a fork, and began to eat. She had no real appetite, but of course it was delicious.

Across the table, Chelsea was horrified to see Laney feeding Harper some of Alice's cake from the end of her fork. It was an intimate act. And seeing Harper laugh as a morsel fell onto her lap cut her to the core. Was Harper seriously going to sit there and let Laney flirt with her? After kissing Chelsea like that. She reached across the table and helped herself to another shot. Her temples throbbing in frustration. She had to do something, but she had no idea what.

"If I were you, I'd warn your *friend* about Laney." Jess tipped her glass in Harper's direction as she spoke.

"What about Laney?"

Jess put her glass down and ran her fingers through her hair. "I know you say you don't care, but you should." She shifted her position and leaned in slightly. "Laney likes to bed women, and she has plenty who throw themselves at her. They're the ones who become her playthings, but they also bore her. It's the women who don't fall all over her, the ones who become more of a challenge to sleep with, that interest her the most. She likes to play a game with those women. Oliver refers to it as Laney going fox hunting, and it couldn't be more accurate, because for her, it's all about the chase. I figure since she's still making a play for Harper, it means she hasn't fucked her yet, so the game isn't over. But just give it time. It's a rare woman who doesn't give in to her. And when they do, she moves on to the next *hunt* without a backward glance."

Chelsea's anger flared. "So you're saying she's playing some sick fucking game and she's not really into Harper? At all?"

"Oh, sweetie, Laney isn't even capable of it. Besides, do you honestly think for one minute she would compromise her position—or her trust fund—to openly be with a woman? I know from my own experience exactly what she's like. Bedding your friend is just a game to her. Something she can boast to Oliver about. I mean, Harper seems sweet, and she scrubs up well, but she's hardly the type to capture a princess. She's not exactly sophisticated." Jess turned back to the table and took a sip of champagne. "No offense."

Chelsea's head began to pound. The air felt thick and suffocating as the walls seemed to close in on her. Her gut had been right this whole time. Laney was a snake in princess clothing. She gulped down the rest of her drink hoping the liquid would cool the rage building inside her. A part of her wanted to call Laney out and give her a piece of her mind, but she didn't want to make a scene and embarrass Harper. Instead, she excused herself to the restroom, bolted through the door and leaned against the sink. She splashed her face with cold water and took deep breaths. Harper was being played, but how was she going to warn her without hurting her feelings? She'd been so clear about finding it hard to trust women, about not feeling good enough. The idea of Laney and Harper together had killed Chelsea, but she had begrudgingly understood why Harper enjoyed the attention.

The door opened, ushering in a group of chatty women, one of whom claimed the space next to her, leaned into the mirror, and began refreshing her makeup. Chelsea grabbed a few paper towels from the dispenser, dabbed her face, and hoped she didn't look as shitty as she felt. She took another deep breath, willing herself to calm down. As she reached their booth, she passed Harper.

"Any idea where the restrooms are?"

Chelsea pointed. "Around the corner to the left." She resisted the urge to follow her.

As Chelsea shuffled into her seat, she could hear Laney holding court, all eyes focused on her. The anger throbbed inside her chest and she tried to make herself calm down.

"I mean, look at Harper and Alice. This is their first trip to Europe, and they're not going to Venice, Paris, or Rome. The furthest they've been is Whitstable. What kind of vacation is that? I said to Harper that next summer she could stay at my villa in the Italian Lakes, and she didn't even know where that was. She's so adorably unworldly. I mean, George Clooney has a villa there for goodness' sake. It's an unmissable stop for anyone coming to Europe. She really needed a better tour guide." Laney turned her attention to Chelsea, her expression hardened as a smirk formed on her lips.

"Tell me, Chelsea, in your not-so-stellar tennis career, did you get to travel much?"

Chelsea felt the heat of her temper rise slowly from her feet.

"I didn't. Not much." She paused. "I might have if my daddy had provided me with a helicopter and a trust fund, but since he didn't…" Chelsea didn't try to keep the hostility from her voice. She had had it with Laney. "At least George Clooney did something useful to earn his villa."

"Someone sounds a tiny bit jealous. It's understandable. But don't despair. Maybe one of the waitresses at your new restaurant will be impressed by the cook paying her some attention and invite you to Benidorm." Laney paused, a malicious expression appearing on her face. "Or maybe a drunken friend, infused with misplaced nostalgia, will take pity, and give you a consolation kiss. But we both know that's all it is. A mistake, one that was instantly regretted. It'd be stupid to think it was anything more than that."

The table fell silent. As if suddenly aware this was something far beyond banter. Chelsea stared at Laney, even though her mind drifted to Harper. Was it true? Was that what Harper had told Laney? Chelsea felt a wave of shame. She had dared to imagine that the kisses meant something, that she had the right to go toe-to-toe with Laney…for Harper. And that Harper might want her to. But Harper hadn't asked for any of it. Worse, if Laney was to be believed, Harper even regretted their kisses. *A consolation.* Chelsea wanted to get out of there as fast as possible.

"You're right. I know my place. But I also know my worth." Chelsea got up from her seat. "And I'm glad I'm not going through life buying friends, never knowing who's interested in me and who just wants to spend my money. It would leave me haunted with…" She searched for the right word. "Inadequacy."

"Wow…" Harper approached the table rubbing and sniffing her hands. "The bathroom's beautiful, and the lotion they have at the sink smells so nice…" Harper paused as she scanned the table. "What'd I miss? Why is everyone so quiet?"

Chelsea walked away from the booth without responding. She didn't trust herself to stay and not make even more of a fool of herself, and the club now felt stifling and claustrophobic. As soon as she burst through the front door, she gulped at the fresh air, and let the unexpected rain wash over her. She closed her eyes and tilted her head to the sky as the pulsing beat of the nightclub's music was replaced with the gentle and rhythmic sound of rain splashing against the pavement. The hand that grabbed her arm startled her. She spun around and faced Harper.

"Chelsea? What's going on? Did something happen while I was in the restroom?"

Chelsea took a breath as she felt the frustration and the alcohol buzzing in her head. She scanned Harper's searching eyes. How could she be so blind to everything that was happening? So completely oblivious to the type of person Laney really is.

"Just your little princess in there…making it clear to me and everyone else what kind of miserable pond life I am. Thought it might be better for all of us if I got out of there."

"Laney?"

"Yes, Laney. She's not what you think, Harper. She's not some sweet princess from one of your romance novels. She may hold a royal title, but she's a total bitch."

"Look, I don't understand what's going on here, or what just happened to make you so agitated, but Laney doesn't deserve to be called a bitch. Self-absorbed and pretentious sure, but not a bitch. She's been a generous friend to me."

"She's not your friend, Harper. She's nice to you just because she wants to fuck you."

"That's enough, Chelsea. I don't know where this is coming from, but I don't like it. Laney is just a cool friend I've made on this trip. You should be happy for me."

"Tell me something, Harper. Do friends feed each other cake and dance with their hands all over each other? And what about me? About us? You kiss me but go running back to her. Are we taking turns, is that what we're doing here? Am I supposed to patiently wait for my go?" Chelsea rolled her shoulders, the tension in her body unbearable. "Well, I won't do that, I'm sorry."

Chelsea had had enough of Laney, and she needed to get Harper to understand so she could get her as far away from Laney as possible. Not just for her own sake but because she didn't want Harper to get hurt by her.

"Don't be like this. I know she can be a little abrasive sometimes, but she's not all that bad. And you're not taking turns. That's an insulting thing to say. I'm being friendly. I'm putting up with her for Alice's sake. Can't you do the same instead of walking out…again? Then we can go home and talk. I know we need to. I'm just confused, and I've been drinking, and I'm probably fucking everything up like I always do, but I'm not trying to. I want to make everyone happy, is that so bad?"

"Look, Harper, this whole thing…" She waved her hand. "The VIP room, the fancy dinners, the helicopter ride, are all part of some sick cat-and-mouse game to try to get you to sleep with her. And once you do." Chelsea leaned closer, her voice barely above a whisper, the panic pulsing in her chest. "She'll drop you in a heartbeat. Job done." She hated saying it, hated the truth of it. "I think that you should leave with me. We do need to talk, but let's do it as far away from her as possible." Chelsea reached for her arm.

"No, Chelsea, just wait. What do you mean it's a game? What the hell are you talking about?"

"Harper…" Chelsea lifted her hands. "I'm so sorry. I'm not telling you this to hurt you, in fact, that's the last thing I want to do. But you need to believe me, it's the truth."

"Well, right now it's feeling pretty damn hurtful." Harper cocked a hip. "And how do you even know this?"

"Jess told me. She said this is what Laney does. She and Oliver call it 'fox hunting.' And she's only interested for as long as it takes someone to sleep with her. That she's not capable of really falling for anyone. It's just a game to her."

"Jess said that?" Harper scoffed. "Of course Jess said that. She and Laney had a thing. She probably told you that story because she's jealous, because Laney didn't want a relationship with her." Harper shook her head, her voice animated. "And I don't believe her. I may be naive when it comes to a lot of things, but I'd like to think I can tell if someone is playing me. And Laney isn't."

"You want Laney to want you?" Chelsea felt the realization hit like an arrow to her chest.

"No, I'm not saying that at all." She took a breath. "Look, I've had a lot to drink, and things aren't making much sense right now, but I know I don't want to leave. I'm celebrating with Alice…giving her the nice time we promised we would give her for her birthday. And I want you to come back inside with me. But this…this hating thing that you have with Laney has to stop. You've been down on her since day one, and I'm getting a little tired of it. I really don't understand why you can't just accept that she's being kind and be happy that someone is being nice to me. Because you know what? It feels pretty damn good to have some uncomplicated attention for once."

"But it's not real, Harper, and I know this sucks to hear, but this isn't like your romance novel. This princess isn't going to give you a happy ending. You're a conquest to her and nothing more. Please." She reached out and gently touched Harper's arm. "I'm on your side."

"No, you're not. Because if you were on my side, you wouldn't be behaving like this. And me spending time with Laney isn't about the damn book, so don't keep saying that. This is you not believing that someone like Laney would be interested in someone like me. Someone you clearly can't see anyone wanting to be with, despite all the angsty regrets you say you have about the past and despite those kisses. Whatever that even was. But if you don't have it in you to believe in me, to want the best for me, then at least have the decency to get out of my way and let me enjoy my trip."

Harper's voice was shaky. Chelsea wanted to reach for her.

"That's not true, Harper. I do believe in you. And I can absolutely see why someone would be into you. I think you're absolutely amazing. I've always thought that." She willed herself to find the right words. It felt like they were on a precipice and if she wasn't careful one of them would fall in. "And I'm so sorry I've never been able to make you understand that. That's on me, I've been stupid." Chelsea took in a breath. "But this isn't you, at least not the Harper I remember. She's making a fool of you. And you can't see that because all you're focused on is the shiny stuff she keeps dangling in front of you."

"How dare you think I would be shallow enough to be influenced by that." Harper now had her hands clenched by her side, her frustration obvious.

"But you are, in your own way. You act like it doesn't impress you, but I think it does. You haven't said no to any of it and you keep going toward it." Chelsea hated saying it, but she hated it even more that Laney's plan to seduce Harper seemed to be working. "You're just like Jennifer in that way. And you know what?" Chelsea felt the realization land. "I was never enough for her either."

She knew she had stepped over the line the moment the words flew out of her mouth. The creased look of pain on Harper's face told her she had caused more hurt than she had intended. But she was angry and she was finally expressing her feelings. And if the anger was mostly because she was messing things up and letting someone as wonderful as Harper slip through her fingers then she couldn't help that.

Harper tilted her head to the sky as the rain came down steadily, soaking them both, and then she glanced back to Chelsea. Under her gaze, Chelsea felt as if she was transparent, that Harper was looking through her as though she wasn't even seeing her.

"I'm sorry, I didn't mean to—"

Harper held up a hand and Chelsea stopped, panic slowly replacing anger. She didn't take her eyes off Harper's face. The rain was streaking down her cheeks, her gaze now focused somewhere past Chelsea's left shoulder. And then, without saying a word, she turned and went back into the club. Chelsea wanted to yell at Harper to come back. To finish this thing that they had started so many years ago.

But as the rain pelted Chelsea, and she stood staring through squinted vision at a door whose color seemed as black as the void she felt stuck in, she lowered her head. Maybe Harper didn't want complicated, maybe she didn't want Chelsea. Maybe she was right, and just like Jennifer, Harper wanted the kind of glitz and glamour that she couldn't offer. But it didn't matter now. She had just ruined any chance they might have had. Her eyes welled and her tears spilled over and merged with the rain.

"Fucking fuck," she grumbled as a low guttural groan emerged from deep within her as the irony of the situation settled in. She had stood in the rain of a thunderstorm fifteen years ago, desperate for Harper to understand just how much she meant to her. They kissed then too. She shook her head and thought about that first kiss in the bed of Harper's old pickup truck and how they retreated out of that rainstorm hand in hand, still hungry for each other. But not this time.

Chelsea shoved her hands deep into her front pockets. She needed to go home, where she felt safe. Where she had learned to retreat when the world became so heavy that all she wanted to do was curl up in a ball and cry until the suffocating pain eased and she could breathe again. And right now, she desperately needed to breathe.

CHAPTER TWELVE

Harper's stomach churned and her heart felt like it was going to beat its way out of her chest. What the actual hell just happened? After they had kissed—Chelsea's kisses unexpected and beautiful, making her body, and heart, react with long forgotten passion—she had dared to believe that they had a chance. But that last outburst? What the fuck? Even with her head swimming in alcohol, she wasn't intoxicated enough not to see how crazy that was. Chelsea claiming that Laney was out to trap Harper was one thing, but coldly comparing her to Jennifer, and accusing her of being shallow, was something else. Chelsea claimed to be trying to save her from being hurt, while hurting her more than she had been in fifteen years—since the last time Chelsea had laid claim to her and then dropped out of sight with hardly a backward glance. She loved Chelsea. It was impossible to deny that, but that didn't mean she needed to put up with being treated like that.

She tried to focus on what Chelsea had said about Laney. She liked Laney, but not in *that* way, and she had no intention of taking things further. Was it fair to say that she had been enchanted by all Laney's attention in the days after they first met? Maybe. But that didn't make her shallow, and it definitely didn't make her a gold digger. She looked back toward the door, expecting to see Chelsea standing there, ready to apologize and explain. She needed to know that the one she had entrusted with her heart so many years ago wasn't going to hurt her and walk away at a key moment once again. But Chelsea was nowhere to be seen.

She headed back to the bathroom to dry herself off, determined not to let the drama derail Alice's evening. She would speak to Laney herself. And later, when she was sober and much calmer, she'd tell Chelsea how disappointed and upset she was—and how damn wrong Chelsea was to think the only thing she liked about Laney was her money.

"What the hell, Harps." Alice leaned back as Harper scooted in beside her. "You're soaking wet."

"I know. I was outside with Chelsea and we had an argu—" She stopped. "Alice, did Laney and Chelsea get into a fight?" Harper whispered, not wanting everyone else to hear.

"A fight? When?"

"When I was in the restroom."

"Oh that. I thought you meant a real fight." She took a gulp of wine and chuckled. "Yeah, Laney was on her high horse and going on and on about how unsophisticated we all were. But I wasn't really paying attention to her because the DJ started playing this song I haven't heard since high school, and I was listening to that more than Laney. But I do know Laney must have said something that set Chelsea off, because she abruptly got up and left. Why? Is everything okay?"

"No, everything's not okay." Harper felt the truth of it land in her stomach like a stone. "I think Chelsea might have gone home."

She once again scanned the club for Chelsea. Disappointment. Anger. Resentment. Harper struggled to gather her thoughts and feelings. Did Chelsea have any intention of coming back to talk about what had happened? Or was she, rather than Laney, the one playing a game, pretending to be interested when she wasn't? She exhaled a frustrated breath. *Damn it, Chelsea.*

The waitress placed yet another round of shots on the table, and Harper knocked one back, hoping it would take the edge off her anxiety as Laney scooted in next to her.

"There you are, I was looking for you." Laney gently brushed her hand over her shoulder, then recoiled. "You're wet."

"She was outside," Alice said.

"What the hell were you doing out there?"

Laney's question went unanswered as Harper began to shiver from the AC as she sat feeling like a soggy dejected mess. She crossed her arms and tried to hug warmth back into her body as Laney leaned in.

"We need to get you out of that dress. I have an apartment right around the corner. You can take a quick shower to warm up, and I'll throw your dress in the dryer on a delicate cycle. We'll be back for more dancing in no time."

Harper hesitated. A part of her wanted to go and find Chelsea and talk about what the hell just happened, to find out why Chelsea had kissed her if she had such a low opinion of her. But she was getting tired of chasing dead ends. If Chelsea really did want more from her, she would manage her ridiculous jealousy and be by her side right now, instead of Laney.

"Come on," Laney said. "It'll only take a few minutes."

"Yeah, all right."

Ten minutes later, Harper stood in a large, overstuffed room on the third floor of a historic-looking condo complex. Two large couches, whose thick cushions matched the design of the room's patterned wallpaper, consumed most of the space. Thick drapes covered the windows, and oversized gold framed portraits of unknown people hung on the walls. The word gaudy came to mind, but maybe that wasn't totally fair. Maybe this was the epitome of tasteful British luxury, even if to her, it was over the top.

"Now then." Laney escorted her to a marble bathroom. She started the shower and pulled a towel out of the closet. "Warm yourself up, leave the dress outside the door, and I'll get you a robe."

"Thank you, Laney, I appreciate this." Harper closed the door between them, undressed, deposited her outfit in a wet ball back outside the door, and slowly entered the shower. The water was warm, and as she immersed her body fully under its spray, she tried to numb her thoughts, as emotions surfaced. Her heart fluttered for Chelsea in ways it just didn't for Laney. And her kisses had left Harper aroused, full of feelings, and confused as hell. She closed her eyes and choked down another wave of emotions. If Chelsea thought she was some kind of horrible gold digger, what chance did they have of starting over, of finding a way back to each other? None at all was the answer that whispered back to her. It was no more likely than her marrying a princess. She had lost herself once again to her feelings for Chelsea and now she was getting hurt all over again. Maybe coming to London was a mistake. As much as she complained about her boring life, there was something to be said about still waters. At least they were predictable and safe.

Harper stayed in the shower with her swirling thoughts—

Chelsea's mouth on hers, her wild accusations about Laney—when she heard an insistent knocking on the door. She dried herself with the ultrasoft towel, and willed herself to sober up, to feel calmer, to have a better handle on her feelings, but none of that seemed within reach. She wrapped herself in the plush robe with a sudden desire to curl up, shut down, and sleep. The extra glass of wine, sitting on the coffee table, waiting for her when she ventured into the main room, would have been welcomed if she hadn't overloaded herself with champagne, birthday shots, and hurt feelings—for now, water was more enticing.

"You were in there so long I was starting to worry." Laney sat relaxed on the couch. Her phone in one hand, a glass of wine in the other.

"Sorry, I love to take long showers."

"I can tell." Laney patted the cushion next to her. "Come, relax." She pushed the wine closer to Harper.

"Actually, a glass of water is what I really need. I'm feeling the effects of a long day of celebrating Alice's birthday and I'm starting to get tired. In fact, I'll probably just head home once my dress is dry. Alice will understand if I don't go back." She had no idea if Chelsea had even gone home, but either way it was where she needed to be.

Laney narrowed her eyes. "Home? Don't be ridiculous. If you're that tired, you should just stay here."

While the offer was sweet, the thought made her uncomfortable. And at the back of her mind, she couldn't help but think about what Chelsea had said. "I've inconvenienced you enough, I should probably just—"

"Stop, Harper, just stop. This isn't an inconvenience. And why in the world would you want to go back home? Chelsea didn't even stick around after those rather dramatic-looking kisses."

"You saw that?"

"Of course I did." Laney scoffed in a biting way. "Nostalgia, fueled by alcohol, obviously. I know you can't possibly be interested in someone so negative and so basic." There was a question there, but Harper didn't want to answer it. "And if we had kissed like that, well, let's just say I would have never left your side. Whatever you might think you have with her, she obviously feels differently. In fact, she seems a bit toxic. One of those people who doesn't want something but doesn't want anyone else to have it either. And she certainly doesn't want you to enjoy yourself, whatever she says. Her jealousy toward me is a very ugly thing."

Her mind whirled. As hard as those words were to hear, she couldn't deny that the argument with Chelsea, and the whole exchange about Laney, had left her feeling some of the same feelings. But the Chelsea she had known was sweet and loving and always had her best interests at heart. It was hard to connect the dots, even harder with the amount of alcohol she'd drunk.

"She's just been through a lot." Harper came to Chelsea's defense. Why, she wasn't entirely sure.

"Well, no matter what she's going through, the fact of the matter is, she didn't choose to stay with you tonight."

"She asked me to go home with her," Harper blurted out, still halfway wondering why she hadn't.

A smile played across Laney's mouth. "And yet here you are."

And yet here I am. The statement echoed in her mind. Was it easier to be angry at Chelsea for all the things she said and the comparisons she made, than to try to untangle the truth behind what she had said about Laney? She leaned forward and began rubbing her temples, a headache starting to pulse. She wanted Chelsea but she wasn't here. And she didn't want Laney, but here she was. And whatever Chelsea said, she had shown Harper nothing but kindness.

She felt the gentle sensation of Laney's hand stroke her back and she became acutely aware that Laney had moved closer to her. "Is there anything you need from me to make you feel better?" Her voice was low and sultry. Harper's eyes fluttered closed for an instant. When she opened them, Laney's face was inches away, her lips parted. Harper felt Laney's breath as she leaned in for a kiss.

Harper jerked away in surprise. "Laney, can we just…it's just…" She exhaled in frustration as her mind wandered back to Chelsea. "It's been a long day, and this isn't what I want. I like you, but not…not like this. Look, I'm sorry, but there's things I need to sort out with Chelsea. We need to—"

Laney held up a hand. "Please don't. I have no interest in any drama you might have going on in your life. I don't do *complicated* in case you haven't noticed." Laney's eyes were hard, and she looked indignant, a strange rigid expression etched on her face. "And this… this thing that isn't what you want…well, I think you might have misunderstood a little what the offer is." She stared at Harper, and then a blink later, softened her demeanor. "And just so we're clear, I'm not all that sure that it isn't what you want. Tell you what, why don't I make you some tea to warm you up while you sit here and relax a little." Laney stood, dimmed the lights with a remote, and turned on some music. "Here's a blanket in case you get cold. We can just wait for your dress to dry and chat…ideally about something other than Chelsea. I've got plenty more I want to ask you. I'm very keen to know you, Harper. Perhaps keener than you realize." The words were accompanied by a tight smile.

"Thank you." Harper willed herself to sit back on the sumptuous couch and relax a little. Laney was right, she couldn't go anywhere until her dress was dry. And she was grateful that Laney had taken the rejection well.

"Maybe we can just cuddle up and watch a movie. See if we can't *thaw you out* a bit more." Laney hit a control pad fixed to the wall on her way to the kitchen and a large screen slid down hydraulically from the ceiling above the fireplace. "A bit ostentatious, I know."

Harper nodded, gazing at Laney through heavy eyes as she muttered her agreement. The warm blanket, the soft lights, and the alcohol in her system were all conspiring to make her feel sleepy. Everything about Laney was ostentatious. *And everything about Chelsea isn't.* She thought about how happy she had been eating cereal with Chelsea in the little café. She let herself close her eyes, let herself go back there, to the café, to the beach at Whitstable, to the kisses they had shared before the wheels had come off. She pulled the blanket higher up her chest and slowly gave in to the blackness of sleep.

CHAPTER THIRTEEN

Chelsea flicked the kettle on to boil and resumed pacing the small living room, buzzing with a nervous stress that remained, even after the long run she'd forced herself to take. She'd gotten up at five, tired of trying to sleep. Her night had been full of thoughts of Harper—of them kissing, of them arguing, of Harper dancing with Laney—and when that loop stopped playing, she settled on tormenting herself with her own stupidity. She had walked away from the club because she didn't trust herself enough to follow Harper back inside without making things a whole lot worse than she already had. She had intended to. She owed it to them both to try to explain her feelings, to ask Harper if the way she had kissed her meant something, and yes, to try harder to convince her she was in danger of making a fool of herself with Laney. But there was something about the way the whole evening had turned out that made Chelsea think that she was the one making a fool of herself. So she'd gone home full of misery and regrets—abandoning Harper in just the way that Harper accused her of always doing.

And now she was waiting for Harper to get up so she could apologize. And somehow find a way to explain that although she was sorry for her behavior, she didn't regret kissing her for a minute. What felt like months ago, Denise had told her to let Harper know she still had feelings for her—to not abandon her to Laney—but she hadn't listened. She had to hope it wasn't too late.

She filled the teapot, brewed a fresh pot of coffee, and checked her watch again, deciding to make Harper and Alice a fried breakfast as a hangover cure. When she'd got up to get water at around two a.m., they weren't yet home, so she guessed they'd had quite a night of it. And besides, she had already promised Alice the chance to try a full English. She opened the fridge and began to take out what she needed. And if she banged the pans a little louder than she needed to—desperate for them to wake up so she could begin to repair last night's damage—she didn't feel that bad about it.

"I need coffee." Alice emerged from the bedroom, flinging open the door dramatically and then wincing as the door thudded loudly against the wall.

Despite everything, Chelsea couldn't help but smile. Alice was wearing yesterday's party outfit, her face was smudged in makeup, and her hair looked like crows had nested in it overnight.

"You look like you had a good night." Chelsea poured some coffee, splashed in some almond milk, and handed it to Alice, who flopped down on one of the dining chairs with a heavy thud and sighed.

"The night was good. It's the morning that's betraying me." She ran a hand through her hair. It got stuck midway.

"It certainly looks that way." Chelsea smiled kindly but couldn't help looking past Alice to the open doorway, waiting for Harper to emerge. Her heart was beating faster than it had during the morning's run. "I was going to make you guys an English breakfast. Perfect hangover food. Sausage, bacon, black pudding, the works. Better than a Bloody Mary any day."

"Sounds great." Alice drained her cup and handed it to Chelsea, nodding toward the pot. "Would you mind? I'd fill it myself if I thought I could make it that far without my head exploding."

Chelsea took Alice's cup and headed into the kitchen. "Do you think Harper is hungry?" Chelsea pointed at the open bedroom door. "Is she awake? Should I pour her a cup too or wait a bit?"

"Erm." Alice looked from Chelsea to the open door. "She's not…I mean, I wouldn't worry about pouring her a cup of coffee." She sat more upright in the chair, turning her body to Chelsea. "She stayed at Laney's last night."

Chelsea felt the words drop like stones into the bottom of her stomach.

"She did?" It was a question, but it didn't need an answer. Of course she did. Chelsea behaving the way she had had almost guaranteed it.

"Yeah, but it's not what you're thinking—" Alice stopped. "At least I'm pretty sure it's not what you're thinking. She was wet from the rain. Though, come to think of it, I don't remember how that happened. Or why. Anyway…" She waved a dismissive hand. "She got cold sitting in the club with the AC on, so Laney took her to her place to dry her dress and get warm."

"Of course she fucking did." Chelsea slumped against the counter. "Fuck." She couldn't believe how stupid she'd been. "Fuck!" This time she said it louder.

She had finally shown herself to Harper, made it clear she still had feelings, warned Harper that Laney was using her, and Harper's response was to finally fuck Laney. It was almost impossible for her to believe it of Harper, but she doubted that a night spent with Laney would have been spent talking about romance novels. And if Jess was right, then Laney would have got what she wanted and now begin the painful process of breaking Harper's heart. Despite Harper kissing Chelsea like it meant something, Harper didn't want her. The reality of that was breathtakingly hurtful—but that didn't mean she wanted Harper to be fucked over by Laney.

"You okay there, Chelsea? You seem kinda upset." Alice's tone was gentle.

"I am. Stupid, I know." Chelsea pushed herself off the counter, handed Alice her refreshed mug, and turned back to the cooker. She didn't want Alice's pity.

"Nah, it's not stupid." Alice took a sip, then rubbed the mug against her forehead. "Look, I know you guys haven't seen each other in a long time, but she really hasn't changed that much. She's never been into casual sex, and she doesn't fall for women very easily. Love always comes first with Harper. I don't get it, 'cause I'm just the opposite, but hey, that's Harps. She has insanely high standards…" Alice knocked on the table. "Chelsea?"

She turned and faced Alice. It was hard. She was embarrassed by how much she had gotten wrong. Harper had kissed her like she meant it—but she clearly hadn't. She'd chosen helicopter rides and lobster fucking thermidor. She wasn't sure how Alice could say Harper hadn't changed.

"I thought you, of all people, knew that about Harper. It took you guys what, like over a year to get it on, and it was obvious to everyone but the two of you the kind of chemistry you had. She had it bad for you, but she had to be sure you liked her in the right way first. I mean, let's face it…" Alice snorted. "You did have a bit of a reputation."

"I adored her." Chelsea whispered the words. She hadn't ever talked to anyone about Harper, about the way she had felt about her. There hadn't been time.

"And she adored you. And she waited for you, y'know? After you left Phoenix and even after you stopped communicating with her. Long past the point I would have. She said you needed space. I know with what you had going on with your brother, I can't really blame you, but she waited a long time for you. In fact, since we're being honest, I'm not really sure she ever stopped waiting for you."

"Oh, I think she's stopped. Sure, Laney has given her every encouragement, but Harper is big enough to make choices. And she's chosen the storybook romance with the princess. It's okay. I mean it's not like I had a lot to offer in the grand scheme of things. I just felt we had a connection and now I feel a bit foolish." She took in a breath, and then another. "I kissed her last night, Alice. And she kissed me back. But then we argued. I told her Laney was using her…Jess told me she was, that her interest was just a game, and I told Harper, but she didn't believe me. Accused me of being jealous—at least she got that right—and I got angry and told her that she was…" Chelsea winced as she remembered. "I said she was shallow, that she was attracted by the lifestyle. I compared her to Jennifer, my ex. The one who spent all my money and walked out." It sounded even worse saying it out loud to Alice. "And then she turned her back on me and I left and came home. I don't know why I'm telling you this. Maybe if I hadn't left…maybe if I'd found a way to not be jealous, to believe that I had a single thing that Harper wanted." Chelsea made herself stop talking. Alice didn't need this. "Sorry, it doesn't matter now."

"Ohhh." One drawn out syllable was all Alice could offer in response. "Now I get it."

Chelsea put far too much oil in the pan, desperate to be busy. She flung in some rashers of bacon and a couple of sausages.

"You know what's funny?"

Chelsea couldn't imagine there was a single funny thing to be said about this whole situation.

"What?" She turned back to Alice.

"Harper definitely has a favorite trope when it comes to romances. I don't. I want over-the-top chemistry, lots and lots of heat and I don't want to have to wait for it either. I'm not like you and Harper, I have no patience. I want instant gratification. In fact, a couple of months ago, one of the book club ladies brought her insanely gorgeous butch friend to our meeting, two days later, we were on our first dinner date, and by nine that evening we were—"

"Alice." Chelsea really needed her to get to the point.

"Hmm?"

"We were talking about Harper."

"Oh yeah, sorry. Anyway, my point is, Harper sort of enjoys ice queens, she can tolerate a rich girl, poor girl trope—even root for a princess and a plain Jane—but the stories she loves the most are all the same. Second chance romances. Every single book she raves about has that theme, and I've never known anyone root so hard for two people to find each other again after an impossibly long time apart than Harper." Alice smiled.

"What are you saying?"

"I'm saying that I'd always assumed that you were Harper's second chance romance. The one she's been waiting for."

"You're assuming. Meaning she never said that?"

"No, not in so many words. But I know Harper, and I know how much you meant to her. I've seen the way she reacts to you, and it's very different than the way she is around Laney."

Chelsea wanted to be comforted by Alice's words, but it was impossible.

"But she's not here, Alice. She's with Laney. And Laney has made it her mission to get Harper into bed. I don't have a right to be hurt by it, but I am. I know I didn't handle any of it very well, but bottom line, I showed her how I felt about her, and it didn't matter. She still spent the night with Laney."

"You showed her how you felt about her by kissing her, arguing with her, comparing her to your horrible ex, and then walking away, leaving her wondering, once again, what's going on. I don't mean to be harsh, Chels, but she's been waiting for years, while you pop up, only to disappear again. Maybe she just got tired of it."

"That's not fair."

"I think it is. And I don't think you have a right to be possessive either. I would bet my cat—the nice one, the orange one, the one that doesn't scratch the furniture—that she stayed at Laney's without doing anything other than sleep drooling on Laney's expensive sheets. Like I said, she doesn't do casual sex." Alice lifted her shoulders in a shrug. "But if she has spent the night making love with Laney, it's none of your business. Maybe this interest in her is a bit too little, too late."

The words were harsh. Chelsea wanted to object, to defend herself, but she couldn't. Alice had nailed it. She had failed once again. Her caution, her fear of not having enough to offer, had cost her a second chance with Harper. And she was way less convinced than Alice that Harper, full of champagne, full of the flattery and attention that Laney was happy to lavish on her, wouldn't allow herself to be seduced. Hell, maybe she was the one doing the seducing. Even at nineteen, she had been the one who had finally made the move that led to them becoming lovers. They'd had one glorious night. A night she'd thought about often. They didn't know that was all it would be, that night it had felt like they had forever stretched out in front of them. She should have found a way back to Harper years before, but she hadn't. And this trip had felt like she had been given an unlikely chance to try again. And she had once again failed to live up to expectations. Jennifer was right to get out while she could.

"You're right. Of course you are. Harper is one in a million, too good for Laney and too good for me. And she deserves happiness with someone who has something to offer her. That's not Laney, but maybe it's not me either." Chelsea wiped an unwelcome tear from her cheek and set to work on the breakfast that she had promised Alice. Her own stomach roiled with the bitterness of how badly she had messed up this second chance with Harper.

Twenty minutes later, Alice was polishing off a third piece of buttered toast, and wiping her plate clean with the crust as Chelsea sipped at her tea.

"That was awesome! Thanks, Chelsea. My stomach's bursting with a food baby, so I understand now why they call it a full English."

Chelsea nodded, her thoughts elsewhere. Today was Friday and she was supposed to be going to Whitstable to sign the contract. Billy had said to expect an early call confirming the provisional appointment they'd made. Yesterday, she'd had half a hope that she could persuade Harper and Alice to go with her. A chance to celebrate something important together before they went home. Today it was hard to even get excited about it herself.

"I bet that's Harper." Alice went to her room to retrieve her phone after it had dinged three times in quick succession.

Chelsea stood and began gathering plates, taking them to the sink and running water into the bowl. She left them soaking and went to her room, not wanting to know what Harper had to say to Alice about last night. She figured, like Alice had said, it was none of her business. She called Billy, impatient for news—and desperate to do something that wasn't just moping around the apartment all day. When all she reached was his voice mail, she let out a deep sigh, left a message, grabbed some clean clothes, and headed toward the shower. She had barely crossed the living room when her phone rang.

"Hi, Billy. Yeah, sorry for calling. Just checking if we're still on for two o'clock?"

As he spoke, Chelsea felt the same awful churning in her stomach that she had experienced when she realized Harper had spent the night with Laney.

"Wait, what are you saying? I thought it was locked in, that it was all a formality? You've got to be kidding me." She couldn't help but raise her voice. She wasn't angry, she was panicking.

Alice came out of her room and moved toward her with a questioning look on her face. She held up a hand.

"I can't afford to pay another forty percent. You know that. It's been hard enough to get together what I needed to meet the original asking price. How the hell can I compete with an offer like that?"

Chelsea's stomach knotted and her head buzzed so loudly with stress that she wasn't sure she was even hearing Billy correctly.

"Sure, I can go to the bank…I can ask, but I'm pretty sure they'll say no." She paused, fighting the urge both to cry and to smash her phone against the wall. "Of course I want it. I just said I'll try to get the bank to help me match the offer. I just can't believe someone came in from nowhere with an offer this good. Are you telling me the truth about this? There's really another bidder? I know that you work on commission, it's in your interest to get me to pay more—"

Alice moved closer. The deep look of concern on her face was a surprise to Chelsea somehow. She hadn't imagined that she would care.

"I know, I know, I'm sorry. I didn't mean to insult you. I'm just…I'm just…" Chelsea took in a deep breath, and then another, she felt close to tears. "Look, I'll go down there now and see the manager in person. It's probably pointless, but I'll try. Can you hold the other bidder off for a few hours?"

Chelsea ended the call and closed her eyes, fighting for composure. She felt Alice's hand on her arm.

"Uh-oh, that didn't sound good. Did someone outbid you for the space?"

"Yeah. And not even for another restaurant. Seems like somebody wants to turn it into a fucking art gallery. I can't believe it. Seems like coming in second is my superpower." Chelsea sounded as bitter as she felt. If she didn't have Harper and she didn't have her dream restaurant, then what the hell came next? Once again, she felt the panic course through her body.

"I have to go to the bank." Chelsea took her clothes back into her room, and then doubled back into the bathroom. She needed to shower, and she needed the time to think. She had one chance to turn this around—and it was a slim one. She closed the door as Alice called something out to her. She heard Harper's name. She opened the door. "Sorry, what did you say?"

"I said Harper is on her way back here. She said she—" Alice stopped herself, as if unsure how much to say.

Chelsea waited for the hammer to drop on any hope she had with Harper.

"She's a bit hungover. She asked if you're around. Maybe you should hang out here a bit and see her. Have some breakfast and talk?"

Chelsea scrutinized Alice's face, not sure she was understanding properly. But she was too proud—too afraid—to ask for the details. Despite everything, she couldn't help but want to see Harper. She pushed the thought away. She had made her choice, and it wasn't Chelsea. And she only had a few hours to try to save her dream.

"I can't, I have to go." She closed the door, stripped, turned on the water, and stepped into the shower. As the water pulsed against her chest, she unclenched her fists and let the tears she had been fighting flow freely. Everything about Harper's dream visit was turning into a nightmare for Chelsea.

❖

"She really brought someone back there?" Alice was as incredulous as Harper had been.

"Yeah, I couldn't believe it. They came out of the bedroom this morning, hanging all over each other, barely dressed. Laney as casual as can be as she asked this woman to introduce herself to me…as though she was making it obvious that she didn't even know her name."

"That's fucked up." Alice shook her head.

"I know, right? And I was still semiconscious under a blanket on her couch, wearing her robe, while this woman is introducing herself. I must have been in a coma because I didn't hear Laney go out, or come back, and I definitely didn't hear whatever it was they did in the bedroom last night. I'm never drinking shots again. I don't care if it's your birthday." Harper drained her second cup of coffee.

"Yeah, well, I might join you on that wagon."

Harper took a moment to pause and reflect as she let the morning fog clouding her mind dissipate.

"It's such a fuck you, Harps," Alice said. "You rejected her and fell asleep on her couch, so she went out and found someone who wasn't going to say no. Then she purposely paraded her in front of you."

Harper nodded. Alice wasn't sugarcoating it, but she was right. It was a horrible thought.

"Maybe Chelsea was right when she warned you about her. I hate to say it, sweetie, but if Laney was at all sincere about her interest in you, she wouldn't have reacted that way to you falling asleep on her."

"Wait, how do you know about that?"

"Chelsea filled me in this morning, and trust me, if Jess had told *me* that, I'd have done exactly what Chelsea did, even if I knew it would upset you."

"I should have known." Harper felt stupid. It was obvious Laney didn't really care about her. She should never have thrown Chelsea's attempt to warn her back in her face with such disregard.

"I told Chelsea she was just being jealous and trying to cause trouble. Told her to stop hating on Laney and to try to be happy that someone actually wanted me." Harper bowed her face to her hands. "Did she tell you I said that?"

"Yeah. She also said she had said a lot of things she was sorry for too."

"She accused me of only liking Laney because she was rich and a princess. Accused me of being just like her ex."

"I know. She said she was angry and upset, and that she regretted it." Alice stood and carried her cup to the sink. "Look, I don't really want to get stuck in the middle between you two, and you know I'll always take your side, but I kinda like Chelsea."

"I know. Thanks, Alice."

Alice came back to the table and put a hand on Harper's shoulder.

"She said she was sad about how things ended last night between you two. And you know how much I hate giving advice…"

"You do realize you always say you hate giving advice, while giving advice." Harper smiled.

"Exactly, so hear me out. You guys need to talk. Seems to me you're both holding back telling each other how you feel, and we've read enough romance novels to know that main characters with any hope of a happy ending need to talk things out. So, my advice is that it's time you two talk, Harper, and I mean *really* talk."

The truth of what Alice was saying hit hard, and Harper felt the prickle of tears.

"I came home to talk. To at least try, and she's not even here. It's like one of us is always on the wrong page."

"Not her fault this time. She was really devastated when she heard someone outbid her on her restaurant space. She said that she's going to the bank and then going to see her sister so they can talk about options within the family. She said she might even go to Whitstable to see the real estate agent and try to persuade him to accept a lower offer with an extended leasing period. She said it's a risk because if she signs on for longer and it doesn't work out, she'll be in trouble financially, but it might be her only option. Anyway, she was pretty upset over it all."

"I already messaged her to say how sorry I am about the restaurant." Harper looked at her phone, the message still showing as unread. "Maybe I should text and tell her I'm here, and that I'll wait for when she comes back, so we can talk."

"Ah, that sounds so romantic, but are you forgetting we have plans this evening."

"We do?"

"Wow, you must have been really out of it last night. Don't you remember? Laney gave me tickets to *La Bohème* for my birthday. She's booked a box for all of us at the Royal Opera House this evening. Ring any bells?"

Harper shook her head.

"Seriously? You raved about how much you wanted to see it for a good five minutes. About how you'd read the book and always wanted to see the opera."

Harper searched her memory. Her head had been full of vodka shots…and Chelsea. But since *Rent* was one of her favorite musicals, and she knew it was a modern reworking of *La Bohème*, she definitely would have raved about wanting to see it. The memory appeared on the horizon but was hazy.

"Kind of."

"Well, we said we'd go. And even though Laney pulled a shit move on you last night, I really want to see it. You said you'd go, it's a birthday gift, and Oliver and the others said they're going too. Come on, we've only got a couple of days left, so we should drink up as many experiences as we can before we leave."

Harper winced; the word "drink" made her stomach turn.

"Trust me, after last night, I'm sure Laney would rather take Felicity than me." Even as she said it, Harper was doubtful. Felicity looked about twenty and would probably rather spend an evening on her phone instead of at the opera.

"Don't bail on me, Harper. Besides, from the way you described it, it sounds like it was a one and done with that woman."

Harper rolled her eyes and groaned as feelings of awkwardness and regret from last night resurfaced. And yet again, as she glanced at Alice, she felt the pressure to please the people who were counting on her. If she promised Alice she would go to he opera tonight, she didn't want to disappoint. She made a mental note to call her therapist when she returned home. It was time to stop being such a people pleaser and instead learn how to speak up for herself.

"Meanwhile," Alice sniffed her armpits, "I really need a shower. Oliver wants to take me out for drinks beforehand, so I'm meeting him at three. Laney said she'd send a car for you around five. I figured between now and then we could walk around the street tents. I want to buy some tacky souvenirs to bring back home." She got up from the table.

"Alice…"

"Oh no you don't. I know that look."

Harper fidgeted. "Would you be mad at me if I don't go to the opera? I feel like I should stay here and wait for Chelsea to get back." She sighed. "I really wish you hadn't told her I spent the night at Laney's."

"Oh yeah, and what was I supposed to tell her, huh?" Alice snapped a bit, then softened her voice and placed her hand on Harper's shoulder and gave it a gentle squeeze. "Look, we don't know when she'll be back tonight. She has a lot on her plate right now. Text her that you want to talk and tell her a bit of what you just told me. Invite her to come, even though I doubt she'll go, but wouldn't it be awesome if she did and sat on your lap the whole time. Ha, bet that would make Laney's head explode."

Harper couldn't help but smile, even though she knew deep down Chelsea wouldn't accept the invite, and it was all her fault. Harper felt her mood sink. Everything was so fucked up.

Alice pulled her into a tight hug. "Okay, I'm off to the shower. Don't overthink this too much. Everything's going to be okay, you'll see."

It was enough to make the tears Harper had been holding back flow freely. "I made such a mess."

"Shhh." Alice held on to her. "You didn't, and even if you did, you definitely got some mixed signals from Chelsea. And from Laney. Look, if Chelsea's meant to be your second chance romance, it'll all work out in the end."

Harper waited for Alice to slowly release her, but when she didn't, she pulled away and even managed a small smile. They looked at each other and communicated the unspoken words that said they'd always have each other's back. "Now go shower, you stink." Harper playfully pushed her toward the bathroom.

God, she loved Alice. In all her Alice-y ways. But she was right, if she and Chelsea were meant to be, it would find a way to work itself out. How, she hadn't a clue. Harper looked down at her phone once more.

The message she sent hours ago, still unread. She'd spend the afternoon with Alice, wait for Chelsea to respond and for the inspiration to figure out what to do next. And if Chelsea didn't come home before five and give them a chance to talk, she'd go to the opera, say a final good-bye to Laney, and make it as clear as she could to Chelsea that she was never in a competition with Laney. Chelsea had her heart. She always had.

Chapter Fourteen

"Simply stunning."

A *thank you* formed on the tip of Harper's lips as she folded herself next to Laney in the back seat of the sedan, but she didn't express it, not really sure if Laney's compliment was directed at her or the dress.

"Jess sent the dress over earlier this afternoon. I wasn't expecting it." She settled in her seat and ran her hands over the smooth silky fabric of the formal one-shoulder black gown. She had to admit that it suited her, and the fit was perfect. "I'm assuming that was your doing, so thank you." An awkwardness fell between them that hadn't been there before. Laney simply nodded before settling back in her seat as the sedan pulled away.

"I didn't want you turning up not looking the part. Everyone who is anyone will be there, and Oliver promised me he'd take it upon himself to sort Alice out." Laney raked her eyes up and down Harper's body in a way that made her feel a bit objectified. It made her uncomfortable. "You know, Jess was like an annoying gnat after we went our separate ways, but I have to admit the woman has impeccable taste in fashion." Laney ran a hand over Harper's knee. "But don't fall in love with it. It's a loaner. Jess's markup on Stella McCartney dresses has been outrageous ever since Meghan wore one for her royal wedding reception, and I refuse to pay a price equivalent to a ransom. I already overpaid for Felicity to have this Tom Ford jacket she really *had to have* today, and even my largesse has limits."

Harper had no interest in owning overpriced dresses. She knew nothing about designers, fashion, or the latest clothing trends. In fact, it had always been easier for her to pair a bottle of wine with a meal than to pair pants with a shirt. "Speaking of…is she not joining us this evening?" Harper wanted to let Laney know that she was perfectly fine with her having someone in her life.

"Felicity? That silly thing?" Laney scoffed. "She can't handle the opera. She probably thinks Puccini is a type of pizza. She's the kind of girl you have fun with, not the kind of girl you take to the opera. Kind of like the opposite of you actually." Laney smiled. It wasn't a kind smile. And even Harper understood the comment for what it was. "Though she is coming to Lake Como with me next week. Got quite excited at the idea of skinny-dipping in Italy. One advantage of her not being American is that she has some idea of the basics of European geography."

The expression on Laney's face was spiteful.

"So, are you going to insult me the entire way to the opera?" Harper felt her temper rise. The day had already been a shitty one. She didn't need this. She had set out intending to be pleasant, to thank Laney for all the experiences she had given her, and to say good-bye politely. As befitted a princess.

"Not at all. Don't be so sensitive. That would imply I had some sort of jealousy or feelings for you."

"Then why are you being like this?"

Laney lifted an eyebrow. "This? This is what I'm like, Harper. I don't have endless patience and I'm not to be taken advantage of. Whatever you think…whatever your cook thinks. The one you seem inexplicably obsessed with despite seeming to want to spend all your time with me, and despite being perfectly happy to wear my dresses and drink my champagne. It's disappointing actually, but make no mistake, no matter what you think, and how you try to come across, you are more like me than not. In fact—"

The jingle of Laney's phone sent her reaching into her purse. She held up her finger, signaling she needed a moment. "Markus, I didn't expect to hear from you until tomorrow." She cradled the device against her ear. "Is everything okay?"

Harper averted her eyes. That was twice in twenty-four hours that someone had accused her of being more materialistic than she ever thought she was. She blinked back the few tears that welled and threatened to spill over. Was she really that shallow? No, she concluded. She knew who she was, despite what others apparently thought.

She filled her lungs and dabbed at her eyes as she tried to distract herself by looking out the window at the scenery—as Chelsea's neighborhood dissolved into what she now knew was Moorgate, with its office blocks and tiny city squares. Laney was in a foul mood, the thick traffic meant they weren't going anywhere fast anytime soon, she still hadn't heard back from Chelsea, and she was acutely aware that their vacation was nearing its end and she would be home soon and back to a boring life full of predictability but empty of joy. She shook off the melancholy that washed over her, as she focused again on her surroundings as they passed a line of people waiting to enter a sandwich shop. She liked England. Amongst its condensed spaces far too full of people and buildings, she found it charming and inviting. And its rich history and beautiful architecture spoke to her, waking up her creative juices. It made her feel invigorated and full of possibilities and she had wished more than once that she could find a way to somehow bottle the essence of the place and take it with her.

And of course, there was Chelsea. She seemed so much more content here. More so than she ever was at college. Her cute little apartment, the vibe of Shoreditch, and so many historic pubs all within walking distance. Harper pinched her phone out of her purse and flicked her eyes at the screen again. She couldn't quite find the words to tell Chelsea everything she was feeling—that conversation needed to take place in person—but she had sent a message asking for time for them to talk, and she'd included a comment about how she'd slept the night through on Laney's couch, hoping it spoke for itself. Her memory of much of the evening was hazy at best, but she remembered their passionate kissing, and every time she did, the arousal felt fresh. She also remembered Chelsea calling her "amazing"—just before she compared her to the ex that she clearly hated. She sighed. She had come here fighting absurd thoughts of possibly rekindling a smoldering ember, but after two weeks of failed attempts, she had surrendered those feelings to friendship. Any flame that took that much effort to ignite, she reasoned, wasn't meant to be. But the way Chelsea had kissed her made her wonder if she should have tried harder.

A distant low roar of thunder snapped her back to the present, and a cold chill washed over her as she focused on Laney's raised voice.

"What do you mean the paperwork will take an extra day? That's unacceptable…I don't care if the banker you're working with is on holiday tomorrow, get someone else to do it. And remind them that I bid forty percent over the current offer, which is above market value for that space, because I expected that to be enough to close this deal in a timely manner." She paused. "Fine, then I'll pay the extra fee to rush the documents through processing. What do I care, I'm not paying for it, the Academy is. And no, I'm not interested in looking at another open space. I want that one, and only that one. Do you understand?" She fell silent. "Well, if there's kitchen equipment in there, then just have someone get rid of it all…yes, that's correct…it's going to be an art gallery, not a bloody restaurant, and, Markus, this all needs to happen fast. I'm presenting the space to the other trustees on Thursday, so everything needs to be completed by then. No, we won't take the chopper for the showing. We'll take the train. It's barely an hour's journey on the express service. I want them all to understand how close and accessible it is to London."

An art gallery, not a restaurant? Laney couldn't possibly be the mysterious person who outbid Chelsea for the space. No. Harper shook her head, and with it the nightmare thought. Laney wouldn't be that cruel. Would she?

"How would I know? I haven't even seen it." Laney snapped, obviously irritated with the conversation. "When have I had time to travel to Whitstable? I just heard about an amazing space available right on the beach, with spectacular views, and I had to snap it up. After all, provincial seaside gallery offshoots are all the rage." Laney held Harper's gaze as she spoke. The challenge in her eyes was unmistakable. "Yes…that's right. Okay, thanks, Markus, I appreciate you coming through for me last minute on this."

Laney ended the call and Harper sat dumbfounded. Enough words were spoken that she didn't have to stretch her imagination very far to connect the dots.

"You're the person who outbid Chelsea on her restaurant?"

The corners of Laney's mouth twitched. "Tell you what. Let's make a rule for tonight, shall we? Let's not talk about her. I'm finding it rather tiresome."

"Laney, how could you? You knew that space meant the world to Chelsea."

"Oh, please. Do you honestly think Whitstable needs another seafood restaurant?"

"It's not about what Whitstable needs, it's what Chelsea needs. That space was about her fulfilling a dream. To finally have the opportunity to live her life's passion. She was going to dedicate that restaurant to her deceased brother."

Laney made a dismissive grunt. "Well, I'm sure there are other spaces available. She can have a go at one of them. Quite frankly, I'm a bit surprised she was able to secure a bid on that location in the first place. She doesn't seem like a person of many means, and Markus tells me it's a prime location."

"Not that it's any of your business, but she was going to sell her flat to make the payments."

"Well, see, there you go. Now she won't have to. I did her a favor."

Harper felt repulsed. Everything Chelsea had tried to warn her about Laney flooded her head like a chorus of strident voices. What the actual fuck?

"Oh, please, don't give me that pathetic 'feeling sorry for her' kind of look. Did you really think I was going to let her get away with talking to me the way she did last night? In front of my friends. She should have remembered who it was she was speaking to. While you were sleeping, I called Markus, and made sure he was the first call the estate agents took this morning."

Laney hesitated, a sneer on her face. Harper steeled herself. She had no idea the depths of unpleasantness Laney was capable of.

"Perhaps if I hadn't had quite so much time on my hands last night, none of this would have happened. But as it was, my *date* for the evening ended up disappointing me and giving me more free time than I would have liked."

"You purposely went after her space—with the intent to ruin her future—because I wouldn't sleep with you? Because she dared to call you out for exactly what you are? You sicken me. I can't believe it took me this long to realize what you're really like." Harper felt a chill in her veins, her head began to spin, but she was determined not to let Laney see how upset she was. "Everything about you is disgusting."

Laney twisted her body around, her eyes fixed on Harper in a hard stare. "Disgusting?" She released the word and laced it with venom. "You didn't seem to think high tea at the Ritz, or a private showing at the Academy, was disgusting. Or being in a beautiful dress that most would kill to wear. Don't fool yourself, Harper, there's a part of you that loves all this. We may have come from different upbringings, but I've seen something in your eyes that tells me we're not that dissimilar. You like what I have. You just hate yourself for wanting it."

"I'm *nothing* like you."

"Oh yeah?" Laney scoffed in her face. "How many times have you left Chelsea or altered your plans to come do something with me? Hmm? No one forced you to take that helicopter ride or spend last night in my apartment. No, Harper, you did it because there was something about this lifestyle that called to you more than the company you were keeping."

"That's not fair. You painted me into a corner and made it impossible for me to say no. I wanted to, I wanted to be with Chelsea. Every time—"

Laney held up her finger and moved it back and forth in a mocking tsk-tsk motion. "No. You did it all of your own free will, so don't you dare point the mirror in my direction because you're suddenly feeling guilty and you're too ashamed to admit it."

"How dare you even insinuate that—"

"I'm not insinuating. I'm stating it as a fact. Don't think for a minute you're better than me. Chelsea thinks I buy people. Well, you let yourself be bought. You spend your time reading your romance novels because you're looking for something that's lacking in your tired little life. And now that you've found it, you're honestly going to try and tell me you're not enjoying it? Please. This lifestyle might come with a price—including never knowing quite who you can trust—but I've made peace with that. Now then…" Laney let out a breath, pinched the bridge of her nose softening the creases in her forehead, and presented an almost comical forced smile. "Let's put this behind us so we don't ruin a nice evening at the opera."

Harper sat in silence as a barrage of thoughts and feelings pounded in her head. She had come to London on the off chance of finding the most important thing in her life that was missing—true love. The part of her, that for the past fifteen years, had never felt whole. Or wholly loved. She had come back for Chelsea. And everything she had done up to now was misguided and wrong.

"Manny, stop the car." She caught Manny's questioning eyes in the rearview mirror. "I said stop the car!"

"Harper, what are you doing?" Laney squared off to Harper. Her expression was strange and somewhat bewildered looking.

Harper turned to her as she opened the door. "You're right about one thing. I came here in search of something I was lacking in my life. And thanks to you, I've found her."

"You can't be serious." Laney's words came out wearily. "But fine, please go and live your pathetic little life. I was tired of you anyway."

Harper hopped out of the car and began to back away, then stopped. There was one more thing. "I'll FedEx the dress back to Jess." Harper leveled her gaze at Laney for what was hopefully the last time. She slammed the door with as much force as she could muster, happy to no longer be breathing the same air as Laney. She glanced at the sky as tears began streaking her cheeks. How could she have been so foolish? So blinded to what was right in front of her. She took a long deep breath, grabbed the hem of the dress, lifting it in a bundle, and started to run. She wasn't sure if Chelsea was home, but if she wasn't, she would wait for her. She had waited fifteen years, what difference did a few more hours make? She had a lot of explaining to do, and she had to hope that Chelsea was willing to let her.

The sedan slowed to a stop beside her and she stopped, breathing heavily, waiting for Laney to step out, to continue berating her. But as fast as the car slowed down, it sped up again, and Harper let out a relieved sigh.

"That's right, fuck off, and keep driving. Ideally off the edge of Tower Bridge." Harper muttered the words under her breath as she hurried in the direction they had just come from and back to the person who was more of a fairy tale to her than a princess like Laney ever could be. The one she should never have doubted. The one she had always loved.

Harper's sense of direction was not great at the best of times, and these London streets felt like a maze. She periodically called out to people for directions and followed their pointing fingers and verbal instructions down streets and around corners until the scenery became familiar and her inner compass took over. As she ran past the murals and familiar street vendors, she rounded the last corner to Chelsea's street and paused at an image as her heart began to beat wildly. There, sitting at a table in front of the cereal shop, was Chelsea. She wore a pair of running shorts and a faded T-shirt. She looked sexy as hell, and all the feelings Harper had for her, that she locked away so many years ago, burst free. This was the woman of her dreams. The woman she had been waiting for. They had only made love for one fateful night. A few hours, hours that in the overall scheme of Harper's life, should never constitute enough time for her to feel like this. But time wasn't always the best measure of love. One night could capture the heart with as much certainty as a love years in the making.

But with each step she took toward Chelsea, doubt rushed in, and Harper wondered if Chelsea felt any of the same feelings. And more than that, what in the world was she going to say to her? How could Chelsea possibly forgive her for acting like such a fool? For not believing her when she had her best interests at heart? Her stupidity had cost Chelsea her restaurant.

Harper approached the table, smoothing one hand down her dress, and running the other hand through her hair, now damp with sweat. She'd been so fixed on getting to Chelsea as quickly as she could that she hadn't stopped to think about what she was going to say.

Chelsea lifted her gaze from her phone to Harper, her eyes wide and full of questions as Harper searched for a sign. Anything that said there was still a chance Chelsea would forgive her. How had she strayed so far away from the one person who'd always made her feel *at home*?

"Hi." She lifted a hand. It was a start, but not much of one.

They needed to have a conversation and sort things out. Feelings were hurt, meanings were twisted, and expressions were misunderstood. She needed to tell Chelsea how sorry she was about everything, and most of all, she needed to let her know, as clichéd as it sounded, that she was the woman she had come on this trip hoping to "meet" and capture her heart. But now was not the time. She moved closer to the table without once taking her eyes off Chelsea.

Chelsea stood and moved to her side of the small table.

"Thought you were at the opera?" She sounded hesitant, but she held Harper's gaze, not breaking eye contact.

"Change of plans." Harper moved even closer. They were inches apart. The smell of Chelsea's lavender shampoo danced across Harper's senses, giving her goose bumps. They gazed at each other, Harper trying to let Chelsea know why she was there.

"And do those plans include me?"

"Yes." She cupped Chelsea's cheek with one hand, grazing her thumb softly across Chelsea's lips, the memory of how soft they were, how warm, causing a tightening low down in her belly, the pulsing between her legs impossible to ignore. She moved her other hand to the back of Chelsea's head, her fingers softly playing with the hair at the nape of her neck, holding Chelsea's gaze, using her touch to communicate the things she hadn't been able to say. The moment she sensed Chelsea's breath quicken, felt Chelsea lean into her touch, Harper brought her lips to Chelsea's. The kiss was not soft, nor was it tentative. It was deep and wanting. And all Harper's doubts disappeared the moment Chelsea pressed herself against her, her kisses just as hungry. She deepened the kiss, moaning when Chelsea parted her lips, allowing her tongue inside. The warm, wet softness was making her throb. Chelsea's hands were in her hair, her breathing heavy and ragged, her kisses demanding, and when she plunged her tongue into Harper's mouth, she felt her knees buckle with desire. Only Chelsea's arm—now around her waist, pulling them closer together, Chelsea's body pressed against the length of her, her breasts crushed against her own—stopping her from falling.

Chelsea was the first to break the kiss between them. She rested her forehead against Harper's, her breathing heavy. When she pressed her lips against Harper's again, the kiss was soft and slow, and everything about it reminded her of the night they had lain in the back of her truck, kissing like that and exploring each other's bodies for the very first time. Harper wanted it to go on forever. And when Chelsea threaded her fingers through Harper's, bringing their hands to her mouth for a tender kiss, Harper felt like she was going to melt.

Harper felt bereft when Chelsea moved back a step, breaking the contact between their bodies. Across the street, a man applauded them. Chelsea blinked and looked at him, and then back at Harper with a shy smile. She held Harper's hands in front of her, using them to make Harper take a step backward.

"You look absolutely gorgeous." Chelsea said it as if to herself. "Truly beautiful. How did I even stand a chance of resisting you?"

Harper felt heat flush her cheeks. It was still a novelty to hear those words spoken about her, but she couldn't deny she liked hearing them. Especially from Chelsea.

"Oh, Harper." Chelsea pulled Harper back into her arms, wrapping her in a tight hug, then resting her chin on Harper's shoulder. "I thought

I'd lost you." She whispered the words into Harper's ear, and Harper felt every part of herself tremble.

"Never." Harper pulled away, placed her finger under Chelsea's chin, and brought her gaze up to meet her. "I'm so sorry for what I did. So sorry for not seeing what was right in front of me all this time."

"It wasn't just you, Harper. I should have never let you go in the first place. I was just so lost and preoccupied with my own pain that I closed off the world and pushed everyone away, even the people I loved. And having you here again has made me realize what a fool I've been."

Harper grabbed her by the waist, pulling her close, joining their bodies together all over again. "We have a lot to talk about," she whispered in Chelsea's ear. "But for now, what do you say we go back to your place and make up for some of that lost time?"

If the heavy release in Chelsea's breath sent heat flashing up Harper's skin, it was nothing compared to what the next few words did to her center.

"I thought you'd never ask."

CHAPTER FIFTEEN

"Chelsea." As they stood opposite each other inside Chelsea's front door, another wave of guilt washed over Harper. "I'm so sorry for what's happened."

Chelsea raised her finger to Harper's lips, silencing her and her thoughts. "Shh. It's okay. Some things aren't meant to be. And losing the restaurant is nothing compared to how I felt when I thought I'd lost you. And I haven't, so…" She placed her other hand around Harper's waist drawing them closer together.

Harper nodded. Right now, they didn't need to talk, they didn't need to rehash all the reasons—or the people—that had kept them apart all these years. Right then, the only thing that mattered was the fact that they were together.

Harper ached to touch Chelsea, to kiss her again. She leaned in and finally touched her lips to Chelsea's. The soft warmth of her mouth made Harper moan slightly. In response, Chelsea deepened the kiss, pressing her body against Harper, the kiss hard and hot. Harper felt the power of it in the heat, the throbbing, between her legs. And when Chelsea parted her lips, Harper dipped her tongue inside, needing to taste her again and glorying at the way that Chelsea moaned in return and pulled Harper even closer. Her hands were now in her hair, and her breathing was ragged.

"We've wasted so much time." Harper placed her hands on the bottom seam of Chelsea's T-shirt and pulled the fabric over her head, then dropped it to the floor. "You okay with this?" She didn't wait for an answer as she raked her nails up Chelsea's stomach, across the twitching muscles, until she reached her breasts. She traced her fingers softly across Chelsea's nipples, feeling how erect they were even through the fabric of her sports bra. A hunger stirred inside her as an urgency to have her desires satisfied took hold. Harper pulled Chelsea closer, wanting to feel the length of her body, feel her breasts, pressed against her own. She bit down softly on Chelsea's lower lip and was rewarded with a deeper kiss, and a low groan, as Chelsea's hands slipped the dress off her shoulder, then grabbed at her ass and pushed them together at the waist. She seemed every bit as desperate as Harper was.

Harper lowered her mouth to pepper kisses softly down Chelsea's neck, and across her collarbone, before pausing to unhook Chelsea's bra. She took it off and dropped it next to the T-shirt on the floor at their feet. She hungrily claimed first one nipple and then the other as Chelsea's breathing accelerated.

Chelsea arched her body into Harper. Her nipples were hard underneath Harper's tongue as she licked and sucked them greedily. Chelsea's moans filled her head, the sound of them intoxicating to Harper. She circled her tongue around Chelsea's nipple one more time before lifting her head and pushing Chelsea back against the front door. The eyes looking back at her were almost black with desire, and when Chelsea reached for her, she let herself be pulled into an embrace. They kissed hungrily, their lips crushed together. Harper reached both her hands down to Chelsea's waist before slipping them inside her shorts to push them down Chelsea's long legs, suddenly desperate to see her naked. She wanted to look at Chelsea's body, sear the image of every inch of her into her mind. It had been fifteen years, and time had transformed Chelsea's body into something even more desirable than she remembered.

"You are so beautiful." Harper tried to damp down her desire to the point where she could actually form words. "And so damn sexy. And I've spent too many years of my life waiting to feel like this again." She cupped Chelsea's breasts and moved her thumbs over her still wet nipples. Chelsea shivered.

"Are you cold?" Harper ceased her motion.

"The cold is not what my body is reacting to."

"Ohhh." Harper grinned as she leaned in and demanded another kiss, their tongues touching. Chelsea moaned. Harper dipped her head again to close her mouth over one nipple and then the other, caressing them with her tongue, desperate to keep tasting Chelsea. She had waited so long for this, and now that they were here, she wanted everything, and all at once. Harper moved her mouth down Chelsea's torso, tracing her tongue across her ribs, and along her abs, before kneeling in front of her.

"Keep that up and I'm going to fall down." The words came out breathily. "But please, don't stop…" Chelsea looked at her with pleading eyes, her body taut, stretched out in bliss.

"You won't." Harper placed her hand flat against Chelsea's stomach, not taking her eyes off Chelsea's face. She swallowed, the desire thick in her throat. "I want to taste you."

Chelsea's eyes widened. She shifted her position wordlessly, opening herself to Harper. Harper nudged Chelsea's knees a little further apart, trailing kisses along the inside of her thigh. When she reached Chelsea's center, she brushed the lightest of kisses against it, letting her hot breath linger, before carrying on to kiss the inside of her other thigh. Her own desire lighting a fire in her core that needed feeding.

"Please, Harper." Chelsea placed a hand on her head, her fingers threaded through her hair.

Harper didn't wait a beat longer. She placed her mouth firmly against the warm wetness of Chelsea's center and stroked her tongue up and down the length of her before finally flicking it across the swollen bud of her clitoris. She teased and probed with her tongue as Chelsea pushed herself off the door and against Harper's mouth. She sucked greedily, feeling Chelsea's orgasm building in the way she panted and murmured. Hearing her name in Chelsea's mouth drove Harper wild. She pressed her hand more firmly against Chelsea's stomach and increased the speed and pressure of her tongue. Chelsea's breathing grew more rapid, her body grinding against Harper's mouth, her legs shaking.

"God, yes. Harper, don't stop." Harper felt Chelsea's fingers in her hair, urging her on, opening her legs wider.

She grazed her fingertips alongside the inside of Chelsea's thigh, the skin soft and smooth. All the time, she teased Chelsea with her tongue, her strokes relentless, Chelsea's breathing and whimpering telling her that she was doing exactly the right thing. She paused for a second before closing her mouth over Chelsea's erect clitoris at the same time as she filled her with her fingers. The cry of pleasure from Chelsea was primal, and Harper loved it. Chelsea pushed herself against Harper's fingers, seeming to want her even deeper inside, hungry for more. Harper fucked her harder, keeping up the rhythm, sliding in and out of Chelsea, the feeling absolutely wonderful, her own body close to orgasm without even being touched. She curled her fingers slightly, pushing deeper inside Chelsea, and increased the speed of her tongue against Chelsea's swollen bud.

With a loud guttural scream, Chelsea came, her breathing rapid, one hand in Harper's hair, the other grabbing for the doorframe. Harper watched Chelsea ride out the wave of her orgasm, her eyes clamped shut, her body shuddering. Her knees buckled, and despite the presence of Harper's steadying hand, she slid down the door until she was also on her knees, face-to-face with Harper. After a beat, and a few deep ragged breaths, she opened her eyes. Harper loved seeing how big and black her pupils were. She could only imagine her own eyes looked the same. The arousal coursing through her own body was hard to control. She was desperate for Chelsea to make love to her.

"Harper…" The word came out with a croak. "Fuck. I can't even speak." Chelsea smiled and the dimple that came with it made Harper swoon. "That was…" Chelsea leaned in to place a soft kiss on her lips. "Incredible." Chelsea kissed her again. "My body has turned to liquid. I might not be able to move again." As she said the words, Chelsea traced a finger along the top of Harper's bra, following the line, before dipping into her cleavage. Harper felt every nerve in her body vibrate.

"I think you're going to have to." Harper pulled Chelsea into a kiss that she hoped made it clear what she wanted—needed—to happen next.

"Well, strangely enough, I think I'm coming around." Chelsea kissed her fiercely, while running her hands up and down Harper's back, lingering on her ass in a way that made her take in a breath. "And I think if we got you out of that dress, I'd somehow feel completely recovered."

Harper smiled. "Oh, I see, you think I should join you in blissful nakedness, huh?" She got to her feet slowly, not taking her eyes off Chelsea. She held out her hands, encouraging Chelsea to stand before taking a step away from her. She let her gaze rake up and down Chelsea's naked body, wanting nothing more than to be able to feel Chelsea's hands and lips on her skin. "In that case, I'm in need of assistance." Harper turned around and lifted her hair.

"It would be my pleasure." Chelsea whispered with hot breath on Harper's neck, and Harper felt herself heat up all over again.

Chelsea clasped the fabric of the dress and eased the zipper slowly down Harper's back, her fingers trailing their way down Harper's newly exposed skin, her mouth following, as she scattered soft gentle kisses down her spine. Harper let the dress fall to the floor and kicked it to one side. She turned back around, standing in front of Chelsea in her lacy underwear, and Harper could see the lust in Chelsea's eyes. She was no exhibitionist, but right then, the act of undressing for Chelsea was an unbelievable turn-on.

When Chelsea stepped forward, reaching for her, running her hands across Harper's breasts, Harper leaned into the touch, bolts of pleasure landing between her legs. Chelsea put a hand at the nape of her neck and used it to pull Harper into a kiss. She gloried in the feel of Chelsea's lips and moaned when their tongues touched. She stepped back, unhooked her bra, and tossed it on the floor. The desire clearly visible on Chelsea's face was something she had waited years to see. Without waiting, she grazed the back of her hands across Harper's breasts, before pinching her nipples gently, and Harper couldn't help the gasp that escaped her.

Chelsea stepped closer to her, capturing her mouth in a passionate kiss. Slowly, without dropping her gaze, she pushed them backward toward the open door to her bedroom and didn't stop moving—or kissing—until the back of Harper's calves gently hit the edge of Chelsea's bed. Harper lowered herself back onto the bed, her body pulsing with anticipation. She had the desire to tell Chelsea how long she had wanted this, how long she had waited. That she had never stopped hoping they'd have a second chance. But as soon as Chelsea lowered her body on top of Harper's, their nipples grazing against each other, their bodies fusing together, Harper's mind emptied of all the words she might have said. The kiss that came next was passionate and fierce. Harper moaned in delight, and just as she had in the truck, so many moons ago, she let Chelsea take control. Chelsea dipped her head to kiss Harper's neck, to trail kisses along her shoulders, gently biting the soft skin above her collarbones, before licking her way, so slowly, to her nipples. Nipples that were hard, erect, and aching to be sucked.

"Your breasts are perfect. You are perfect..." Chelsea said the words in between pauses as she drove Harper wild with everything her mouth was doing. She lifted her head from Harper's breasts. "I never once forgot how beautiful you are. Or the way you made me feel." Her gaze was intense.

Harper tried to reply. To form a coherent sentence that communicated to Chelsea that she felt the same. But her actions were making Harper's body ignite with desire, and it was impossible to speak. Her brain was completely swamped with the feel of Chelsea on top of her, her leg pressed between Harper's thighs.

"Fuck." The word escaped Harper's lips as nothing more than a whisper as Chelsea's mouth tormented her nipples beautifully. She closed her eyes and arched her back. Every fiber of her aching to feel Chelsea inside her. "Please," Harper whispered as she pushed herself against Chelsea's thigh, made slick with her own wetness. She moaned as the pressure against her center sent a wave of arousal through her body. "I don't want to wait any more." It was the truest thing she had ever said.

Chelsea lifted herself up, making room to reach down and slide Harper's panties down her thighs and past her knees. She kicked them off before pulling Chelsea back down on top of her, kissing her hungrily, gasping with pleasure as Chelsea pushed her tongue inside her mouth and slid her hand down Harper's torso. Harper's desire for her was obvious in the way she opened her legs. She was past pretending this wasn't what she was desperate for.

Chelsea stroked her center in long, sweeping movements, gliding her fingers through the wetness. On each upward stroke, she made sure her fingertip brushed against Harper's clitoris. She kissed Harper hard, cupping her breast with her free hand, pinching the nipple between her fingers.

"Uhhh." Harper couldn't stop the moan from escaping. She lifted her hips off the bed, pushing herself against Chelsea, her insides like molten lava.

"Yeah, I seem to remember you liked that."

Chelsea's fingers never stopped moving. Her mouth now closed over Harper's breast, driving her just as crazy as the rhythmic strokes between her legs. Harper closed her eyes and tightened her stomach muscles, stiffening as she tried to control her desires. If Chelsea continued to tease her like that, she would come any second. But that wasn't what she wanted. What she wanted was those same fingers to stop skating around and slip inside and fill her.

"I want to fuck you—"

"Please." Harper said the word like a growl. She felt her orgasm coming. She tensed her muscles, trying to hold back the climax. She wanted Chelsea in her when she came. "Yes, please."

Harper exhaled as she felt Chelsea's fingers enter her, sending a surge of electric arousal through her body. She arched her back, pressing her center as hard as she could against Chelsea's hand, before giving herself over to the oblivion she knew was coming. She closed her eyes as a new layer of sweat formed on her skin, and every time Chelsea thrust deeper, she moaned louder. Her body rocked back and forth with each thrust as she reached out both arms, grabbing at the sheets on Chelsea's bed, bunching them in her fists.

"I want to make love to you like this forever." Chelsea's whispered words lit the fuse to what Harper had been waiting for. As she got to the edge, she rocked faster and pressed harder against Chelsea's hand, feeling Chelsea's fingers deep inside her. As Chelsea's thumb grazed across her clit, Harper gave in. Her insides contracted, and she cried out, and her orgasm came in a burst of vivid color and light, her body bucking with what felt like fifteen years of pent-up intensity. She tightened her muscles around Chelsea's fingers, not ready for her to withdraw, riding out the wave of her climax. A moment passed, then two. She let out a contented breath and slowly opened her eyes. As the pulsing subsided, Harper relaxed her muscles and Chelsea gently withdrew her fingers, then dropped to the bed next to Harper.

"That was…" Harper took Chelsea's hand and laced their fingers. "Wonderful."

She smiled, her muscles feeling like Jell-O. The orgasm was still causing every nerve in her body to vibrate. They were side by side on their backs, breathing heavily as the air cooled the sweat beading on their skin.

"It was." Chelsea turned to her before bringing her hand to her mouth and planting a soft, tender kiss on the center of her palm. It was a touch that caused Harper to feel an entirely different set of feelings from the ones she had been feeling moments ago. Pleasure, yes. Tenderness, of course. But also—she couldn't deny it—love. They stayed motionless for several minutes, until Harper's breathing calmed and her heart rate slowed. She leaned on her elbow and gently let her fingers glide over Chelsea's torso, watching her muscles twitch under her touch.

"You keep that up," Chelsea said, "and I can't be held responsible for what might happen next."

"I remember us lying naked like this in the back of my old truck." Harper continued tracing circles across Chelsea's skin, not heeding Chelsea's warning. "I'm pretty sure this got me into trouble then as well." Harper felt a wave of sadness wash over her. "It felt like we had so much time to discover each other…but of course, we didn't."

"Not enough time." Chelsea hesitated. "Then, or now."

"I really fell for you. When we were finally together…I can honestly say it was the best night of my life." Harper lifted herself up onto an elbow, running her fingers through Chelsea's hair, then down her jawline and across her luscious mouth. "I know we should talk, but I want this," she leaned in and pressed her lips to Chelsea's, "to carry on forever. It feels so right somehow."

"You used the past tense." Chelsea frowned before leaning in for a deep, slow kiss. Harper felt everything shift again, her body responding to Chelsea's lips, to her tongue, in ways she had forgotten were even possible. She could get used to feeling this way. "And I'm kind of hoping that *this* might turn out to be the best night of your life." She smiled, but Harper knew that underneath the smile, and the words, Chelsea was asking for reassurance. She felt some of the same need.

"In case it's not obvious enough, the way I feel about you is very much present tense." She took a breath. "There's no one else—there never really has been. And in case you still need to hear it, even after all this," Harper dipped her head to circle Chelsea's nipple with her tongue, "I was never interested in *her* like that." Harper couldn't bring herself to say Laney's name. "And you were right, she's a monster. Perhaps even more than you know."

Chelsea lowered her eyes without responding and Harper chided herself for bringing it up. A beat passed before Chelsea looked back up at her. And when she did, her face was full of emotion. "It seems like we have a lot of lost time to make up for. We can't do anything about the past. But the present," Chelsea took in a breath, "and the future… this time, we can make sure they're ours."

"We can," Harper responded, her voice thick with emotion. "We just need to be better at talking, at saying what we want."

"We do." Chelsea lifted an eyebrow. "I mean, right now, for example, I want to…" Chelsea pushed Harper gently onto her back. She kissed her softly while running her hands across her breasts, leaving Harper trembling and throbbing as her arousal reignited. "I want to make some more memories." Harper gasped as Chelsea raked her nails up the inside of her thigh and began to stroke her center. She threaded her hands behind Chelsea's neck and pulled her closer to capture her mouth in a hard possessive kiss. When Chelsea entered her, she closed her eyes and saw herself in the back of her truck, parked on that mountainside, and felt once again like all the scattered puzzle pieces of her life had finally come together.

CHAPTER SIXTEEN

Chelsea woke and stretched, the sore muscles in her legs a happy reminder of the hours of making love with Harper. Harper's head was resting on her arm, and her leg was lying across her torso. They were naked. They had fallen asleep unwillingly sometime after three, finally too exhausted to carry on. It had been a night full of magic. Harper's sudden appearance, the hours they had spent making love, the long, slow shower they had taken, even the pizza they had ordered in. Everything had been perfect. The soft sound of Harper's breathing against her neck was wonderful. She imagined herself waking up like this every day and then felt a flush of sadness. In two days, Harper was leaving. They had wasted time—because of Laney, yes. But also because of not saying what they really needed to. What little talking they had done last night made it clear that each of them had their own reasons for holding back, for not feeling like they had enough to offer.

Harper shifted position, moving her head to Chelsea's chest, her arm now thrown possessively across Chelsea's body, hugging Chelsea even in sleep. It was a glorious feeling. She stroked Harper's hair softly and tried to shake away the negative feelings that lurked at the edge of her consciousness. The ones that kept trying to get her attention. Worrying about her future—and forcing herself to find another restaurant site—was something she would do after Harper left. She pushed away her sadness at the thought of them leaving each other again. Not daring to imagine how she was going to cope. For now, she just wanted to drink in every moment they had left.

"Hi, gorgeous." Harper said the words sleepily, without lifting her head from Chelsea's chest. She began to softly kiss the skin where her head lay and then shifted position slightly so her lips could reach Chelsea's breasts. As Harper closed her mouth over her nipple, Chelsea felt the pleasure flush through her body, landing with an insistent throb between her legs.

"Well, good morning to you too." Chelsea tipped her head back as Harper's expert mouth and tongue teased her breasts, deepening her arousal to the point where talking would be impossible. She reached down to still Harper's movement, to gently frame Harper's face with her hands, until she lifted her head and gazed up at her, her face carrying a frown.

"You don't want me to—"

"Oh, trust me, I do." Chelsea leaned down and placed a tender kiss on Harper's lips. "I can't think of a single thing I want more." She took in a breath. "But I think we need to talk."

The effect of those words on Harper was immediate. She pulled herself up to a sitting position on the bed, her arms hugging her legs defensively. Chelsea reached for her, but Harper pushed her hands away.

"Is this where you tell me I fucked it up? That you can't forgive me because you lost the restaurant? Last night you said you didn't blame me, that it wasn't my fault." She wiped a few spilled tears off her cheek. "She did it to punish you because I didn't sleep with her. I had no idea she would do that…that she was so sick and competitive. I'm so sorry."

"Harper, Harper. Stop. It's not that." Chelsea reached for Harper again. This time she allowed Chelsea to pull her into an embrace. She moved position, shuffling back against the headboard, so that she could nestle Harper between her legs, wrapping her arms around her possessively. "I hate her. And I'm going to be wishing every bad thing in the world happens to her for the rest of my life—but I don't blame you. How could I?"

Chelsea had been boiling with anger when Harper had finally told her it was Laney who had taken the restaurant from her, but in the hours since, she realized that Harper choosing her mattered more to her than anything else. Yes, she had set her heart on Whitstable, on that particular space, but she had given her heart to Harper all those years ago, and now they were together. She just had to find out what Harper's version of them being *together* was.

"I'm mad at myself for not handling some things better. Actually, a lot of things."

"So am I." Chelsea murmured the words into Harper's mouth, pulling her into another kiss, deeper this time, wanting. She had to find a way to tell Harper how she felt. When she pulled away and looked at Harper, the unmistakable need on her face made Chelsea's insides tighten. She stroked strands of hair away from Harper's forehead and marveled at the feeling that she was able to touch her that way, that they were naked in each other's arms. It had to mean something.

"I'm scared."

"Of what?" Harper's beautiful blue eyes looked up at her with concern.

"Of what happens next." Chelsea didn't know what to say. She had never been an optimistic person. Life had taught her that dreams had a habit of turning into nightmares, and she couldn't help but feel that, for them, their circumstances might mean that the love she had for Harper would not be enough. "I never imagined that we'd find each other again, but now that we have, I don't want to lose you. And…" She forced herself to ask the question. "And I don't really know what this is. Or what we do now?" Chelsea didn't know what she was going to do if Harper didn't feel the same way.

"Oh, Chelsea." Harper smiled and Chelsea felt her heart lift. "Last night was amazing. No one has ever made me feel the way you do. With you," Harper lifted her face to touch her lips softly to Chelsea's, "there are so many feelings. Finding you again, and spending time together—well, it's made me realize just how much I've missed you. Going through life without the person you're meant to be with can be exhausting. Being with you these past couple of weeks has reminded me of what we could have had, and how much I loved you."

"Loved?"

"Love. How much I *love* you. I don't think I ever really stopped."

Harper had just said exactly what Chelsea wanted to hear. She wanted to be reassured by it, but she couldn't let herself.

"I love you too. And I didn't dare to imagine you would feel the same way." Chelsea took in a breath. "But is it enough?"

"How can it not be?" Harper gazed at her, her expression open and hopeful.

"I just mean…I don't know. You're leaving in two days. We'll be a continent apart again. You have a career—"

"A job. And it's a job I hate."

"And I have to find some way to earn some money, to start over with some new idea, some new place. I don't have the means to come and visit, not right now. What if we lose each other again? We'll go our separate ways and life will get in the way again. Our track record isn't great." Chelsea had spent the last thirty minutes worrying about all of this, the words coming out in a rush.

"Well, the Universe hasn't exactly conspired to help us over the years." Harper closed her hand over Chelsea's, teasing her fingers out of the clenched fist, and holding her hand tenderly. "But I'd like to think of this as our second chance. The one we're meant to take. Fate brought me to London, it even threw a princess in my path, and yet here I am…in your bed, in your arms. And I don't intend to throw this chance away." Harper held her gaze, offering a wide smile. "We can do this. If we really want to."

"I really want to."

"I don't have to be back at school for another month. We can start with that. I can delay my flight home." Harper turned her body to fully face Chelsea. "If you'd like me to."

Chelsea felt the tension in her chest start to dissipate. "I would *really* like that." It was a start. It gave them time to figure things out. "And maybe we'll find that Phoenix really needs a new seafood restaurant."

She saw Harper react. It was just a flash of something, but it suggested she didn't like the idea.

"Sorry. I'm not presuming. It was just a joke." Was it? Chelsea wasn't sure. She knew she'd follow Harper anywhere to avoid losing her again—but maybe Harper wasn't there yet. She didn't want to scare her off. "I just meant I could maybe visit you too, if I got my shit together here—"

"It's not that, it's just…"

Chelsea waited, her heart beating in her throat.

"I really like England. Maybe it's the bearable temperatures, the insane amount of history, the cute red buses…maybe it's even the chocolate stout…I don't know, but I could really see myself spending more time here." She hesitated. "I feel so stagnant in my life right now.

I can't even motivate myself to finish one of the half dozen manuscripts I've started. What if the second chance I came to England for wasn't just you but a chance to try something new? *With* you. Is that crazy?"

Chelsea felt her heart swell with love and happiness. "No, not crazy. It sounds wonderful. And maybe this sounds crazy, but I always felt that maybe we were meant to be. If it wasn't for Ryan, if we hadn't lost our way, I kind of imagined you could have been my happy ever after. And I know that makes me sound like one of those romance novels you love. I don't care."

"Oh, you mean one of those novels you read without telling me, because you thought it would ruin your cool?" Harper laughed, poking a finger into her chest.

"Yeah, one of those."

"Well, who knows, maybe I'll write you one. About two misguided souls who may have found each other in Phoenix but couldn't find the true meaning of their lives until they reconnected one glorious summer in London."

It sounded like a book Chelsea would love to read.

"It's not always this glorious in summer. And it rains a lot in the winter." She kissed Harper softly. "And in the autumn." She pulled Harper closer to her, deepening the kiss, her hands in Harper's hair. "And in spring actually."

"Well." Harper got up onto her knees and pushed Chelsea down onto her back. "I can think of a lot of things to do inside when it's raining, so if you're trying to dissuade me, you need to try harder." She dipped her head to capture Chelsea's nipple in her mouth, her nails scratching softly up and down the inside of Chelsea's thigh.

In one movement, Chelsea slipped her arm around Harper's waist and flipped her over onto her back. She leaned above her on her elbows, and the look of arousal on Harper's face was all the encouragement she needed. She captured Harper's mouth in a deep, hard kiss while pushing her leg between Harper's thighs. The groan of desire from Harper was delicious. She moved rhythmically, pushing her thigh against Harper's center. Harper opened her legs to her. And Chelsea let her hands roam over Harper's breasts, grazing the nipples, already knowing what drove her wild. She teased, massaged, and pinched until Harper started to writhe against her, her breathing becoming ragged.

Chelsea slipped a hand between Harper's legs and stroked

Harper's clitoris steadily. It was swollen and erect, her center wet with arousal. When she felt Harper push her hips up off the bed, straining to meet her hand, Chelsea pushed her fingers gently inside Harper and then, as Harper opened herself up further, buried them deeper and began the gentle, rhythmic thrusting that had Harper gasping her name, and arching her back, wanting everything that Chelsea could give her. Chelsea could feel Harper was close to losing control. She grabbed at Chelsea wildly, pulling them closer in a rocking movement that matched the rhythm of the thrusts. She increased the speed and depth of her fucking, brushing a thumb against Harper's clitoris with every thrust.

"Fuck. Yes. Fuck. That. Don't stop. I'm coming, I'm. Coming." The words came out of Harper in a staccato rhythm, each sounding like it was swallowed as fast as it emerged. And then she wrapped her arms around Chelsea, and came, crying out noisily, Chelsea too slow to clamp a hand over her mouth, hoping against hope that Alice was still asleep. Harper clung to her, panting, the shudders subsiding, and when her muscles finally relaxed, Chelsea withdrew her hand. Harper nestled in her arms and Chelsea felt the currents of arousal dancing around her own body, like electricity. She kissed the top of Harper's head. This, wherever this was, this was where she wanted to be.

As Harper murmured against her chest, Chelsea pulled the covers over them, ready to let Harper sleep. She wasn't sure the insistent pulsing between her legs would give her the same opportunity, but having Harper wrapped around her was reward enough.

"Guys, guys!" Alice accompanied the words with a series of sharp knocks on Chelsea's bedroom door.

"We're sorry for waking you! We're sleeping now. Go back to bed," Chelsea shout-whispered back through the closed door, feeling a flush of embarrassment at the idea they had been loud enough to wake Alice. Harper shifted in her arms, lifting her head, a puzzled expression on her face.

"Can I come in?" A beat passed. "I'm coming in."

Alice flung open Chelsea's door at about the same time that Harper and Chelsea scooted back against the headboard, pulling the covers up around their necks. Without hesitating, and with an expression on her face that said something terrible had happened, Alice shuffled with hunched shoulders to Harper's side of the bed and flopped down next to her.

"I've been so fucking stupid." Alice was fighting back tears. Chelsea had never seen her this serious…or upset.

"Alice, what happened? What's wrong?" Harper sounded as worried as Chelsea was.

Alice presented her phone. "The video's up. But instead of making me look like a Cinderella, he made me look like one of the ugly stepsisters. I didn't realize he was videotaping that time he challenged me to eat a plate of food…ten bites in ten seconds, or when I grabbed a shirt that was obviously too small but I didn't realize it until after I put it on and then couldn't get it back off." Alice let out a huge sob. "I feel so humiliated. I told everyone I know to watch the episode. And he fucking betrayed me." She buried her head in one of Chelsea's pillows.

"It can't be *that* bad." Harper took the phone from Alice and pressed play on the video. They watched it in silence. The only sound in the room was Alice's distressed sniffling. Chelsea couldn't quite believe it. She knew Laney was a snake, a monster even—after what she'd done to "her" restaurant—but she had imagined Oliver was more benign. A clown, sure. A total waste of space, but nowhere near as dangerous. But this? It was as bad as Alice had said. Shots of her with her arms swaying erratically in the air as she tried to squirm out of a shirt that was obviously the wrong size, were followed by a close-up of her horribly mispronouncing words from a restaurant's menu. All of it cut with a sardonic and cruel voiceover from Oliver, interspersed with cutaways of him snickering. Every scene, every edit, made Alice look ridiculous and goofy.

"He makes me look like I have no class, like I'm a dumb fuck."

"Stop. You're not a dumb fuck." Harper looked distraught. "But I don't understand. I mean, you and Oliver seemed to get along so well. He seemed genuinely fond of you."

"I really liked and trusted him. He was like a brother from another mother. And all the time he knew he was going to do this to me." Alice puffed out her breath as she held a faraway stare. "I called him, and he didn't understand why I was so upset and said that I just needed to roll with the punches, because it was going to get him a lot more views than his other videos." Alice's eyes welled with tears all over again. "He sounded like a complete stranger. I asked him to take the video down and he laughed at me…he actually laughed…and then he reminded me about the release I signed."

Alice's phone rang, and as she took the call, Chelsea took the chance to grab a couple of T-shirts so she and Harper could stop worrying about flashing Alice. It sounded as though whoever was calling was trying to make Alice feel better about the video. It wasn't working. Alice began pacing up and down the room, getting angrier. Chelsea couldn't help but feeling that anger was what Alice needed to get hold of now.

"Do you think Laney had anything to do with this?" Harper spoke quietly, a distraught look on her face. "I mean, think about it, she and Oliver are thick as thieves."

Chelsea pulled Harper closer. "Two nasty, inadequate, unpleasant individuals who can't be happy unless they're making someone else miserable. I hope karma really is a bitch, and she hits them hard." Chelsea was getting in touch with her own anger. Having Harper in her arms had softened the blow of losing the restaurant, but now the reality of what Laney had done—the depth of her spitefulness—made her feel rageful.

"That was Jess." Alice rubbed her eyes. "She said she saw the video and was sorry. She said Oliver can always be a bit vicious, but he's never taken it to this extreme. She asked if there's anything she can do. She suggested that Laney might have had a hand in it. But I don't understand why Laney would interfere with Oliver's video?"

"Maybe if I hadn't gone toe-to-toe with her, if I hadn't made her mad, jealous, whatever"—Chelsea felt instantly guilty—"this wouldn't have happened."

Alice glanced from Harper to Chelsea, head tilted with a look of confusion. "I don't get it, what am I missing?"

"There's something else, Alice." Harper sounded serious. "Something we haven't told you."

"Yeah, I know, you guys finally got together. As if the loud orgasms weren't the first clue, you both being naked in bed together kind of gave it away. Congratulations, by the way."

Chelsea was happy to see Alice get some of her old snark back.

"Thanks, but I'm not talking about that. What you don't know is that—" Harper took in a breath. "Laney was the one who outbid

Chelsea for the space in Whitstable. Because of…well, actually, there isn't any because of. It wasn't because of me or because of Chelsea. She's just a nasty vindictive bitch, and I can't believe I ever imagined she wanted to be a friend to us."

"Wait…what? Really?"

Chelsea nodded. She was angry enough now by all of it not to trust herself to speak.

"Oh man, I'm so sorry, Chelsea. That's horrible. Way worse than what Oliver did to me. In fact…" She trailed off and began tapping her phone against her thigh as she arched a brow and stood in a frozen stare.

"Uh-oh." Harper turned to Chelsea. "Things are about to get weird."

"You know what? Jess just offered to drive the getaway car for me if I wanted to burn down Oliver's house. I'm not suggesting that, but I can't believe we can't do *something*. I mean, look at us, we're three smart and powerful women. Four if we include Jess. Surely there's a way we can do something about this."

Chelsea felt like Alice was right. She was sick of expecting the knocks and just taking them when they arrived. Laney had got away with her nastiness and games for far too long, and in Oliver, she had a willing accomplice.

"What about if I speak to Laney, ask her to pull out of renting the restaurant, and ask her to persuade Oliver to take down the video?" Harper sounded serious.

"No!" Alice and Chelsea said the word in unison.

"It's what she wants. She'll want you to make contact, to beg, and then say no. It's all a power play for them." Chelsea had never been so certain of something being a terrible idea.

"I agree with Chelsea." Alice nodded seriously. "They're probably both having a good laugh at our expense. So let's get some breakfast and coffee and think about our options." She moved toward the door and pointed at Chelsea. "That means pancakes." She moved her finger and pointed at Harper. "And that also means no dilly-dallying, which means no more sex. I know your parts were rusted over, but they have to be good and greased by now, so chop-chop, I'm hungry."

"Alice!" Harper scolded, and despite everything, they laughed.

❖

"And she'd definitely lose the trust fund. It would hurt her in the pocket, which is all she and Oliver seem to really care about." Alice speared another pancake with her fork as she finished setting out her plan.

"Alice, we are not outing Laney." Chelsea poured herself another cup of hot coffee, needing to wake up her senses. She didn't regret a single minute making love to Harper, but she couldn't keep up with Alice. She was on revenge plan number four, and all of them sounded terrible. "I don't care how much she deserves to hurt, we just don't do that kind of thing. It wouldn't stop with Laney. Imagine how it would get played out in the press, all the homophobia, all the suggested shame."

"I agree with Chelsea. It's not anything we should even be considering." Harper reached across and squeezed her hand, the loving look on her face making Chelsea feel a bit weak at the knees. Despite Harper having her own clothes in a room barely five yards away, Chelsea had insisted she wear one of her hoodies to breakfast, and Harper looked distractingly cute in it.

"I know, I know." Alice sounded frustrated. "That was a shitty thing to suggest. But I'm the only one coming up with plans here. You guys need to do less swooning over each other and more vengeful planning."

"Oh, trust me, I've got vengeance in mind." Chelsea meant it. The more they had talked about what happened, the angrier she felt.

"Hey, I have an idea," Harper said. "It's probably crazy, but hear me out." She hesitated. "We'd need Jess to pull it off, and I'm not totally sure whose side she's really on."

"Oh." Alice snorted. "She's on our side. She told me she's not going to work with Oliver anymore, and that she's had it with Laney too. She's just too toxic to be around. She doesn't need the additional exposure from either of them. Her boutique is doing fine."

Chelsea had a memory of Jess saying something along those lines in the club.

"Well, she'd need to be willing to put up with her for one more visit." Harper put down her coffee and leaned forward.

"And?" Chelsea and Alice both leaned in expectantly.

"Laney presents a false image of herself and gets love and adoration from a public that seems to adore her—and loads of perks from everyone who wants to be associated with her because she's a royal. We know she's a spoiled and spiteful person, but to everyone else, she's a sweet princess, seen with her family at functions, and doing charity work for the cameras. Charity work that, by the way, she says over and over that she hates doing. But she knows it pays the bills. Her trust fund is linked to her staying out of trouble and performing all the expected royal duties, duties which she despises."

Harper hesitated, seeming unsure. Chelsea willed her to find the good idea they needed.

"Jess's boutique has cameras all over the place. I remember seeing them when we were there, and I overheard her tell Oliver a story about some sour-faced customer complaining to her friend when Jess wouldn't exchange something that was damaged. She'd gone into the back room to print out a copy of the return policy and the security camera recorded the woman admitting she'd damaged it herself. So, since her system obviously captures sound, I was thinking that if we could persuade her to invite Laney over—"

"We could set her up," Alice said. "Get her to say something incriminating on camera. We can hide in a back room, or somewhere, and listen while Jess eggs her on. And we can record something we can use to blackmail her with." Alice offered her hand to Harper for a high five. "I love it. You're a genius. It'll be like *Ocean's Four*, with me as Sandra Bullock." She paused. "But I thought you said we shouldn't out her."

"I'm not talking about outing her, Alice. I'm talking about something else, something that would tarnish her public image, make people turn against her. Maybe Jess can help us figure out how to trigger her. If we get her on video saying how much she despises being a royal, how much she hates shaking hands with the general public, we can tell her we'll leak it, and she'll think she's going to lose her trust fund, and all that stuff she gets from being a princess. Then she'll give us what we want."

"And what do we want?" Chelsea wasn't sure she liked this idea. It felt reckless somehow. And it would bring Harper—all of them actually—close to Laney again. She was really hoping to never have to see her again.

"I was thinking about that." Harper held up her fingers. "One, we need her to pull her bid for the restaurant space. She could easily find another space somewhere else to present to her charity." Chelsea felt her heart pounding in her chest, but next to her, Harper sounded calm and certain. "Two, she needs to convince Oliver to take down Alice's video. Immediately. And destroy all the footage. We're not blackmailing her for money. We're just trying to *incentivize* her to do the right thing."

"How's Jess going to get Laney to her boutique?" Alice asked.

"Don't know. For that, we're going to have to rely on Jess." Harper sounded hopeful.

"And will Jess do it?" Chelsea couldn't believe she was even entertaining the idea, but they hadn't come up with anything better, and she hated the idea of Laney getting away with everything she'd done.

"There's one way to find out." Alice stood up from the table with her phone in her hand.

CHAPTER SEVENTEEN

Alice held the door open as Harper filed into Jess's boutique, last night's evening gown in hand. Chelsea and Alice came from behind and flanked her.

"May I help you?" A woman in a tight black dress sauntered over to them.

"I've got this one." Jess appeared from seemingly out of nowhere and approached. With a flick of her finger, she wordlessly summoned them to follow her into the back room. It was a small somewhat sparse space with several semi-full wardrobe racks and a few neatly stacked boxes against a far wall. A small kitchenette and a sleek glass and black metal desk that housed a typical computer and printer setup sat off to the other side. The center space consisted of four folding chairs prearranged in a circle, seemingly waiting for them.

"I have several high-resolution cameras that give me a clear view of the entire store." Jess herded them over to the desk and pointed to the four black-and-white squares that equally divided the computer's screen. "And each camera is equipped with multidirectional mics because I like to hear what my customers say when they think no one is listening. It helps with marketing decisions, and more than once, I've overheard patrons plotting a theft that luckily, we've been able to thwart." Jess turned to the group. "Trust me, nothing much gets by the eyes and ears of this equipment."

Harper nodded as she thought back to the day she and Alice were shopping at the store and cringed in memory of the snarky remarks they made about the overpriced merchandise and unappreciated designs. "Impressive." She shook off the twinge of embarrassment as she handed over the dress. “Thank you for meeting with us and thank you for this. It truly is a stunning dress.”

“I had a client in here yesterday looking for a Stella McCartney in this size. I’ll let her know one just came in.” Jess took a moment to trail her fingers down the material as though it were as fragile and beautiful as a blooming flower before gently hanging it on a rack. “Now then.” She turned. “Let’s talk about what you need me to do.” She gestured toward the chairs, and they each settled into a seat.

“I take it Alice told you about my restaurant?” Chelsea was the first to chime in.

“She did. I’ve always known Laney could be vindictive when she doesn’t get her way, but from what Alice has told me, this is a new low even for her.” She faced Harper. “You turning her down must have really gotten under her skin. I don’t think I’ve ever known anyone who could resist her charm, or…” She paused, seemingly searching for the right word. “Advances. So, good for you.”

Not the word Harper would have used. Manipulation seemed much more appropriate.

“Well, someone else had my heart, so it wasn’t that hard to say no.” Harper reached over and gently squeezed Chelsea’s hand.

“Your heart was never what she was after.” Jess smiled grimly before focusing on Alice. “And as for you, I’ve known Oliver for years, and I’m sorry as hell he’s hurt you with this video. He has a good side to him, at least he used to. But ever since he and Laney have become friends, I’ve noticed him wanting to follow in her footsteps more and more. He adores her and craves what she stands for. It’s a pity, really.”

“I trusted him,” Alice muttered, a look of hurt etched on her face. “I thought we were friends.”

“Sometimes with Oliver, he straddles a thin line between friendship for fun and friendship for personal gain. Lately it’s hard to tell, but one thing’s for sure, they both could use a good dose of their own medicine.”

“So, are you in?” Chelsea raised a questioning brow.

“All in, and it just so happens I have the perfect bait to lure Laney to the shop.” Jess stood and walked toward a lone dress hanging on a wardrobe rack as though it commanded the attention of a centerpiece. Even without having the full effect of a body or mannequin to display it in all its grandeur, Harper could tell it was something special.

"This exquisite dress was designed by an up-and-coming designer who has become the buzz of Paris. She goes by the name Chantal, and I've had my eye on her for a while. In fact, I showcased some of her designs years ago, when she was trying to get herself noticed. When I heard she was releasing some of the original designs from when she was first starting out, I contacted her, and she was kind enough to grace me with three. One just happens to be Laney's size. Trust me, when I let her know I have a one-of-a-kind Chantal in my shop that happens to be her size, she'll be here in a heartbeat."

"Then what? How do we get her to say something incriminating? Something that would really embarrass her if it was ever leaked." Chelsea locked eyes with Jess. "How will you do that?"

Jess let out a slight chuckle. "In case you haven't noticed, Laney loves to talk about herself. Most of my clientele does. In fact, the only thing Laney loves more than money is herself. The second thing Laney likes to talk about is her family. Or should I say *bitch* about. All the conversation will need is a nudge in the right direction, and Laney will fall off the cliff all by herself. Ladies, leave this one to me." Jess grabbed her phone off the desk, snapped a couple of pics of the dress, and sent a text. "There, now all we have to do is wait for—" The ding was immediate. "Ah, and there it is." She glanced at the screen. "She'll be here within the hour. Meanwhile, tea anyone?" Jess said with a satisfied grin as she ventured over to the kitchenette.

Harper approached. "Thanks, Jess. But are you sure you want to go through with this? You'll lose your friendship with her."

Jess turned, leaned against the small counter, and sighed. "What friendship? I'm nothing more than Laney's fashion supplier. Granted, there was a time last year after a weekend at her family's chateau in France, where I…" She trailed off seemingly lost in thought. After a beat, she cleared her throat and waved a dismissive hand. "Anyway, I was just one lover among many. Nothing more than a notch on her belt, a conquest in the game of catch and drop she likes to play."

Harper could tell from the look on Jess's face that she had fallen for Laney. She fought back the urge to give her a hug. Paying Laney back like this might not completely heal her wounds, but hopefully it would provide some form of satisfaction.

Forty-five minutes later, a subtle chime from the computer announced the front door had opened, and Harper focused on the upper left square of the monitor capturing the image of Laney walking into the store.

"Looks like it's showtime." Jess got up and tapped on the computer's keyboard. "I turned up the volume so you can hear better. Don't come out until you have what you came for. If Laney suspects this is an ambush in any way, you'll never get what you want."

They nodded in agreement.

Jess grabbed the dress, took a moment to settle herself, and walked out as they scooted their chairs around the desk.

"I'm going to record this as well." Harper pulled out her phone and hit the video icon as they watched and listened to the conversation unfold.

Jess approached Laney, leaned in, and gave an air kiss toward each of her cheeks.

"How the hell did you get your hands on a Chantal?" Laney widened her eyes and extended her arms as Jess handed over the dress.

"I've been showcasing her designs for years. So, when I reached out, she graced me with three, in gratitude for being one of the first shops to carry and promote her designs."

"I have to hand it to you, Jess, you've always had an impeccable eye for fashion." Laney pressed the dress against her front as she meandered over to a full-length mirror.

Jess flanked her. "You'll look exquisite in this."

"And no one else has this design?"

"No one else has even *seen* this design. It was one of a handful she made when she was first starting out and has kept from the public until now."

"How much?" Laney asked without taking her eyes off the mirror as she repositioned the fabric a little higher on her body.

"Does it matter?"

Laney puffed a laugh. "Not in the slightest. That's the benefit of a royal trust fund. If I want something, I get it…and this magnificent dress is something I definitely want." Laney handed it back. "Put it on my tab, won't you, Jess. I simply must have it."

"It's as though Chantal designed it specifically for a princess," Jess said as she hung the dress on a hook by the register, placed a plastic bag with the store's logo over the material, and tied off the bottom. "Do you have an event coming up where you can wear it?"

"I have the perfect one in mind, where there'll be plenty of press and cameras. It's a charity auction with proceeds going to help rough sleepers."

Harper turned to Chelsea for clarification. "What are rough sleepers?"

"The homeless."

"Oh." Harper nodded as she refocused on the screen.

"Papa has been really pushing me lately to make more appearances with the family at events that benefit the less fortunate, but honestly, what we need is to figure out a way to completely get them off the streets and, you know, send them somewhere far away. You have to admit, they're a bit of an eyesore. All over Mayfair, completely ruining the vibe. How can you enjoy dinner or the opera when you have to step over them on the way out?"

Harper grabbed Chelsea by the arm. Beside her, Alice fist-pumped the air. It was enough, it had to be. The comment was nasty, and unforgiveable. The audio was impressive enough to pick up the deep breath that Jess took in, before turning slowly back to Laney.

"Times are tough right now for a lot of people, Laney. Something I'm sure you wouldn't understand because you're too busy spending money you've never had to work for."

"Really? You don't think going to charity functions and pretending to care about causes—and people—I could give two shits about isn't work?" Laney scoffed. "Please, do you know how many hands I shake every year, and how physically ill it makes me?" Her phone dinged and she glanced down. "That's Oliver. I need to get going. I bumped into the most fascinating woman from Australia yesterday. I'm taking her for tea at the Ritz this afternoon, and Ollie's joining us. I'd invite you too, but you know, you have your store to run, and I know you don't approve of my pastimes."

Jess stepped in between Laney and the door. In the back room, Harper held her breath.

"I saw Oliver's video of Alice. Rather cruel the way he made her look, don't you think?"

"Really? I haven't watched it." She plucked a chocolate ball from the silver platter that sat next to the register, unwrapped the gold foil, and popped the dark confection in her mouth. "Cruel in what way?" she mumbled as she chewed.

"He made her look like she was coarse, mocked her weight, her manners…a bit of everything really. Made her seem like a pantomime character."

Laney chuckled. "Well, I'm sure that wasn't much of a stretch. I mean, you worked with her. The way she presents herself begs for that. And while I may have mentioned to Ollie that to increase his viewership, he had to be willing to do some rather uncomfortable things, it's all his own work. It may seem cold-hearted, but you have to agree, Alice was the perfect person to start the new approach with."

Harper placed a protective arm around Alice and squeezed. "She's wrong, Alice. You know that, right?"

Alice shrugged, but Harper could sense the words had already inflicted pain. "I think we've heard enough." Harper got up from her seat and flung the backroom door open. It was time to shut this down.

The stunned look on Laney's face was almost humorous, and if Harper hadn't been so disgusted, she might have reveled in it. "Harper? What are you…" Laney trailed off as Alice and Chelsea stepped out of the room and lined up beside her. "What are all of you doing here?" She turned to Jess, a look of confusion on her face.

"They came by to return the dress I loaned Harper." Jess shrugged.

"I see," Laney said as she averted her eyes. A beat later, as though a spell were cast or a stage light suddenly illuminated her, she shifted her expression and demeanor to one of charm.

"Well, what a wonderful surprise. I figured you'd be on your way back to the States by now." Laney focused her attention on Harper.

"Alice leaves tomorrow." Harper kept her tone flat and void of emotion.

"Ah, well then, safe travels." Laney grabbed the dress. "Don't mean to cut this short, but I'm terribly late for a luncheon."

"Not so fast, there's something we need to discuss first." Harper stepped in front of her blocking any quick getaway Laney was hoping for.

Laney's face fixed in a stern expression. "Oh, I don't think there's anything you and I need to discuss."

"You need to withdraw your bid from Chelsea's restaurant."

Laney leaned back and cocked a hip. "And why on earth would I do that? It's the perfect spot for a gallery, and while it might be unfortunate, it is absolutely not my problem that Chelsea doesn't have the means to pay for what the space is worth. Now excuse me while I tend to other important matters."

As Laney stepped around her, she presented her phone and as the dialogue she recorded reverberated in the room, Laney froze, then slowly turned around. She glared at Jess.

"Oh don't give me that look, Laney, you know my security equipment is running all the time. You should be more careful."

"It'd be a real shame if this recording gets leaked. I mean, what would your family and the citizens of this lovely country think about how their princess feels about homeless people, or how she feels disgusted even shaking the hands of ordinary people? I imagine it would be very bad for your image…and your bank account." Harper sounded every bit as malicious as she felt.

"You wouldn't dare." Laney's words were laced with scorn.

"Harper might not, but I would." Alice stepped forward. "After what you just said about me, don't even think for a second I wouldn't. And this isn't just about withdrawing your bid on Chelsea's restaurant—that's first, but then you need to tell Oliver to take down the video as well."

"I am not his keeper."

"Oh, but I think you are. And you're obviously the reason why he's chosen to be so spiteful. He's your little puppet, so pull his strings. Or this video will be online before the door hits your ass on your way out of here."

Laney's face contorted with anger as deep lines formed on her face. For a moment Harper thought she was going to explode in a tirade of profanity. "Okay, fine." She spit through clenched teeth. "I'll talk to Ollie at lunch and then I will…" She pinched the bridge of her nose as she exhaled a breath. "Withdraw my bid on the space."

"Now, Laney. Call your agent. We want to be sure you do it." For the first time in a long time, Harper took control, and the feeling that pulsed through her veins was like an adrenaline rush.

Laney huffed, as she retrieved her phone from her purse. "Markus, hi. Yes, I'm well, thank you. Markus, dear, seems as though there's been a bit of a…situation come up. I need you to withdraw my bid on the Whitstable space. Yes, right now…yes, I know you've been working hard on it, but I need you to withdraw my offer. Oh, and, Markus, I'll still need a place to present to the trustees in a few days, so you'll need to find me another space that is equally spectacular. Not in Whitstable. Somewhere else coastal. And of course I'll make it worth your while. Thank you, Markus."

She disconnected the call. "Happy now?"

"Once Oliver takes down the video of Alice, we'll destroy this copy of you telling the world how much you despise the people you're supposed to serve, and we'll all forget we ever met each other." Harper felt Chelsea slip an arm around her waist. She welcomed the support, but she was doing just fine.

"You even think of releasing that recording, and I'll make sure to turn your life into a living hell." She turned to Jess. "And you...you and I are finished."

"Thank God." Jess turned her back on Laney and walked away. Laney scowled at her retreating form, turned, and stormed out of the store.

High fives, cheers and hugs were exchanged. If Jess had let them, Harper was sure they would have carried her in the air like a trophy winner. As Jess moved toward the backroom to fetch some champagne and glasses, Chelsea's phone rang. They all stood still, breaths held, watching Chelsea intently.

"Hi, Billy...what's up? The other bidder just pulled out...really? Why, of course I still want it. Yes...yes, I'll be right there to sign the paperwork. And, Billy, thanks."

Harper wrapped Chelsea in a full hug, whirling her around happily before walking over to Jess.

"I don't know how we'll ever repay you," Harper said. "I really hope this doesn't come back to bite you."

"Laney was the one I struggled to get over. When it suited her, she quite liked to make me feel like there was a chance of something. But now I've seen her for what she really is, and it's going to help me properly move on."

"Well, maybe someday, she'll grow up and realize what a great person she let slip through her fingers."

"Maybe by then I'll have found someone who looks at me the way Chelsea looks at you."

Harper extended her hand to Chelsea, brought her in close, and placed a soft kiss on her lips. "Looks like we got your restaurant back," she softly said through a smile as they broke the kiss.

"You know, I've never been to Whitstable, and I'm very partial to oysters, so…when your restaurant is ready, maybe I can join you for opening night?" Jess sounded almost bashful.

"It would be my pleasure to have you as my guest." Chelsea stepped forward and offered Jess a hug. "I can never truly repay you, but I can promise you this, a table will always be waiting for you and your meals will always be on the house."

❖

"You're sure you're okay with me staying an extra month?" Harper fussed to Alice again as Chelsea pulled the rental car curbside at Heathrow.

"Stop already, I'll be fine," she said between grunts and groans as she peeled herself out of the back seat of the car. "Seriously, could they make these things any smaller?" She pulled and yanked two large suitcases, an overstuffed tote bag, and a backpack from the trunk, extended the handles, and secured the tote over one and the backpack around the other. "Besides, you two need to make up for lost time," she said as she dug into the tote, pulled out her neck pillow, and clasped it firmly in place. Gone was the face completely covered in makeup and clothes that looked tailor made. Instead, Alice had on a loose-fitting powder blue T-shirt with "London" spelled out in sparkly sequins across the chest, pink capri pants, flip-flops, and oversized sunglasses. Cinderella had turned back into the old Alice. The one Harper loved so dearly.

Chelsea rounded the car and hugged her. "I'll miss you."

"Good, 'cause that means you'll have to get your ass back to Arizona soon and come see me. And you…" She pointed to Harper. "I'll see you back home."

Harper pulled her into a big hug as Alice softly spoke. "Told you this trip would be magical. Aren't you glad you listened to me?"

Harper leaned out of the hug. "I never doubted it for a minute."

"Pfft. Yeah, right. Okay, you two lovebirds, I need to get going," she said as she walked backward, wheeling her suitcases next to her. "I wanna get checked in and still have enough time to get a drink before the flight."

"Alice, watch out!" Harper called a bit too late, as she watched

Alice collide with a short-haired woman who was wearing faded jeans and a pink T-shirt that had "Princess" written across the chest in sparkly letters.

"Holy shit, I'm so…" Alice trailed off as Harper watched a pause fall between them before they lifted their sunglasses in unison and smiled at each other.

"Tell me you're not a princess?" Alice said.

"What?"

Alice nodded to her shirt.

"Oh, this." She laughed. "My grandma always called me her little princess when I was a kid, so for my birthday last year, she gave this to me. Definitely not an actual princess."

"You have no idea how glad I am to hear that." Alice extended her hand. "I'm Alice."

"Julie. Nice to meet you, and so sorry about crashing into you like that."

"No worries." They stood frozen for another beat. "So, you um… you heading in?"

"Yeah, I'm flying to the States to visit my grandma, hence the shirt."

"Oh yeah? Whereabouts?"

"Arizona by way of New York."

"No shit. Flight 2302?"

"How did you…"

"We're on the same flight. Huh…" Alice said as they shuffled toward the doors. "You, uh, you wouldn't by chance want to get a drink before we board?"

"Actually, I'd love a cocktail. Or two. Flying always makes me anxious."

"Me too." Alice turned back to them and waved. The look on her face suggested she was going to enjoy this long flight a little more than the last one.

"Wow," Harper said as she and Chelsea returned to the car. "I didn't see that one coming."

"Looks like Alice found herself a princess after all," Chelsea mused as she pulled away from the curb and merged with the ebb and flow of traffic.

"Yeah, kinda spooky."

"Maybe this trip is gonna be responsible for two happy ever afters." Chelsea pulled Harper into a kiss. A kiss that Harper would have let last a lot longer if it wasn't for the impatient beeping of the cars that wanted them to move.

Thirty minutes later, the claustrophobic feeling from the congested traffic loosened its grip and as the cityscape turned to beautiful, lush landscape, Harper powered down the window and inhaled a deep breath. The temperature was mid-eighties, and although the humidity was high, the air didn't scorch her lungs like the dry high heat of the desert.

"Sure you don't mind spending the day in Whitstable?" Chelsea said as Harper turned to her.

"Are you kidding? I love it there."

The call had come early that morning, notifying Chelsea that the keys to the space were ready to be picked up from the real estate agent. They figured they could drop Alice off at Heathrow and have enough time for a nice seaside lunch before they had to meet up with the estate agent. Harper settled further into her seat and tipped her head back to gaze at the scenery as she thought about the past three weeks.

It had been a crazy ride, with more twists and turns then she ever wanted to repeat, but she wouldn't change it for anything in the world. Chelsea was about to live her dream, the two of them were together, and Alice was the face of a video viewed over two million times. In the end, Oliver had refused to pull the episode but did agree to re-edit it and present Alice in a very favorable light. And according to what they could tell from the online comments and likes, the new version seemed more popular than the old one.

Chelsea reached for her hand and brought it to her lips for a soft, tender kiss before giving her a smile that made her feel weak at the knees. And Harper wondered if maybe there was something to the magic of romance novels after all. After all, she finally got her slow burn happy ever after romance, even if it had taken fifteen years to unfold.

EPILOGUE

"Hey, I don't want to break your flow, but it's nearly time." Chelsea put her hands on Harper's shoulders, massaging gently.

"Really?" Harper looked up at her, stretched, and then peered at her laptop. "Wow, that last couple of hours flew by." She pulled Chelsea down onto the bench next to her and leaned in, planting a soft kiss on Chelsea's lips, a kiss Chelsea deepened when Harper parted her lips and reached a hand into her hair. The touch of Harper's tongue against hers ignited something they definitely didn't have time for right then. She made herself pull away, happy to see Harper was just as aroused, her eyes a shade darker than normal.

"I guess time flies when your juices are flowing." Chelsea waggled her eyebrows and was rewarded with a laugh. It was a sound Chelsea had always loved.

"Yeah, and I think I finally nailed the sex scene."

"I'm happy about that." Chelsea couldn't help but smirk. "But do you have any idea how hard it is for me, in the fine tradition of every British person ever, not to turn those innocent remarks of yours into smutty double entendres? You really think you can say something like 'I nailed the sex scene' and not have me make reference to this morning? When you absolutely nailed m—"

"Chelsea!"

"What?" Chelsea lifted her hands, a picture of innocence.

"You're making me blush."

"Oh yeah?" Chelsea pointed at the laptop. "You can write heat like this, but you expect me to believe I can make you blush." She shuffled closer on the bench, wrapping her arms around Harper, kissing her neck softly from behind. Harper moaned happily and leaned back into Chelsea's chest. They sat like that for a while, just looking out at the sea. It was almost seven, and the sun was about ready to give it up for the day. The sky was glowing a beautiful orangey red, and despite May being a week away, it was warm enough to sit out.

"It's such a great spot. You were so right about this place." Harper sighed. "I love our life here." She turned her face to Chelsea's. "And I love you." Chelsea felt her heart lift. In the months since they'd finally come together—after fifteen ridiculous years of waiting—she had never got used to Harper saying that to her.

"I love you too." Chelsea kissed Harper and felt her arousal like an electric current that ran down her body and landed between her legs. "And I'm glad you're happy here. I was worried you might miss home, miss the weather, the big city life."

"Are you kidding?" Harper frowned. "Everything I need is here, and by everything, I mean you, of course." They kissed again, slowly, tenderly. Chelsea didn't ever want them to stop. "I'm getting used to a whole new definition of rainy days, and since London's only an hour away by train, so we can have as much big city as we want."

"Fifteen minutes…" Chelsea whispered the words into Harper's ear, taking the opportunity to nibble it softly. "By helicopter."

"You did not just say that?" Harper laughed and thumped Chelsea's thigh. "Bad girl!"

"I mean, the restaurant's going pretty well, you sold your book to a publisher, so if we save hard enough for the next hundred years, that helicopter might be within reach." Chelsea smiled. And then laughed. "Imagine picking Alice up at Heathrow in a helicopter. Do you think she'd be pleased or moan the whole way home about the quality of the air conditioning?"

"Both, I'd guess. You know Alice. She'd probably also complain that the color of the helicopter didn't match her outfit." Harper grinned.

"Well, I've learned my lesson. I am not taking a car to the airport next week. We can meet her and then all jump in an Uber."

"I'm really getting excited to see her. It's been too long."

"It has."

Harper had gone back to Phoenix after their blissful summer together to formally quit her job and pack up everything she thought she needed to move to England. Despite how good everything seemed, Chelsea had been a bundle of stress and anxiety, worrying Harper might have second thoughts once they were apart and she was back home. But eight weeks after they had said a loving good-bye, Harper returned and installed herself in Chelsea's new Whitstable flat, helped her open the restaurant, and even found a part-time job lecturing on English literature at the local university. It couldn't have gone better. It was almost like the Universe was helping them make up for lost time.

"I hope she likes the restaurant...and the menu. She was one of my favorite people to cook for."

"She loved your cooking. Oh..." Harper pulled a newspaper from under her laptop. "That reminds me, Janey dropped this off while you were inside. Said she's happy to be friends with a local celebrity. It's really a great write-up." She opened the newspaper and put it in front of Chelsea. "And I have to admit, you look super cute."

It was one of those free local newspapers made up mostly of adverts, and Chelsea saw herself looking back from a photograph, arms folded, wearing chef whites. She scanned the article. It referenced the opening of the restaurant, praised the food, and talked about Ryan. The pride she felt was mingled with the sadness she always felt when reminded of her brother.

"I think we're now definitely one of Whistable's celebrity sapphic couples. The restaurantcur and the soon-to-be romance author." Chelsea folded the newspaper and put it back under the laptop before the breeze took it off onto the beach somewhere.

"Definitely." Harper raised a hand for a high five. When Chelsea made contact, Harper didn't let go, pulling her hand into her lap and grazing it with her thumb. "But one of many. I had no idea how many lesbians lived here." Harper's eyes grew wide. "When I advertised the book club, I honestly expected that maybe just one or two would reply."

"And yet here I am, opening on a Monday evening just for you to host all those romance lovers at Whitstable's number one sapphic book club. Seafood canapes at the ready. Prosecco chilling nicely."

"Whitstable's *only* sapphic book club." Harper laughed.

"Hey, don't knock it. My marketing course is giving me new skills I am happy to pass on." She glanced at her watch. "But, Harps, you really need to get ready. You know Janey and Kim always arrive early."

"That they do." Harper moved away from her, gathering up her phone and laptop busily. Chelsea missed feeling the press of her back against her chest. She pulled Harper close to her again, not ready to let her go.

"What's this month's book about?"

"It's set in Miami and it's about two female band members who are flung back into each other's lives years after the band split acrimoniously. I really liked it. It's sweet…and kind of sexy. And it has this flashback in the prologue that is so full of heat, Alice will love it. She always hates those slow burn books that make her wait for the sex."

"Okay, now I'm interested. Maybe I need to start attending." Chelsea nuzzled at Harper's neck. "When you write our story, make sure we have a hot and horny prologue that has us in the back of your truck doing all of the glorious things that we did when we were supposed to be watching the sunset."

"Oh, I will." Harper gave her a smile that was equal parts sexy and shy. "And I have a couple of other chapters that will be inspired by our more recent adventures. One of them will start with me finding you eating cereal while you look drop-dead gorgeous in those sexy shorts you're so fond of."

"I like the idea of that." Chelsea turned Harper's face to hers and grazed a finger across Harpers lips. "So how long did your girl band lovers have to wait for their second chance?"

"Five years."

"Five years?" Chelsea captured Harper's mouth in a hard, hot kiss. "Five years doesn't count as waiting." She pulled Harper closer, feeling the press of her breasts against her own, biting down softly on Harper's lower lip. She was rewarded with a deep intake of breath and Harper's hands in her hair, pulling her into a hungry, passionate kiss.

A loud, exaggerated cough sounded from just over Chelsea's shoulder. "I know we're early…" Janey stood next to the table arm in arm with Kim. "But I didn't think we were *that* early. Do you two lovebirds need us to walk around the block again?" Janey lifted her eyebrows and smirked.

They broke their kiss and Chelsea slowly got to her feet, trailing her fingers across the back of Harper's neck, not quite ready to lose her to her friends.

"Hi, Janey, hi, Kim. No, you're okay. We can wait. It's not like we haven't had the practice."

Harper got to her feet and stood next to Chelsea, slipping an arm around her waist and leaning in sweetly. "And you know what they say?" She gazed at Chelsea. It was a look that promised everything. "The best things in life are always worth waiting for."

About the Authors

MA Binfield is stranded on that little island off the coast of France known as the United Kingdom. It's a magical place, with endless mugs of tea and lots of the kind of weather that makes you stay home to read and write. MA is tall and hopelessly romantic. She is fond of the ocean and boiled eggs, and loves writing about women loving women.

Toni Logan grew up in the Midwest but soon transplanted to the land of lizards and saguaro cactus. She enjoys sunset hikes, traveling, and spending time with family and friends. Toni also writes erotic romance as Piper Jordan.

About the Authors

[illegible]

[illegible]

Books Available From Bold Strokes Books

All This Time by Sage Donnell. Erin and Jodi share a complicated past, but a very different present. Will they ever be able to make a future together work? (978-1-63679-622-2)

Crossing Bridges by Chelsey Lynford. When a one-night stand between a snowboard instructor and a business executive becomes more, one has to overcome her past, while the other must let go of her planned future. (978-1-63679-646-8)

Dancing Toward Stardust by Julia Underwood. Age has nothing to do with becoming the person you were meant to be, taking a chance, and finding love. (978-1-63679-588-1)

Evacuation to Love by CA Popovich. As a hurricane rips through Florida, so too are Joanne and Shanna's lives upended. It'll take a force of nature to show them the love it takes to rebuild. (978-1-63679-493-8)

Lean in to Love by Catherine Lane. Will badly behaving celebrities, erotic sex tapes, and steamy scandals prevent Rory and Ellis from leaning in to love? (978-1-63679-582-9)

The Romance Lovers Book Club by MA Binfield and Toni Logan. After their book club reads a romance about an American tourist falling in love with an English princess, Harper and her best friend, Alice, book an impulsive trip to London hoping they'll both fall for the women of their dreams. (978-1-63679-501-0)

Searching for Someday by Renee Roman. For loner Rayne Thomas, her only goal for working out is to build her confidence, but Maggie Flanders has another idea, and neither is prepared for the outcome. (978-1-63679-568-3)

Truly Home by J.J. Hale. Ruth and Olivia discover home is more than a four-letter word. (978-1-63679-579-9)

View from the Top by Morgan Adams. When it comes to love, sometimes the higher you climb, the harder you fall. (978-1-63679-604-8)

Blood Rage by Illeandra Young. A stolen artifact, a family in the dark, an entire city on edge. Can SPEAR agent Danika Karson juggle all three over a weekend with the "in-laws" while an unknown, malevolent entity lies in wait upon her very skin? (978-1-63679-539-3)

Ghost Town by R.E. Ward. Blair Wyndon and Leif Henderson are set to prove ghosts exist when the mystery suddenly turns deadly. Someone or something else is in Masonville, and if they don't find a way to escape, they might never leave. (978-1-63679-523-2)

Good Christian Girls by Elizabeth Bradshaw. In this heartfelt coming of age lesbian romance, Lacey and Jo help each other untangle who they are from who everyone says they're supposed to be. (978-1-63679-555-3)

Guide Us Home by CF Frizzell and Jesse J. Thoma. When acquisition of an abandoned lighthouse pits ambitious competitors Nancy and Sam against each other, it takes a WWII tale of two brave women to make them see the light. (978-1-63679-533-1)

Lost Harbor by Kimberly Cooper Griffin. For Alice and Bridget's love to survive, they must find a way to reconcile the most important passions in their lives—devotion to the church and each other. (978-1-63679-463-1)

Never a Bridesmaid by Spencer Greene. As her sister's wedding gets closer, Jessica finds that her hatred for the maid of honor is a bit more complicated than she thought. Could it be something more than hatred? (978-1-63679-559-1)

The Rewind by Nicole Stiling. For police detective Cami Lyons and crime reporter Alicia Flynn, some choices break hearts. Others leave a body count. (978-1-63679-572-0)

Turning Point by Cathy Dunnell. When Asha and her former high school bully Jody struggle to deny their growing attraction, can they move forward without going back? (978-1-63679-549-2)

When Tomorrow Comes by D. Jackson Leigh. Teague Maxwell, convinced she will die before she turns 41, hires animal rescue owner Baye Cobb to rehome her extensive menagerie. (978-1-63679-557-7)

You Had Me at Merlot by Melissa Brayden. Leighton and Jamie have all the ingredients to turn their attraction into love, but it's a recipe for disaster.(978-1-63679-543-0)

Appalachian Awakening by Nance Sparks. The more Amber's and Leslie's paths cross, the more this hike of a lifetime begins to look like a love of a lifetime. (978-1-63679-527-0)

Dreamer by Kris Bryant. When life seems to be too good to be true and love is within reach, Sawyer and Macey discover the truth about the town of Ladybug Junction, and the cold light of reality tests the hearts of these dreamers. (978-1-63679-378-8)

Eyes on Her by Eden Darry. When increasingly violent acts of sabotage threaten to derail the opening of her glamping business, Callie Pope is sure her ex, Jules, has something to do with it. But Jules is dead…isn't she? (978-1-63679-214-9)

Letters from Sarah by Joy Argento. A simple mistake brought them together, but Sarah must release past love to create a future with Lindsey she never dreamed possible. (978-1-63679-509-6)

Lost in the Wild by Kadyan. When their plane crash-lands, Allison and Mike face hunger, cold, a terrifying encounter with a bear, and feelings for each other neither expects. (978-1-63679-545-4)

Not Just Friends by Jordan Meadows. A tragedy leaves Jen struggling to figure out who she is and what is important to her. (978-1-63679-517-1)

Of Auras and Shadows by Jennifer Karter. Eryn and Rina's unexpected love may be exactly what the Community needs to heal the rot that comes not from the fetid Dark Lands that surround the Community but from within. (978-1-63679-541-6)

The Secret Duchess by Jane Walsh. A determined widow defies a duke and falls in love with a fashionable spinster in a fight for her rightful home. (978-1-63679-519-5)

Winter's Spell by Ursula Klein. When former college roommates reunite at a wedding in Provincetown, sparks fly, but can they find true love when evil sirens and trickster mermaids get in the way? (978-1-63679-503-4)

Coasting and Crashing by Ana Hartnett. Life comes easy to Emma Wilson until Lake Palmer shows up at Alder University and derails her every plan. (978-1-63679-511-9)

Every Beat of Her Heart by KC Richardson. Piper and Gillian have their own fears about falling in love, but will they be able to overcome those feelings once they learn each other's secrets? (978-1-63679-515-7)

Fire in the Sky by Radclyffe and Julie Cannon. Two women from different worlds have nothing in common and every reason to wish they'd never met—except for the attraction neither can deny. (978-1-63679-561-4)

Grave Consequences by Sandra Barret. A decade after necromancy became licensed and legalized, can Tamar and Maddy overcome the lingering prejudice against their kind and their growing attraction to each other to uncover a plot that threatens both their lives? (978-1-63679-467-9)

Haunted by Myth by Barbara Ann Wright. When ghost-hunter Chloe seeks an answer to the current spectral epidemic, all clues point to one very famous face: Helen of Troy, whose motives are more complicated than history suggests and whose charms few can resist. (978-1-63679-461-7)

Invisible by Anna Larner. When medical school dropout Phoebe Frink falls for the shy costume shop assistant Violet Unwin, everything about their love feels certain, but can the same be said about their future? (978-1-63679-469-3)

Like They Do in the Movies by Nan Campbell. Celebrity gossip writer Fran Underhill becomes Chelsea Cartwright's personal assistant with the aim of taking the popular actress down, but neither of them anticipates the clash of their attraction. (978-1-63679-525-6)

Limelight by Gun Brooke. Liberty Bell and Palmer Elliston loathe each other. They clash every week on the hottest new TV show, until Liberty starts to sing and the impossible happens. (978-1-63679-192-0)

Playing with Matches by Georgia Beers. To help save Cori's store and help Liz survive her ex's wedding, they strike a deal: a fake relationship, but just for one week. There's no way this will turn into the real deal. (978-1-63679-507-2)